The Urbana Free Library

To renew: call 217-367-4057
or go to "*urbanafreelibrary.org*"
and select "Renew/Request Items"

3—12

	DATE DUE	
	MAR 17 2012	
	APR 02 2012	
	MAY 13 2012	
	JUN 06 2012	
	JUL 25 2012	
	AUG 18 2012	

ANY DAY NOW

ANY DAY NOW

A NOVEL

TERRY BISSON

OVERLOOK
New York, NY

This edition first published in hardcover the United States in 2012 by
The Overlook Press, Peter Mayer Publishers, Inc.

141 Wooster Street
New York, NY 10012
www.overlookpress.com
For bulk and special sales, please contact sales@overlookny.com

Cataloging-in-Publication Data is available from the Library of Congress

Design and typeformatting by Bernard Schleifer

Manufactured in the United States of America

1 3 5 7 9 10 8 6 4 2

ISBN 978-1-59020-709-3

Family and friends:
If you hope to find yourself in these pages,
you will be disappointed. If you dread it,
you will be relieved. For I made it all up.

"Graves from which a glorious Phantom may
Burst to illumine our tempestuous day."
—SHELLEY, "England in 1819"

For the Old Man, the Beatnik Daddy, once again.

ONE

"HE'S JUST A LITTLE BOY."

"But I can't see out the back."

"What are those big mirrors for?"

"They're for looks, Lou Emma. Not for looking out."

"Shhhh. I think he's asleep."

"He's pretending."

Clay was just a little boy. He knew his name. He knew to keep his eyes closed so they would think he was sleeping, wasn't listening, wasn't there. That was his first trick. More would follow. He lay up in the back of the car, a '39 Mercury coupe, june bug green, under the slanted glass. It was perfect, like a little bed. Like it was made for him.

Soon they were talking of something else in low voices in the soft light from the dash. *Dash.* Clay liked that word.

His mother's voice was soft and familiar, like cotton cloth. His father's voice was sharp and strange, like steel or plastic. It came from far away.

The little boy opened his eyes. The one-eyed moon looked back. The world below it was dark. Light bounced off running posts and signs. The world was flat. The moon was round. The car made a singing sound. Tires, motor, radio. It made the world go by. The big trees, far away, went slower the farther away they were.

It was all moving, just right. It was perfect.

"He's not pretending," his mother said. "He's just a boy. A little boy."

Calhoun was small.
Owensboro was big.

"This is it," his father said. They had a new house. It was just like all the others. They were all new, all in a row. The trees in the front yards were all small, like children. Wires held them up. The trees in Calhoun had been big. He had lived in a big house with his aunts and his cousins. Now he had his own room.

"He's not used to you yet," said his mother.

His father was home from the War.

"He'll get used to you," said his mother.

"What was the War like?" he asked one day.

"It was like nothing," his father said. "It was like a lot of big gray steel nothing." He had been on a ship.

"Don't tell him that," his mother said.

"Why not," his father said. "It's true."

Jimmy Spence lived two doors down. He was sixteen. His father was a dealer. Jimmy had a '49 Ford. It made a rumbling sound like the '39 Merc. He liked to drive fast through the puddles and splash the kids playing.

Everybody laughed but them.

There were no sidewalks. The neighborhood was too new.

Jesse and Yancey were twins. They lived next door. Clay hated them.

"Your daddy's a Yankee," they said. "He talks funny."

"Your daddy's a hillbilly," said Clay.

"No, he's not."

Yes, he was. Clay had heard his mother and father talking about it. It was one of the few times they agreed.

The second grade school was new. There was a ditch between the playground and the tobacco field. There were crawdads in the muddy water.

The teacher's name was Miss Wilson. She was pretty. Nice too. She let the boys catch crawdads and bring them into the classroom in a coffee can. Clay and Bobby Lee caught the most. Bobby Lee was his best friend.

On Monday they were all dead and the room smelled bad but Miss Wilson didn't care. She opened all the windows with a crank.

It was Science, she said.

Fourth grade was another school, all the way across town. They had to ride a yellow bus. The driver's name was Porter.

All the kids liked Porter. He taught them songs.

MacArthur, MacArthur, he's our man!
Throw old Truman in the garbage can!

"Where'd you learn that?" Clay's mother asked.

Clay didn't know who MacArthur was, or Truman either, but he knew better than to tell on Porter.

"From Bobby Lee," he said.

Bobby Lee's father owned a drugstore and a picture show. Every Saturday there was a cowboy movie and a serial too. Clay and Bobby Lee got in free.

Clay's mother picked them up after the show.

"How was the show?" she asked. "Did the cowboys win again?" She was smoking a cigarette. The cowboys always won.

"The niggers threw popcorn," said Clay.

"The what?"

"The niggers in the balcony," Bobby Lee explained. "They eat the popcorn and then they flatten out the boxes and sail them down to try and hit us. It doesn't hurt though."

Clay's mother let Bobby Lee out at his house, then stopped

the car again at the end of the block. She lit another cigarette and said, "Don't you ever let me hear you say that again."

"Say what?"

"*Nigger.* That's a white trash word. That's white trash talk. You're a Bewley and don't you forget it. We've always had colored help, colored people around, in Calhoun. We don't use that word."

Clay had a little sister. Then she died. She was zero years old.

Now he had his own room again. His mother sat up late, crying and smoking. His father was in the garage, listening to the radio. He listened to the radio a lot. He had a shortwave.

Clay read airplane books under the covers with a flashlight. His favorite was the Curtiss P-40, the Warhawk.

On Sundays, after church, they went to Calhoun.

Calhoun Mama lived in the Big House, on the banks of the Green. There were old cars all around the barn and empty whiskey bottles in the rafters of the tobacco stripping room. A BB gun to keep cats out of the milk.

Calhoun Mama sat in a rocker by the window, with her legs straight out, like white sticks, all wrapped up. All the kids had to say hello and remind her of their names. The curtains were always closed.

All the aunts and cousins were there. Sometimes Uncle Ham cooked squirrels. They were like chicken but all dark meat. The boys looked for buckshot with their teeth, then played in the sweet-smelling barn, where the burley was hanging.

They sat on the big green tractor. From the barn door Clay could see the bridge and the cars speeding over, one at a time. Two out of three were Chevrolets

ф

There was a new boy in the fifth grade, Emil, pronounced "a meal." He was a Yankee, from Chicago. He talked funny but Clay liked him. He knew all about airplanes. Bobby Lee liked him too. Emil had all the Oz books. He kept them on a shelf in his room, in order.

There were thirty-nine in all. Clay had never dreamed there could be so many.

They formed an Oz club. You had to read all the books, in order. They built a clubhouse under an Osage orange tree and each took a name. Bobby Lee was Tik-Tok of Oz, Emil was Peter Brown, the American boy, and Clay was Ojo.

"When we grow up and get out of here, we'll find Oz," said Bobby Lee. Nome, Alaska, was suspect.

Owensboro seemed suddenly small. Now they saw it for what it really was: a shadow of the real world.

On the first Saturday of every month all the boys in Owensboro, it seemed like anyway, went to the icehouse on Ninth Street. An old colored man on the porch gave haircuts for a quarter. The icehouse had a big old-fashioned porch like in a Western and the boys all lined up. It only took sixty seconds and all the boys looked alike when he was done. Only white boys of course. They were all ten. The iceman's grandson took the quarters. He was thirteen and mean-looking and black as night. He had already failed two grades.

The boys were all afraid of him.

There was a girl with a shovel behind the Loyals' garage.

"Who are you?" Clay asked.

"None of your beeswax," she said. She was tall for a girl and skinny.

She was burying a bird. That seemed more interesting than hide-and-seek. It was a little gray thing. There was no blood and nothing was broken. The only thing wrong with it was that it was dead.

"How did you kill it?"

"I didn't. I found it. Maybe it just died."

"If it was a cat, it would have eaten it. There would at least be blood."

It seemed better without the blood. Even more dead.

She handed Clay the shovel. They wrapped the bird in a paper bag. Ruth Ann put a ribbon around it, but that didn't seem right. That was her name. They put a little cross on the grave.

"I wonder if he died from the inside out," Clay said.

"Maybe he just didn't belong here," said Ruth Ann. "Do you think there's a heaven for birds?"

"I guess there would have to be. What about a hell?"

"Brrr." They shivered and looked at the tiny grave. Had they sent a bird to Hell?

They decided to dig it up in a year, to see what it looked like. Clay looked for Ruth Ann the next day but she was gone. "She's our cousin," said Yancey, the only one of the Loyal twins who had any sense. "She lives in the country."

"She had a pony," said Jesse.

"It died," said Yancey. "Her daddy didn't feed it right."

In 1953, Hillary and a Sherpa were lost on the descent from Everest. It was on the radio but nobody in Owensboro noticed except for Emil and Clay and Bobby Lee. Sherpas were colored helpers.

They went through all the mountain climbing books in the library: Annapurna, Everest, Hunt and Shipton. The Matterhorn, gleaming with ice like a cruel tooth. On Saturdays, while the other boys were getting haircuts and playing baseball, they hiked out to the strip mines and climbed the shallow clay cliffs—Camp One, Camp Two—all the way to the summit, which was just a flat spot.

It was hot, with flies, but you could see all the way to the Ohio, slick as silver in the sun.

"The Amazon," said Bobby Lee. Defying the cornfields.

Clay was in a movie. It was called *Kentucky Rifle*, and it was shot in Indiana, across the river. They hired kids from Owensboro as extras. Clay got in because his Uncle Ham rented the cars for the movie stars. They all wanted Lincolns.

Being in a movie meant standing around a lot. The kid in the movie was a child star from Hollywood. In between shots, he pointed at Clay and Bobby Lee and motioned for them to follow him.

They went behind the sound wagon and all smoked a cigarette. First he tore the filter off. Nick was a movie star. He taught them to French inhale. Bobby Lee threw up.

Burt Lancaster was the grown-up star. He thrilled the mothers by teasing them.

"They hired you guys because you are used to going barefoot," said Nick. He thought they were all hillbillies. He was fifteen but he looked eight. "Cigarettes stunted his growth," said Bobby Lee, who didn't like him.

After that Clay smoked with Nick and a poor kid from the trailer park. His name was Harl. He was a year older than Clay.

"If the movie is about Kentucky," Clay said, "how come they are shooting it in Indiana?"

"What's the big difference?" said Nick.

"I'll tell you why," said Harl. "Because nothing ever happens in Kentucky."

Bobby Lee was a Baptist. Clay was a Methodist. Methodists were better than Baptists but only a little. On Sundays Clay wore scratchy pants and sat in a pew between his mother and his Uncle Ham.

They all stood up to sing. His mother sang too loud. His father never went to church at all.

Emil's favorite airplane was the F4U Corsair with the gull wings. Then he moved away. He took his Oz books with him.

Clay washed cars at his Uncle Ham's lot after school. Fifty cents a car. An old colored man washed the engines. His name was Hosea but everybody called him Hosey. He ran the engines to dry them off.

"Hear that, honey?" he would say.

"Hear what?" Clay would lean over to listen.

Hosey would roll a cigarette and smile. He rolled perfect cigarettes, out of a little pouch tied with a string. He had one gold tooth. Clay liked the way he called him honey. He liked leaning on the fender and smelling the sweet Bull Durham and watching the engine idle, making the water drops fade.

"Hear what?" he said again. "I don't hear a thing."

"Zactly," said Hosey. "That's a flathead for you. Quiet as a possum at midnight."

"Happy Birthday," said Clay's father.

"Oh boy," said Clay. The engine, a Cox .049, came in a plastic box. The plane, a little plank-winged U-control P-40, came in a cardboard box.

"How did you know this was my favorite?" Clay asked. But his father was already gone, back to the garage. Clay could hear the radio.

The best place to fly it was at the other edge of town (Owensboro was all edges), where there were lots of vacant lots and the houses were mixed with trailers, and littler than Clay's.

The .049 was hard to start. It made a wet sound when Clay flipped the prop.

A boy was in the front yard of a double-wide, working on a motorcycle. The yard was full of junk. He walked over without saying hello. Clay remembered him from the movie. He looked tough now. He had a flattop.

"Sounds like it's flooded," he said. He smelled it, then turned the prop so the port was open and blew in it, hard. It started.

He stuck out his hand for Clay to shake. "Harl," he said. "*Kentucky Rifle.*"

Clay flew the plane till it crashed and broke the prop, then went over to look at the motorcycle. It had a big yellow tank and fat wheels.

"It's a K-model," said Harl. "It's my brother's. He's in Korea. I'm taking care of it for him." Clay nodded like he knew.

Harl's sister was sitting on the porch, smoking a cigarette. Her name was Donna. She wore short shorts. They were narrow between her legs and Clay could see the little pink arc of her panties, peeking out.

"Getting your eyes full?" she asked.

"No," said Clay even though he was. "I'd better be heading home."

That night he lay in bed and thought about the flattop, the motorcycle, the little arc.

Mostly the little arc.

Clay's father didn't like guns. Clay's mother said it was because of the War. Clay liked guns though.

Uncle Ham took Clay and his cousin Junior squirrel hunting in the Panther Creek bottoms. Junior didn't like hunting but his father made him go. There were no panthers but lots of squirrels. Uncle Ham carried a 12 gauge and the boys both had .22s. Junior's was a pretty little Remington pump and Clay's was a single-shot Stevens. All you ever got was one shot anyway.

Uncle Ham let the boys take the first shot, and miss. Then he would blow the squirrel out of the tree with his 12 gauge. The boys had to pick up the squirrels and put them in the bag.

"I feel sorry for the squirrels," said Junior. He was whispering so his father wouldn't hear.

"I don't," said Clay, even though he did, a little. His cousin Junior was a sissy. Clay was afraid of being a sissy too.

One day Clay hit the squirrel. Ham didn't have to shoot. It fell from the hickory tree like a stone.

"Good shot, Clay," said Ham.

"How do you know it wasn't me?" asked Junior.

"I just do," said Ham.

That same day they jumped a deer. In those days deer were rare. "It's like seeing a unicorn," Clay said. He had been reading about unicorns.

"There aren't any unicorns," said Junior.

He hated his father.

Illinois was neat. Kentucky was messy.

They went north, once every summer, to visit Clay's father's parents, near Decatur.

The world got flat and wide until it was a table under the sky. The sky itself was filled with clouds marching from west to east. The dirt on the roadside was black. The roads all met at right angles. Every twenty minutes there was a neat little town with tall trees and big houses lined up on a rumbly brick street. Leaving one town, you could see the next on the horizon, a little clump of trees and a grain elevator, like a skyscraper.

"Here's my little man," Grandpa Martin would say.

"I saved some magazines for you," Grandma Minnie would say. They were stacked on the porch for Clay to read, a spring and summer's worth of "Life in These United States" and "Increase Your Word Power."

"Humor in Uniform" was good too.

There were more issues of *Reader's Digest* in the attic, all different and yet somehow all the same. Each had a condensed book in the back, but Clay didn't know what to add to it to make it any fun to read. Water? Milk? Books apparently weren't allowed downstairs, especially after they had been read. Clay's father's old high school textbooks were in a pile under the little triangular window. *Exploring Our Modern World* was best. There was a camel crossing the desert. Seattle harbor with its forest of masts and steamers mixed. A man with a hoe looking up at a dam being built. Was that the world my father expected? Clay wondered. None of it looked like Illinois, or Kentucky either.

The *Reader's Digest*s were piled in years. Illinois was all in squares. Grandpa Martin had a Cadillac. Then they both died in the fire and the house was gone and Illinois was gone. They never went back.

Clay never learned what happened to the Cadillac.

"What's this?"

"Science fiction," said Bobby Lee.

They were smaller than regular books and they weren't in the library. They were paperbacks. They appeared on the racks in Bobby Lee's father's drugstore, different ones every month. They had rocket ships on the cover.

The Oz books were for little kids. These weren't.

They cost a quarter but Bobby Lee and Clay didn't have to buy them. They could read them as long as they didn't bend them up and then put them back on the rack.

It was like the picture show.

Clay's Uncle Ham owned the Ford-Lincoln-Mercury dealership. He gave Clay's father a job in the office. Now they had a new car every other year. It was always a Ford, never a Mercury or a Lincoln.

Clay loved cars. They made sense. They were like ladders,

leading up: Ford, Mercury, Lincoln; Plymouth, Dodge, DeSoto, Chrysler, Imperial; Chevrolet, Pontiac, Oldsmobile, Buick, Cadillac. And there were ladders within ladders: Firesweep, Firedome, Fireflite; Monterey, Montclair; Special, Super, Roadmaster.

They were like grades. Clay was in the eighth, going on ninth. Everything got bigger, newer, higher every year. It was the way the world worked.

Clay's mother smoked Kents, only halfway down. They were like long white grubs in the ashtrays. Clay stole the long butts and smoked them by the window in his room, reading late, after dark.

"Buy your own cigarettes," his mother said. "They will stunt your growth. So will that stuff."

She mistrusted paperbacks. He was reading Heinlein, Simak, Arthur C. Clarke.

"See that old Ford?" said Clay's Uncle Ham. It was a 1949 Ford two-door with bad paint. It was at the back of the lot by the fence next to the funeral home.

Clay had noticed it before. It reminded him of Jimmy Spence's hot rod, except it didn't have duals.

"Like it?"

"Yes, sir," Clay said. He always called his Uncle Ham *sir*. He was his mother's big brother.

"It's yours when you turn sixteen, boy."

That was only a year away.

"You have to pay me for it though. Fifty dollars."

Still a good deal, Clay thought.

"Want a ride?" It was Harl, the kid from the other edge of town.

He had pulled up on his motorcycle in front of Clay's house. Clay was mowing the lawn. He shut off the mower.

The motorcycle was idling: *potato, potato, potato*.

"Sure," he said.

"Just where you two going?" Clay's mother asked.

She was standing in the doorway, smoking a Kent.

"For a ride," said Clay, getting on the back. Harl didn't say a word.

"No, you are not," said Clay's mother. She was wearing her terry cloth bathrobe even though it was two in the afternoon. It was Saturday. "He's not old enough to have a motorcycle."

"It's his brother's," said Clay. "He's in Korea." He held on to the seat underneath his legs. He wasn't about to put his arms around Harl. "Let's get going," he whispered. "My mother thinks you are a delinquent," he added, after they got going.

"So what," said Harl. He had traded his flattop for a duck-tail, called a DA. They rode around the town but stayed off the big streets. "No plates," said Harl, back over his shoulder.

"He's not in Korea," said Clay's mother when he got back. "He's in jail."

"So what," said Clay.

It was after midnight the night Clay finished *Against the Fall of Night*, by Arthur C. Clarke. He turned out his light and carried his shoes out the door on tiptoes. His father was in the garage with the shortwave; Clay could hear it crackling and mumbling. His mother was asleep in her chair in the living room.

The whole neighborhood was asleep. The whole town was asleep. Only the streetlights were on, and they ended at the end of the street. He pulled on his shoes and went to Bobby Lee's house. It was only three blocks away.

"Wake up," he said, tapping on Bobby Lee's window. "Let's go."

"Where? What time is it?"

"Midnight!"

"It's too late. We'll get in trouble."

"So what," said Clay. He gave up and went on alone. It was summer. The bugs were loud. Owensboro was all edges. The town ended at the end of the street. He walked out into the darkness, between the long rows of burley tobacco, still only waist high. He kept his eyes on the ground until he was far out in the field. Then he looked up.

There was the Universe. It was all stars. He lit a Kent and watched the smoke drift up into the Universe. Nobody in Owensboro even knew it was there.

He finished the cigarette and turned back toward town. *In this universe the night was falling . . .*

TWO

CLAY'S MOTHER DIDN'T LIKE HANK WILLIAMS BECAUSE HE WAS A hillbilly. She liked Elvis though, in spite of it. So did all the girls in Owensboro. So did all the girls in the world. They liked James Dean too.

In Owensboro it was football players, movie stars, and cars, in that order. Bobby Lee tried out and made the team. He even started, twice. Now he had a girlfriend, a cheerleader; her name was Mary Beth. She was a Baptist.

Clay tried out for football but didn't make the team. But that's okay, he thought. I'll have a car in three months. He had already saved thirty-four dollars, washing cars.

High school was different. All the kids were older now. The boys had ROTC, one day a week. The uniforms were scratchy like church but Clay liked the guns. He got on the rifle team. They shot .22s.

ROTC was integrated and the colored boys from Lee, the colored high school, came once a week. One of them was called Ice.

"I know you," said Clay. "From the icehouse, the haircut porch."

"So what," said Ice. He hated school and white boys too.

Clay was sixteen. He gave his Uncle Ham fifty dollars and Uncle Ham gave him twenty back. "For gas," he said. The '49 Ford was his.

It was a Tudor, with gray felt seats. It was hot inside. He rolled down the windows and opened the hood for the first time.

It was a six. He tried not to look disappointed.

"Don't worry about it," said Hosey. "Those flathead sixes got a lot of grunt off the line."

"They do?" Clay wasn't so sure. Plus it knocked a little, and smoked a lot.

"Rings," said his Uncle Ham later. "Get Hosey to help you. Those niggers love flatheads."

"Colored," said Clay.

Uncle Ham grinned. "Where'd you hear that, boy? Don't tell me. My little sister. Your mother."

Mary Beth was a cheerleader. The kids all hung out at her house after school. Clay too, because he was a friend of her boyfriend, Bobby Lee. The others were all on the team.

"Libby likes you," Bobby Lee said. She had just broken up with her boyfriend, John S., the second team halfback.

"You sure?" Clay asked.

"I have it on good authority," said Bobby Lee. He was beginning to talk like that.

Libby was a little fat but her father was the mayor. She had big tits. They played 45s in the basement at Mary Beth's and danced. "*Everyday it's a-gettin' closer.*" They pressed against him. "*Goin' faster than a roller coaster.*"

Libby kissed with her mouth closed. It was like kissing a basketball. One night all the girls were weeping. James Dean had been in a car wreck.

"What if he had been killed?" said Mary Beth. She shivered.

"We would always remember him anyway," said Libby. "Like Buddy Holly."

"He would be dead though," said Bobby Lee.

"Don't say that," said Libby. "Don't dare say that."

"Arthur C. Clarke is dead," Clay said. He had seen the article in *Time*. "I will always remember him."

"Who is he?" Mary Beth asked.

"A writer," said Bobby Lee.

"That doesn't count," said Libby.

Clay walked home alone. *In this universe the night was falling.*

Clay pulled the head and dropped the pan. The valves looked okay, according to Hosey. One rod was loose. He unbolted the rod caps and pushed the pistons out of the top of the block with a broomstick. He broke the glaze and reamed the ridges; Hosey showed him how. He fitted the inserts and torqued the rod caps. Every time he got stuck he would call out to Hosey, who would come over to his corner of the shop and shake his head and say, "Honey, you in a world of trouble."

Then he would roll a cigarette and show Clay what to do.

"See? Those niggers love flatheads," Uncle Ham would say.

"Colored," said Clay, very quietly.

The Dairy Drive-In, or DDI, was on Fourth Street, out at the edge of town.

The cars cruised through, on display: a '55 Chevrolet, a '56 DeSoto, a Ford T-bird. Clay's '49 Ford, with a shot of primer, fit right in. He never opened the hood so nobody knew it was a six.

He even had a girlfriend to fill out the front seat. They didn't talk much. Libby liked to fool with the radio. She liked the Everly Brothers. Who didn't?

Her father wouldn't let her go to the drive-in movie. They would sit and sip their Cokes and watch the cars roll through the DDI. Then they would kiss, then go home.

One Saturday night Harl rolled through on his K-model. Clay waved at him; you were not allowed to honk at the DDI.

Harl pulled over and they leaned on the hood and smoked a cigarette. Libby stayed in the car, sipping on her Coke and listening to the Everly Brothers. "Cathy's Clown."

"What's under the hood?" asked Harl.

Clay opened the hood; he didn't know why.

"A six is not so bad," said Harl, combing his DA back with his fingers. He had a black leather jacket. The sleeves were too short.

"They have a lot of grunt off the line," said Clay.

"Split the pipe, for duals, nobody needs to know."

"Good idea," said Clay.

"Doesn't he live in a trailer?" Libby asked as Harl rode off. "He's a delinquent."

"So what," said Clay.

Bobby Lee made first team. He was almost All-State. Mary Beth let him look up her cheerleader skirt. Harl was in the band. That didn't count for much. Clay was on the rifle team. That didn't count for anything.

The Owensboro Sportscenter was now integrated, even the pool. Especially the pool. The colored came in and all the white girls went away. The boys too, even Clay.

There was a ditch behind the DDI. It was filled with water and, as far as Clay knew, even crawdads.

The boys hung around and smoked cigarettes and drank beer out of cans in paper bags. "Those damn niggers," they said.

Clay didn't say anything. He kept his mouth shut.

Round Man was the captain of the football team, a senior with a yellow Bonneville, bright as an Easter chick. He was drunk. He had whiskey in a paper bag. Early Times.

He skipped and fell into the ditch, then lay on his back in the muddy water, laughing. His teammate Danny Rose joined him.

"No niggers here!" they said, splashing their arms like swimmers. Snow angels in the mud.

"You show them, Round Man," said Clay, but quietly.

Clay and Ice both made the ROTC rifle team. The sergeant let them smoke behind the building. He gave them a cigarette for each bull's-eye. None of the other boys ever got one. When Ice didn't get one, Clay shared his.

"Aren't you afraid I will nigger-lip it?" Ice said. "Don't you white boys worry about that?"

"No," said Clay. "I don't mind colored."

After that Ice brought his own cigarettes.

The new carhop at the DDI looked familiar.

"I remember you," said Clay.

"You do?"

"We buried a bird together."

"We did?" she said. "What can I get you two?"

"She goes to County High," said Libby.

"So?"

"So. A hillbilly."

"The Everly Brothers are hillbillies," said Clay.

"I have to be home by eleven," said Libby. "I have a civics test tomorrow."

After he broke up with Libby, Clay wasn't invited to Mary Beth's anymore. He had had his chance.

He bolted a split pipe behind his single glasspack and parked at the DDI alone. Some boys took off the air cleaner so that the carb would howl when the pedal hit the floor, but not Clay. He knew what the engine looked like inside. Hosey had showed him what sand and grit could do.

The front seat looked better empty. The new carhop was still tall and skinny.

"It's Ruth Ann," she said when she took his order.

"Huh?"

"You were trying to remember my name. I saw you."

"You're right. Mine is Clay." He stuck out his hand but she didn't shake it. She had an order book in one hand and a short pencil in the other, with no eraser. She wore a wide twirly skirt with felt hot rods sewed on it.

"Clayton Bewley Bauer," she said. "I just pretended not to remember you. I was working. And you were with some girl."

"She was just a friend," said Clay.

"I'll bet."

She worked Fridays and Saturdays. On Saturday night she handed him a note with his Coke.

It was folded four times. It was an invitation to a hayride.

Methodists had dances. Baptists had hayrides.

The wagon was pulled by a tractor, a John Deere A, just like the one in Calhoun Mama's barn. It went around Miller's Lake, out by the strip mines. Everybody sang while the tractor kept time: *pooka pooka pooka*. Clay put his arm around Ruth Ann while she was singing "Old MacDonald." She had narrow shoulders for such a tall girl. Every time the wagon bounced he allowed, and she allowed, his hand to brush against her breast, and she settled into his arms. Soon they were singing "My Old Kentucky Home" and his fingertips were brushing against the top button of her blouse.

"Don't get ahead of yourself," she said, flicking them away. "*'Tis summer, the darkies are gay . . .*"

Junior was in his second year at Vanderbilt. He had learned to soften his *R*s. "College AhrOTC is really cool," he said. "We fahr M1s, not just .22s."

He showed Clay how to read a contour map. They were at the dealership, and he spread it out on the hood of a new Lincoln.

He was wearing his ROTC uniform. Uncle Ham was proud. "Pay attention, Clay," he said. "My boy here knows what he's talking about. He'll be serving his country soon."

"Already," said Junior. "We train all the time."

"There's a man in every boy," said Hosey, mysteriously. "And a boy in every man."

Even though he was retired he hung around the shop every day, leaning on a broom and giving advice.

"The sad fact is," said Clay's mother, "he's your uncle's only friend."

Ruth Ann carhopped weekends. She had to babysit Sundays and Mondays while her mother made light bulbs at Ken-Rad. Her father drove a forklift at the MidSouth Burley Auction Floor. On Thursday nights Clay would pick her up at her little house, which was like a trailer without wheels, white, facing the highway, and they would drive through the DDI, then out Fourth Street to the edge of town and beyond: across the rattling iron bridge where he and Bobby Lee went to shoot their .22s, to the low bluff over Panther Creek where a house had burned years ago and the owner's ghost, it was said, still prowled.

Tuesday nights, the same.

They would sit on the hood of the Ford and smoke Winstons and wait for the ghost, which never came.

Owensboro was just a glow in the distance. The bugs were loud. The flathead six ticked as it cooled. The Universe high overhead was silent and watchful. "There are people out there," Clay said.

"People like us?"

"Vast intelligences."

"I like that better."

"You do?" Clay kissed her, experimentally, and it wasn't like Libby at all. It was called French kissing.

Ruth Ann said, "I wondered when you were going to do that."

"Fall in, men."

There was a rifle match in Louisville, a hundred miles away. They met on Saturday morning at the high school, in uniform, two white boys and two colored. The sergeant stuffed them all into a green '55 Chevy that said US ARMY on the side. A six.

They stopped in Cloverport, a little town on the Ohio River, for breakfast. "The US Army is buying," said Sarge.

"Bacon, Sarge?" asked Ice. He liked it when they called him Sarge. Bacon was always extra.

"As long as it's on the menu," said Sarge. "The US Army is good to go for bacon."

The waitress looked embarrassed. She was watching from across the room. Then she approached and Clay already knew what she was going to say.

"I can't serve colored," she said. "I'm sorry."

"These are not your local hillbillies," said the sergeant. "You are dealing with the US Army, young lady."

"I can't serve colored," she said. "I'm sorry."

"Well, then, sorry it is," said the sergeant. "Suit your hillbilly self. Fall in, men. About-face, we're out of here." They all stood. He always called them men.

They lost the match and drove back on the Indiana side, even though it was longer. Clay had never seen a white man stick up for colored before.

No one said anything about it. Ice quit the rifle team. Clay was now number one. But he quit the next month.

"This is the widest river in the world," said Harl.

"How's that?" They were driving over the bridge. The Ohio was almost a mile wide in Owensboro, but Clay knew that the Mississippi was wider, not to mention the Amazon, the Orinoco.

According to the *World Book*, the Ganges at its delta was a hundred miles wide, and yellow muddy color washed out of its mouth for a hundred miles into the sea.

They were heading into Indiana. It was Saturday night.

"It separates the North from the South," Harl said. "The light from the dark."

"We're still closer to Nashville than New York," said Bobby Lee. He was riding shotgun. Mary Beth was at a Baptist church affair.

The North here was nothing but a long bottom of muddy cornfields and coon hunter swamps for six arrow-straight miles along the levee, all the way to the 4-Way, the all-night truck stop where 231 crossed 60.

Everything in Owensboro closed at midnight by law, even the DDI. The long counter at the 4-Way had its own little jukebox, chrome and glass like the dashboard of an Oldsmobile, where you leafed through the available songs by flipping stiff little pages. It was like a book of metal.

In Owensboro songs were a nickel. Here they were a dime, or three for a quarter. Same songs: Everly Brothers, Marty Robbins, Ernest Tubb.

"Give me a quarter," said Harl. He still had a DA.

"Mister Gimme," said Bobby Lee. They argued a lot.

Harl played the same song three times: Dinah Washington, "What a Diff'rence a Day Makes."

"Jazz makes the difference," he said.

"That's not jazz," said Bobby Lee. "Hear the violins?"

"It's in the phrasing," said Harl. He played clarinet in the high school band. He had convinced the band director to subscribe to *DownBeat*.

The song played again.

"Wish they had some Brubeck," said Harl. He cocked his head and drummed on the table.

"What's 'brew beck'?" asked Bobby Lee.

The song played again. The waitress came over.

"You can't play the same song over and over," she said.

"Who says?"

She pointed with her chin at two truckers down the counter. They were grinning like fools.

"I say," said Bobby Lee. He put another quarter in the jukebox and asked the waitress, "What do you like?"

"Marty Robbins is always nice."

Harl groaned.

"Marty Robbins it is."

And Marty Robbins it was.

Jazz was the new thing. "Not that old stuff," said Harl. "Modern jazz."

Brubeck, for example. Ahmad Jamal. The Unbroken Record had some, in a section between Show Tunes and Songs of Faith. Clay, who had money, would buy one, and Harl would steal one, slipping it into the same album cover. Then they would listen to them at Clay's house. Clay had a hi-fi. He had gotten it with the money from washing cars, which had gone up to a dollar apiece. He was also washing the engines now that Hosey was retired. Hosey just watched and rolled him cigarettes when his uncle wasn't looking.

"Where's the tune?" Clay's mother asked. She was standing in the doorway of his room.

"It's all improvised, Lou Emma," said Harl. She had decided she liked him after all. She insisted he call her Lou Emma. It made her feel younger, she said.

"Improvised," she said. She found a Kent in her bathrobe.

"They don't have to follow the tune."

"Not like the rest of us, huh?" said Clay's mother, Lou Emma. "One of you boys got a light?"

"What are you doing?" Ruth Ann asked. They were parked. It was raining so they couldn't sit on the hood. Clay was going through the dial, left to right: nothing but rock and roll and country.

"Looking for jazz," said Clay. He finally found some Jimmy Reed somewhere in the 1500s.

"Nigger music," said Ruth Ann.

"Don't say that."

"Why not?"

"It's prejudiced," said Clay. "But it's good stuff anyway. Listen to that beat."

"The words are stupid."

"They're supposed to be."

"You have a funny explanation for everything," said Ruth Ann. "I like that."

"You do?" Clay kissed her. She had a way of sticking her tongue in his mouth as if she were looking for something. Clay liked that.

"What's with these grades?" asked Clay's mother. She was fanning herself with his report card, even though it wasn't hot.

"Nothing," said Clay.

"Nothing is right. You better shape up or you'll never get into Vanderbilt."

"I don't care about Vanderbilt," said Clay.

"Sure you do," she said. "You're a Bewley and all the Bewleys go to Vanderbilt."

"You didn't."

"I didn't have to go to college." She laughed, and pointed toward the garage. "I married a Yankee."

"It's raining."

"Sssshhhh," said Harl.

He and Clay were hiding in the bushes outside Dr. Rhodes's elegant home on Griffith Avenue. It had a circular driveway.

Dr. Rhodes's son was home from New York, where he had gone away to college and then quit. They were throwing him a party. Harl and Clay were planning to steal some beer from the cooler on the back porch.

The colored servant came out to get some beer, then went back in.

"Now," said Harl. "We make our move."

They opened the cooler and took out four beers each, two in each hand. There was also a bottle of gin. "Should we get the gin?" Clay asked.

Harl didn't answer. The door had opened. A man was standing in the door.

He had a little beard. Clay had never seen a beard before except in pictures. He was also wearing tennis shoes with no socks, and he was grinning.

"Who are you?" Clay asked. He couldn't think of anything else to say.

"The prodigal son," he said. "Better I should ask who are you, and what the hell do you think you are doing?"

"N-nothing," said Harl, putting the beer back. "Are you a beatnik?"

"What do you know about beatniks?"

"I saw the pictures in *Life* magazine," Harl said.

"That stupid rag," said the beatnik. "Take two. Put the gin back."

"Yes, sir," said Harl.

"Take two more. And don't call me *sir*. I'm not your father. Now make yourselves scarce before someone else comes out here."

"Yes, sir."

THREE

THE NEXT DAY WAS SUNDAY.

Clay's mother went to church and sang in the choir. It was the only thing she did.

Clay's father was in the garage. Clay could hear the radio.

Harl came by at eleven. He had two record albums under his arm. "Let's go," he said.

"Where?"

"Dr. Rhodes's."

"Are you kidding?"

"They'll all be gone to church."

"So what's the point?"

"Beatniks don't go to church."

Clay parked on the street and they walked up Dr. Rhodes's long curved drive. It didn't seem right to park the old Ford right in front of the house. It had columns like *Gone with the Wind*. He was almost hoping nobody was home.

"Ring the bell," said Harl. "Go ahead."

The door opened and there he was, with his little goatee. "You two look vaguely familiar," he said.

"Do you dig jazz?" Harl asked.

The Rhodeses' living room was huge. It was full of nice stuff.

The beatnik sat them down on the rug and gave them each a beer. "Now what's this really all about?"

"We brought some sounds," said Harl.

"Are you really a beatnik?" Clay asked.

"Could be," said the beatnik. His name was Peter Rhodes but he called himself Roads. "R-O-A-D-S," he said.

"So what are you doing in Owensboro?"

"Killing time. Same as everybody else."

"Do you like jazz?"

"Don't be stupid. Who are you guys? Let's see what you've got."

Harl handed him the two albums. The beatnik, Roads, took the records out and studied them, as if he could hear what was in the grooves without a record player. He wore tennis shoes with no socks.

"Brubeck," he said. He shook his head and sailed the record across the room. It landed on the couch. Then, "Ahmad Jamal." It landed on the floor and slid against the wall.

"Hey," said Harl.

"This shit is not jazz."

"It has to be real jazz," said Clay.

"So what's real jazz?" Ruth Ann asked. They were sitting on the hood of the Ford with the motor cooling underneath, still warm on their bottoms.

"Felonious Monk, Charles Mingles, Billy Ladyday," said Clay. "Very experimental stuff. But it has to swing. White people don't do it as well. Coal Train is good."

"I'll bet they have hi-fi, the Rhodeses. Like the house."

It was the biggest house in town. Even bigger than Uncle Ham's.

"Stereo," said Clay. "Two channels for realism. So anyway, after that, we listened to Horace Silver and I don't remember the rest of the names. Charlie Parker. He is the absolute best, the god. The Bird."

"Bird? Like the bird we buried."

"Exactly. He's dead too. That's the motto of the beatniks: 'Bird lives.'"

"We should have put that on the gravestone."

"It was a cross. Sticks."

"We forgot to dig it up."

"Too late now."

"Maybe not."

The Loyals had moved away, but the house was unchanged, with the garage behind it. They parked on the street, out of sight of Clay's house, and walked casually back between the drives.

The cross was gone. Weeds everywhere.

"Hopeless," said Ruth Ann. Clay put his arms around her from behind and put his hands over her tiny breasts.

"I wondered when you were going to do that," she said.

Dr. Rhodes's big rug looked soft but it was hard. They sat on it in a circle: Harl, Clay, and Roads, plus Bobby Lee, who had come along out of curiosity.

"R-O-A-D-S," said Roads. "Jack Kerouac gave me that name. One night at the Cedar. He was drunk and so was I. Do you know who he is?"

"I do," said Harl. He even raised his hand.

"Then you begin," said Roads. He handed Harl a paperback book, already opened to the first page.

They took turns reading *On the Road*. By the middle of the afternoon they were at the Bear Mountain Bridge and it was raining, and Roads sent them home.

"My old man will be coming home," he said. "He won't want to find a bunch of beatniks on his expensive rug."

"I thought he was a jazz musician," said Ruth Ann. They were parked out near Panther Creek.

"He's a poet," said Clay. "Jazz and poetry kind of go together though. He was going to college in New York when it happened."

"What happened?"

"When he quit. Dropped out."

"Quit college or quit poetry? Was that what he was studying, poetry?"

"You can't study poetry. That's why he quit. Except old stuff,

I guess. He was pre-med or pre-law or something, and then he dropped out. He knows Kerouac and everybody."

"Who's that?"

"He's a novelist but a poet too. Jazz and poetry kind of go together. They often play while the poets are reading."

"That sounds confusing."

"There are lots of beat poets," said Clay. "And jazz musicians too. We've been reading some of them at his house. They're in little-bitty books. Plus we're reading *On the Road*. That's Kerouac's most famous. It was written on one continuous roll of paper."

"Scroll?"

"Roll."

"Like toilet paper."

"No, not like toilet paper. You can come too if you want to."

"I have to babysit. Besides, it doesn't sound like something for girls."

Bobby Lee dropped out of *On the Road* in Denver. "It's not as good as Heinlein," he said. "Not even."

"It's different."

"Even the cars are stupid. A Hudson?"

"Hudsons were fast in those days."

"I like it," said Harl. "It's realistic."

"It's the way things ought to be," said Clay.

They were on the road in Nebraska, roaring through the Platte Valley on a flatbed truck, struggling to light a cigarette in the wind one afternoon, when Dr. Rhodes himself walked in and right by them without a word, then came back and deposited an ashtray in the center of their circle.

It had a deer on it, smoking a cigar.

"He's a fairy," said Clay's mother.

"What's that?" Clay knew what that was.

"You know what I mean."

"So what."

She lit a cigarette. "One day he'll make his move. I don't want you going over there."

It took eight afternoons after school to read *On the Road.* Then they read "Howl." That was even less of a story, and even more realistic.

Then Harl dropped out. He had a part-time job at the Unbroken Record. They didn't know he had been stealing from them.

Then Roads got a job. "Come see me," he said. "I'll be working at the 4-Way, nights, eleven to seven. It's in Indiana, across the river."

"Up North."

Roads laughed. "Is that what you think? So be it."

"Let me see it."

"What?"

"That book you were reading. I saw it hidden behind your American Literature book."

Mrs. Brodie had stopped Clay on the way out of English class. She was blocking the door.

Clay handed her the book. It was *Evergreen Review.* She leafed through it and sniffed.

"I thought it was a comic book," she said, handing it back. "I was wrong. But I'm still concerned. Yesterday you were sleeping in class. Have you been staying out late?"

"No, ma'am. I mean yes, ma'am."

"Make up your mind, Clayton Bewley Bauer." She stepped aside to let him through. But not quite. She smelled of talcum powder and her hair was piled up in a bun. "You march to a different drummer, I see. A nonconformist. That takes courage and originality these days."

"Yes, ma'am."

"But you still have to hand in your paper on 'Miniver Cheevy.' Have you started it yet?"

"Yes, ma'am. I mean no, ma'am."

"You have promise, Clayton Bewley Bauer, but having promise is not enough."

"Does your mother know you're out this late?"

"My mother doesn't know anything," said Clay. "My mother thinks you are a fairy."

Roads wiped the counter and laughed. "A good fairy or a bad fairy?"

"You know, a queer."

"Faggot," said Roads. "It's called a faggot. There's no such thing as fairies. Not since Yeats, anyway."

"Uh-huh," said Clay. Yeats was a poet. The 4-Way was almost empty at one in the morning. Roads was the fry cook but all he served was coffee, this late. And wiped the counter till it shone.

"So are you?" Clay had learned (the hard way) that Roads liked direct questions; that way he could give indirect answers.

"Tell your mother I'm a poet. Lots of poets are fags. Look at Ginsberg. 'Fucked in the ass by saintly motorcyclists.'"

"Right." Clay nodded. But he was surprised. He had thought that referred to some kind of fighting.

Two truckers came in and sat at the far end of the counter. Roads took them two coffees; they didn't have to ask. Roads had shaved off his beard. No one knew he was a beatnik except Clay.

Roads wiped his way back down the counter to Clay. "We all are everything. Including your mother, who is a very shrewd lady in her way. Tell you what, we poets could use her help."

"What?"

"Take a look in her medicine cabinet. You'll find some little heart-shaped pills. They're orange. Next time you come over, bring me four."

Clay pretended to be shocked. "You want me to steal."

"Bingo."

φ

"I don't get it," said Ruth Ann. "Midol or something? Your mother's pills?"

"It's called decks," said Clay. "It keeps you awake. We stay up all night."

"Oh, I get it," said Ruth Ann. Her Uncle Jay drove a truck. "Doing what?"

"Talking. About everything. Poetry. Jazz. Roads took two and I took two. We talked about Dylan Thomas. He's a Welsh poet."

"Welch?"

"From Wales. King Arthur, you know. Decks is cool. It makes everything brighter even at night, and we drank coffee all night. For free. He's a counter man at the 4-Way, over in Indiana. It stays open all night."

Up North . . .

"That's even better. So he's a dope fiend."

"All the beatniks are dope fiends," said Clay. "It's part of the deal."

"How come you dropped out of Columbia?"

"I decided I needed to get an education." Roads put a mug of coffee in front of Clay. No saucers. Two truckers from Ohio came in, arguing about dogs, and left, still arguing about dogs. Truckers almost never talked about trucks, Clay had noticed lately. But poets talked about poetry. Clay put four orange pills on the counter, lined up like football players, and Roads scooped up two and popped them as he touched up coffee down the counter like a priest giving Communion, with a word for everybody, but most of his words for Clay, perched at the far end with a book and a pack of Camels.

"When you are in college you don't have time to read. You don't have time to listen to music, much less generally just get down with life and groove on what's happening in the world around you."

Clay nodded. "Or write poems."

"*Write* poems?" Roads laughed. "You don't *write* poems. At least a real poet doesn't write poems. The poet is a bird dog. He finds them. He flushes them out. He plucks them out of the air. There's one there!"

"Huh?"

"Lift up that book."

It was e.e. cummings and Roads swiped under it with his gray-white cloth. He liked swiping the counter.

"Whoops. It got away. But you get the idea."

"He's a big phony," said Bobby Lee.

"Who? Kerouac?" They were still arguing about *On the Road*.

"Roads."

"He is not."

"Sure he is. He's always making things up. He's like the Wizard of Oz."

"So?" said Clay. "And since when is that so bad?"

The 4-Way was the only twenty-four-hour restaurant between Indianapolis and Nashville. Roads worked the eleven-to-seven, which was perfect. Clay would come in after he took Ruth Ann home, and stay till two or three in the morning, then tiptoe in past his mother asleep in her chair and his father in the garage.

His mother never missed the dex, which he had finally learned to spell. Also *pot* was not *pod*.

Breakfast was available twenty-four hours a day: two eggs and home fries, $.75, or $1.25 with bacon or sausage. No grits in Indiana, north of the Ohio. Roads gave away coffee but that was all. Clay had to pay for breakfast, even if it was just a donut.

"When do you write your poems? Find your poems. Can I read some?"

"Later, maybe. I'll think about it. I'll bring one in one night."

But Roads never did.

"Can I show you one of mine?" Clay asked.

"Lay it down. Let's have a look at it."

It was about Death and Loneliness.

"That's a damn good start," said Roads. "I think you've got the spark."

The spark!

"But your lines are too long, too many adjectives. Forget Ginsberg and go your own way."

"That's the way it came out."

"Then look out and bring one in. Making them up is not always the thing, you know. Poems are everywhere, you just need to find them. They're all around, you know."

Clay nodded. As if he knew.

"They blow in the door"—

The door had just opened—"or roll in on the wind. They stick to you like burrs on a hound and you peel them off and write them down."

The jukebox clicked into action. Buddy Holly. *"That'll be the day . . ."*

"There you go!" said Roads, and he wiped the counter and made it shine.

Clay missed his prom but went to County High's. Ruth Ann wore her mother's old wedding dress.

"What is it?"

"Just read it."

She read it. "I don't get it."

It was almost summer. The bugs were already loud. They were sitting on the hood of the Ford, looking at the glow of Owensboro in the near distance. "It's a poem," said Clay. "I wrote it a couple of days ago."

"A poem. You did?" Ruth Ann sounded skeptical. "I guess

you showed it to your poet friend already."

"He said he thought it was pretty good. But I didn't write it for him."

"I thought it was a list," she said. "At first."

"I wrote it for you."

She sat up straight and turned to face him. "You did?" The moon was very bright and she read it aloud. "It's song titles."

"Some of the lines are," said Clay. "I wanted it to be romantic. I wrote it for you."

She looked at it, looking down, and folded it up until it was very tiny, as small as a ring.

"So that means I get to keep it?"

"Sure," said Clay. "I have another copy."

"Come here, stupid," she said.

After, they sat on the hood and smoked cigarettes and waited for the ghost. He had burned himself up in the house on purpose. They had even given him a name: Old No Show.

"What you got?" asked Roads.

"*Walden*. I have to write a paper on it," said Clay. "It's for English. I think it's kind of old-fashioned."

"Don't be stupid," said Roads. "He was one of our guys."

Clay liked that: *our guys*. It was a quiet night, or rather morning, at the 4-Way. Roads was behind the counter. Clay was on his usual stool. Two truckers were hunched down over their coffee at the far end of the counter.

"Thoreau was all about traveling light," said Roads.

Clay nodded, trying to look light.

"And what's that, another poem? You're loaded down with papers tonight."

"It's my application for college. I was hoping, wondering, if you would write me a recommendation. My grades aren't all that good."

"For college! Let me see that?"

Clay turned it around and slid it across the counter.

"Vanderbilt? You must be kidding. Why would they listen to me?"

"You're a poet."

"I'm a fry cook. Put that thing away."

Clay put that thing away. Then, on his way back over the bridge, he dropped it into the river.

Graduation was like church. Clay hadn't been in a while. Bobby Lee was salutatorian. Libby was valedictorian.

For his summer job, Clay had a bay in the shop. Hosey came out of retirement to pose as his assistant. That was Uncle Ham's idea, to spare the regular mechanics the hurt of seeing a "nigger" over a white man, even if the man was a boy.

Not that Hosey did much more than share his tools and lean on his broom.

"Honey, you in a world of trouble," he would say, rolling a cigarette and shaking his head whenever Clay was stumped. Then he would tell him what to do and watch him do it.

The flatheads were falling away like leaves. It was mostly OHV, all Fords and Mercurys of course. But brakes were still brakes and points were still points.

"That nigger can still teach you a lot," said Ham.

Hosey's toolbox was an ancient thing. None of his wrenches were matched, and it made reaching for them easier. The 3/8 combination was a Bonney, the 7/16 a Wright, the 1/2 a Proto, the 9/16 a Craftsman, the 5/8 a Wayne, the 11/16 a Thorsen, and so forth.

"Here, you can use my Cadillac, honey," he would say, pulling out his worn and shiny Snap-on 3/8 driver.

"Snap-on dresses up a box," he would say.

"That's going to break your heart," said Ruth Ann.

"Don't be silly," said Clay. He had just told her that Roads was leaving for New York. "That's where he belongs."

"Just like you belong in college."

"Not me," said Clay. "I'm not going."

"You're not going to college? You told me everybody in your family went to Vanderbilt."

"I complained about it, remember? I have different plans."

"You do?" They were in the front seat of the Ford. "You like fixing cars?" She sat a little straighter and looked him in the eye.

"It's more intellectual," Clay said. "It's problem solving. You have to think. It's not like school, where you just remember what somebody is telling you. You're not going to college either."

"That's different." She already had a full time job at The Southern Kitchen.

"Is it?"

"So you're going to, what, settle down, get a job, get married?" She reached for a Winston from the pack they shared; Clay always tore the filters off his.

She lit the wrong end; she had never done that before.

"Can you keep a secret? Cross your heart?"

She crossed her heart.

"Roads is heading back to New York because he got a letter from a friend who has a sailboat, a yawl."

"You all what?"

"It's a kind of sailboat. Anyway, they're going to fix it up and take it down to the Caribbean, maybe Cuba. There are lots of islands, and a small crew, mostly poets and painters, could get by pretty cheap, in different ports."

"Why is that a secret?"

"Because I'm going with them, if it works out. There are other ways to get an education besides sitting in a classroom memorizing what somebody tells you."

"Who is that a secret from? It's not a secret from me."

"From my mother, until it works out. Why should it be a secret from you?"

"Never mind."

She put out her cigarette and unbuttoned her blouse. She took off her bra and put it in the glove compartment, then buttoned her blouse back up. It was their routine. Clay had never noticed before how bright her eyes were, even at night.

The bugs screamed, as if they had just discovered how short their lives were going to be.

"I don't get it," said Clay's mother. "It's August. We should have heard from Vanderbilt by now."

"They must not have wanted me," said Clay. He was checking the mailbox too, looking for a letter from Roads.

"Then you would have gotten a rejection letter," said Clay's mother. "And they don't reject Bewleys anyway. Your cousin Junior's a senior as we speak. You're a legacy."

"Daddy went to Illinois."

"He's a Yankee. You're a Bewley. I'm going to talk to Louise Brodie. She gave you a recommendation, I know. Are you sure you sent in that damn application?"

Harl was gone.

"Drafted?"

"He joined," said Clay.

"Anything to get away," said Bobby Lee. "He sure hated high school. And Owensboro."

He handed Clay the pistol. They were sitting on the iron bridge in the Panther Creek bottoms, shooting at beer cans, which they provided.

"Got him," said Clay.

"You're an idiot," said Bobby Lee. "I would give anything to go to Vanderbilt."

"So go. You have the grades."

"And give up a football scholarship to UK? My old man would shit."

"You hate football."

"They don't know that. Yet. Got him! Seriously, what are your parents going to say when you tell them you're going to sail around the world with a bunch of beatniks on a yacht?"

"It's not a yacht, it's a yawl. It's none of their business any-way."

"You'll never hear from so-called Roads anyway. He's a big phony. He was just amusing himself with you, and Harl too."

"We're all just amusing ourselves," said Clay.

"You even talk like him."

"So is that so bad?"

The letter never came.

"I have this dream," said Clay. "There's this place way up high, it's like on a cloud, except you have to drive to get there, way up this winding road, like a mountain but with no trees, and it's all blue, light blue, and when you get there, there is this big sign, huge letters just floating there."

"Like the JESUS SAVES," said Ruth Ann. "Like that one on the hill behind the Holiness Church on the way to Maceo."

"More like the Hollywood sign," said Clay. "But that's the idea. And it's like I belong there, everyone was expecting me, only I can't read the letters. I don't know what it says. But nobody seems to care."

"Dreams are funny," said Ruth Ann. "Not funny ha-ha. Funny weird. Like you."

"What do you mean by that?"

"Come here and I'll show you."

"What's this?"

"Your acceptance into college," said Clay's mother. His father was standing there beside her. It was like a family meeting.

"Gideon? Where's that? I never heard of it. I never applied."

"You never applied anywhere. I called Vanderbilt and checked."

"They must have lost the application."

Lou Emma Bewley of Calhoun, Kentucky, granddaughter of

the Confederate lieutenant governor who had never officially served because the state had never successfully seceded, fished a bent Kent from her bathrobe and lit it with a TVA Zippo, a gift from her husband, who was already on his way back to the garage to listen on his shortwave radio for a signal that never came.

"They don't lose applications."

"Sure they do. They might, anyway."

"Harl had more sense than you. At least he's doing something somewhere."

"Let me have one of those."

"My name is Jimmy, I'll take what you gimme. Here. I talked to Mrs. Brodie, your long-suffering English teacher. The one who gave you an A even though you never completed the assignment she gave you on that writer Walden."

"*Walden* is the name of the book."

"Which you never bothered to read."

"I read it, I just never finished the paper," Clay said. Roads had made him read the book. Thoreau was full of pronouncements, like Roads.

"The point is, A, you are a Bewley, and B, you are going to college. You are not going to hang around Owensboro and work in your uncle's shop and marry some trashy tramp. Mrs. Brodie pulled a string or two. She went to Gideon. She's also a Yankee, you know."

"Also?"

"You need a haircut."

"I knew it all along," said Ruth Ann. "You don't belong here."

They were sitting on the hood, waiting for the ghost. Old No Show.

FOUR

THE BUILDINGS WERE REPRODUCTIONS: IMITATIONS FROM ANCIENT universities, down to the gargoyles, convincing until you saw the cornfields stretching off into the distance, as square as new pages. If it had been tobacco and beans, Clay thought, it would have been Owensboro.

But it wasn't. It was almost Minnesota.

Gideon students were the brightest in the Midwest, with a smattering of talent from the Northeast, the ones who didn't get into Swarthmore or Dartmouth. This meant not that they would be burning to discuss jazz piano, beat poetry, and the size of the Universe—as Clay had anticipated, had hoped—but rather that they were intent on getting into the maximum med or law school with a minimum of B's on their records.

It was a drag.

Clay had been there for a week and hadn't made a single friend. His roommate was a Kingston Trio enthusiast.

And then, there they were. Crossing the campus on a diagonal, a few yards ahead of him. Pretending not to, he fell in behind.

Two guys—boys? men?—with hair longer than Clay's, one with sideburns, the other with thick intellectual glasses like Buddy Holly or Allen Ginsberg. The third was a girl with long straight hair almost hiding a tiny face, wearing a filmy skirt and cowboy boots.

Clay followed in tennis shoes and the weird corduroy sport coat he had found at a yard sale looking sufficiently beat. No socks. The taller of the two guys was carrying record albums. Mulligan? Monk? Mingus? One was dark blue, so Clay began whistling the head from Coltrane's first album for Blue Note as a leader, *Blue Train* (four stars, *DownBeat*).

"Hey, man. Isn't that Coltrane?"

"Why, yeah," as a matter of fact it was, and by the time they reached the Student Union they were four, the only exemplars of their strange new race on campus, and by the end of the day they were more than friends. Ira was a Jew from the Bronx with a straight-A average from Bronx Science and no more interest in science, he said, than science had in him. Mark was from Rochester, where his father was a rabbi. Lena, from Long Island, called herself a JAP in some sort of joke that Clay didn't get until years later. They were all four, even though they never would have admitted it, in love with Ira: even Ira himself, who towered over them all with his film-star jaw, perfectly unruly hair, and radio voice. He even already had his own show on the campus station. "Blue Train" was his theme.

"Kentucky," Ira said. "*Don't get above your raisin'.* You dig Flatt and Scruggs?"

"Of course," said Clay, though he didn't. "Marty Robbins too."

"Who's Marty Robbins?"

Ira played blues on a gutstring acoustic with a cigarette tucked under the tuners and wore chambray shirts like a Daviess County bean and tobacco farmer—and that was now the style. The Beats were over. The kids from New York, the hip ones, dressed like kids from County High, only with longer hair and softer, sharper Jewish eyes.

I saw Louise Brodie at Winn-Dixie and she said the snow stays on the ground all winter at Gideon and once they saw the aurora borealis. That was rare though. I mailed the coat and shoes you left. "My name is Jimmy, I'll take what you gimme."

Φ

"Dig," said Ira. It was a low, blue sound, like nothing Clay had ever heard.

"Clifford Brown?" Clay had learned from Roads to listen, to pay close attention. It was a strange sound, cold and aloof.

"Miles Davis," said Ira. He had only made two albums but Ira had them both. "He was killed in a car wreck. If he had lived, he might have been even greater than Clifford. He might have been the man."

"I can dig it," said Clay, and so he did.

Sociology was about biology. Biology was about society. History was about politics. Physics was about the Universe. Art history was about form, which was a function of history, not to mention religion.

"Form follows function," Dr. Winters said, "and the function of Art is to open doors. Even the doors the powers-that-be want closed. Especially those doors."

To demonstrate that he had been paying close attention, Clay stationed himself in the hallway the next morning and opened the door for Dr. Winters with a flourish.

"I've seen you fellows around," he said. Clay was letting his hair grow. It was almost as long as Ira's. "You are an artist, I presume."

"A poet," said Clay.

"Remains to be seen. I see you've got the flourish down."

Your father has a new radio. I call it his calliope. When I was a little girl a steamboat came every spring, a showboat with minstrel shows and barbershop quartets, cotton candy and ice cream. The calliope was a kind of steam organ. You could hear it miles away, long before you saw the boat coming around the bend. By the time it got there, all the kids in Calhoun were down at the landing, and the grown-ups weren't far behind, putting things away, locking up the cows, putting the pies on the windowsill.

φ

"Cool," said Ira. "*Steamboat comin' 'round the bend.* I never knew what a calliope was. Your mother writes every week?"

"She's lonely," said Clay.

He folded his mother's letter and put it away. He kept them all in a blue folder with his poems.

"Like that," said Lena.

They were in Clay's room, in Garon Hall. She was standing by the bed in just her underpants; her breasts were small, like Ruth Ann's. She placed Clay's hand between her legs. It was after eleven thirty; she had to be back in the women's dorm, Clarendon Hall, in twenty minutes.

"Like that," she said. "Yes." Then she started to laugh. Then she started to cry.

Jews stick together. Southerners, Clay learned, don't. The only other Southerner at the school was, like Clay, from the Border: Cape Girardeau, Missouri, a little town a hundred miles south of St. Louis, just above the bootheel.

Cape was a senior, with little to say to freshmen. He edited the campus literary magazine, *Prairie Voices*, from his room in Wyatt Hall, which he hardly ever left.

Clay stuck his poems under his door. He signed them, "A fellow Southerner."

Three days later, Cape laid them on the table at the Student Union, then walked out without a word. He always wore a suit and tie. They were rejected, with a note: "It doesn't matter where you're from. What matters is where you are at."

"There's one scary dude," said Ira, admiringly.

NUCLEAR WINTER, said Ira's sign. Clay's was a line from a poem: AFTER THE FIRST DEATH, THERE IS NO OTHER. Lena's said, HANDS OFF CUBA. Mark didn't carry one.

They were protesting the Cuban missile crisis. There were only four of them. They walked in a little circle in front of the Student Union. It was starting to rain.

"Go back to Russia," said a student passing by.

"You wish," said Lena. Her uncle was one of the founders of the Fair Play for Cuba Committee. The demo, as she called it, was her idea.

"Go back to Russia," said a passing football player. Mark looked embarrassed.

"Fuck you," said Ira. "Fuck the pink pig you rode in on."

They marched for half an hour exactly and then stacked their signs outside the Student Union. While they were inside someone pissed on them.

"Yours didn't make sense anyway," said Lena. "If after the first death there is no other, then why bother?"

"It's from Dylan Thomas," Ira explained.

Junior is in North Carolina, at Fort Bragg. He is now a commissioned Second Lieutenant, whatever that means. And Ham is as proud as a dog with a bone. Your father is as ever.

Lena was Ira's girl first. Then she was Clay's. Then she wasn't anymore. "What's the problem?" Clay asked.

"You're always in a hurry to get back to the Student Union," she said.

"Together. With my girl."

"I'm my own girl," she said. "You're all your own guys, aren't you?"

One night the door of Clay's room clicked open. He was in bed, reading. It was after eleven, but only a little. Had Lena reconsidered?

She hadn't. It was the football team, six of them. They pushed open the door and three of them held Clay down while the other three cut his hair with electric clippers, taking turns. They didn't even bother to wear masks.

The professors were outraged. Some of the students too. "Who did it?" the dean asked.

"I don't know," said Clay. "They all wore masks." He was a celebrity. The last thing he wanted was revenge. Instead of shaving his head he wore the clumps and streaks like a badge of honor.

"Where are we going?" Clay asked.

"Cape's room," Ira said.

Clay was impressed. That was by invitation only. In his room, receiving guests, Cape wore a dressing gown.

"So they struck," he said. "They've been muttering for months."

Clay shrugged. Cape poured three drinks, from a decanter. The glasses said Old Forester.

"This place is awash in ignorance," said Cape. "Your mangy dog look is a rebuke to them."

"*The worst are full of passionate intensity,*" said Ira, brushing his chestnut locks out of his eyes with two fingers.

"I hear you're a Southerner," said Cape.

"Western Kentucky. Calhoun." That sounded better than Owensboro.

"Never mind where," said Cape. "The South is a state of mind. I have something for you."

He opened a cedar box. Inside were two cap and ball dueling pistols with ivory grips.

"You're kidding," said Clay.

"Not at all. One's for you too, Ira. Keep it by your bed."

"Cool," said Ira. "Is it loaded?"

"Cap only, no ball. Just cock it. The click will be enough for our local clowns."

Cape handed them each a pistol, butt first, then closed the

box, crossed the room, opened the door. The interview was over.

"I hear you're a poet," he said as they were leaving.

The click was enough.

Two nights later, just after midnight, Ira's door clicked open.

Click.

And clicked shut.

Even Jews go home for Christmas.

There were no trains to Kentucky so Clay had to take a bus. His hair had grown out and he had smoothed it into a burr. It was shorter than when he had left and his mother thought that was a "good sign." Bobby Lee had stayed at UK for an extra credit paper. Clay had two papers overdue already, but he had left his books at school. On Tuesdays and Thursdays Ruth Ann got off work at ten. He picked her up at The Southern Kitchen and they parked at Old No Show's.

"What happened to your hair?" she asked. "When you left you were letting it grow."

He told her. "The place is awash in ignorance," he said.

"Maybe you don't belong there either," she said.

Christmas Day was warm. Clay's father was coughing a lot. He could hear him in the garage.

On the *Today* show it was snowing in New York. On New Year's Eve he stayed home. On New Year's Day he went to the 4-Way and leafed through the metal pages of the jukebox.

THAT'LL BE THE DAY

BORN TO BE WITH YOU

WHAT'D I SAY?

HELLO WALLS

BYE BYE LOVE

"Having trouble making up your mind?" a trucker down the counter asked.

φ

Almost Minnesota was deep in snow. Clay saw his name in print for the first time. Cape had published four of his poems in *Prairie Voices*. His hair was almost long again and people knew who he was. That was a new feeling.

Ira was used to it. He sang delta blues in the Student Union lounge and got all A's. He was especially good in drama. Dr. Sloane cast him in all the plays. He usually got the lead. "He says I'm a natural," Ira said.

"A natural show-off," said Lena.

They were back together.

Junior is in Germany. He says it's just like a foreign country. That's a joke. He writes to me as well as his father. Imagine that.

"What's this?"

"Biology," said Ira. "The doors of perception." It was peyote, little cactus buds, scattered in a box like little green cupcakes. Ira had ordered them from Texas and they had arrived in the mail.

WAKE ME, they said, rattling in the box like little round sleeping lizards. EAT ME.

That night, for the first time, they saw the northern lights. They ran outside and ran circles in the snow. They walked Lena to her dorm in circles. The girls had Hours. The boys didn't. Mark got cold and went to bed. Ira and Clay lay outside on cardboard and studied the lights in the sky.

They had been reading *Don Quixote*, the Putnam translation. It was required and now Clay knew why: there were windmills everywhere.

It was a postcard, forwarded from Owensboro. A picture of a jackalope, with snow-covered mountains in the background.

"BEAUTY IS BEAUTY, TRUTH TRUTH" was scrawled on the back.

"Is that from your mother as well?" asked Ira.

Clay told him about Roads. "He's the reason I'm here," he said. "In a weird sort of way."

"Cool. He's your calliope."

"What do you mean?"

"*Steamboat comin' 'round the bend.*"

"It was supposed to be a yawl," Clay said.

I could have gone to college but got married instead. Don't make the mistake I made. There, I said it. Your father would agree.

Things were changing. The snow was melting. There was plenty of dex for the tests and the papers, but Clay had a hard time getting up for the classes in between. Even literature. Clay never dreamed he could hate spring so.

"This is such bullshit," he said.

"What is?" They were at the Student Union, in their usual booth.

"All this," said Clay. "Classes. Exams. Papers nobody ever reads."

"The ivory tower," said Ira.

"Exactly," said Clay. "The Little College on the Prairie. Studying science instead of doing it. Studying literature instead of writing it. Studying history instead of making it."

"You're just mad because Winters gave you a C," Lena said.

Clay had only written three words in his exam booklet: "Form follows function."

"I thought he would dig it," he said.

There was a knock at the door.

Clay sat up in bed and reached for Cape's pistol. This was the vow they had made: never to be taken again.

"Come in," he said. The door opened and he cocked the pistol with a loud *click*.

Two heads appeared anyway. Long hair, and one with a scraggly beard. "Clayton Bewley Bauer?"

Clay nodded.

"The poet?" asked the one with the beard. "*Prairie Voices?*"

Clay nodded again. He lowered the hammer and put the gun away.

"Name's Ernest, and this is Paul." They had read his poems in New York and driven halfway across the country to meet him.

"You read my poems in *Prairie Voices* in New York?" It seemed like a dream as the two crowded into the room, hairy, disheveled, electric with energy and excitement.

"It's on all the newsstands in the Village," they explained. "So new and so original, we had to meet you. Do you have any other poems?"

"Well, I've been working on some stuff . . ."

"Could you, would you, read them to us? We're on our way to San Francisco, we're poets ourselves, and . . ."

And it was almost midnight but Art was all about opening doors, and here they were swinging wide. It was indeed like a dream.

Clay gathered up his blue folder and followed them downstairs, through the empty lounge, to the front steps.

"Outside," insisted Ernest (the bearded one). "Under the stars. Plus, we have a bottle of wine."

Clay read the four poems from *Prairie Voices*, and his listeners snapped their fingers instead of applauding so as not to wake the sleeping students.

"Here's a new I've been working on," Clay said. "Inspired by my friend Ira."

"Ira!? A nice Jewish boy?"

"Not exactly," said Clay. "A blues singer."

"Another troubadour!" said Ernest. "Perhaps we should wake him."

"It's way too late," said Clay, regretting that he had changed the subject from his poems. "It's called 'Windmills' . . ."

He began to read, and then he heard a strange, familiar sound: Ira's voice, matching his, word for word. Two long-haired heads stuck up from the shrubbery: Ira and Mark. They were both laughing.

It was all a joke. Ernest and Paul were high school friends of Ira's, and they had stopped by to visit him on their way back to New York from Minneapolis. Ira had put them up to it. Clay didn't mind. "Pass the wine," he said, slipping his poems back into the folder.

"*A loaf of bread, a jug of wine, and* . . . here you go," said Ira, passing a skinny joint to Clay who had never tried it before, who was the only one not stoned. It was just as he thought, had expected, had hoped it might be. "It's all windmills," he said. And he read the poem anyway. And even finished the wine.

"Hear that?" Ira said. It wasn't exactly a question.

They were sitting outside under the Promise Tree, the big poplar on the quad where, it was rumored, boys gave rings to girls. It was after midnight. They had just finished Ira's radio show, signing off with the tragical, almost legendary Miles. They were smoking a joint.

"Hear what?"

"Calliope, man," said Ira. "Can't you hear it?"

"*Steamboat comin' 'round the bend.*"

"Believe it, man. And all we have to do it get on."

"I can hear it," Clay croaked, holding his breath the way Ira had showed him.

In this universe the night was falling.

Spring was mud and wind. The prairie grasses were showing through it, waving in it. It was howling across the flat roof of the Student Union and tracking up the floor.

"There's a world waiting out there," said Clay, knocking the mud off his shoes. "A world where real things happen to real people."

He slipped into the booth with Ira and Lena, the wind singing through his veins.

"I do believe we've heard this song," said Ira.

"I mean it. If I had twenty bucks, I would hit the road, stick out my thumb, go where the wind takes me."

A hand appeared over the back of the booth. Dropped a twenty on the table. It fluttered down in slow motion like a falling leaf.

Hesitating for only a moment, Clay picked it up. "It's a sign," he said.

The football players in the booth behind just laughed.

"You're sure," said Ira. He looked dismayed. "You're sure you want to do this?"

"I have to," said Clay. If the moment came and you didn't seize it, what did that say about you? His clothes were in an old guitar case, along with his copy of *The New American Poets*. Mark had added an Irish sweater actually from Ireland.

"We'll miss you," said Lena. It even sounded true. They were at the edge of the campus, where the highway swooped by, barely brushing the lawn like a long white wing.

"I'll stay in touch," said Clay.

All the familiar words were sounding weird this afternoon, like a crow's soft cry.

"Calliope," said Ira, giving Clay an awkward hug. "Listen for it. I'll be on the boat, looking for you."

That meant he would be first but Clay didn't mind. Ira was writing a phone number on a twenty-dollar bill, just above the point of the pyramid.

"Here." It was Ernest's in New York.

New York!

Clay stuck out his thumb. A car sped by, a '58 Chevy two-door. Then a Dodge; then a pickup, hay in the back. Then a Buick stopped.

He ran for it, careful not to look back.

FIVE

"IT'S ME, MOTHER. I—"

"You what?"

"I dropped out of school."

"You what?"

"I'm somewhere in Indiana. I'll call you when I get to New York."

"You what? Wait till your father hears about this."

"Gotta go. There's my ride."

The part about the ride, he was making up. The rides were few and far between. Then he got a ride all the way to Pittsburgh with a Mexican from Los Angeles who had been promised a job in a steel mill. His name was Claudio and he was traveling alone. His wife's name was Felicidad and he had two sons, Rubio and Julio, ages eleven and nine, both good boys. He drove a '59 Chevy Biscayne and kept an S&W .38 special in the glove compartment.

In Pittsburgh Clay caught a freight all the way into the Newark yards, and a bus across the unexpectedly reedy swamps into New York City. That was in the morning, just after rush hour. He was feeling proud of himself for hopping a freight when he arrived at the Port Authority bus station. His socks were filled with cinders. His guitar case suitcase was tied shut with string.

New York! He hesitated in the doorway on Eighth Avenue, looking out at the street, jammed with cabs and jammed with people, all rushing uptown. He was just about to dive in when a young man in a suit brushed past him with a sneer. "Hello, clowns."

Clowns? *How did he know that we were so many?*

ɸ

"The poet? Come on then. In."

Ernest lived in a fourth-floor walk-up on the Lower East Side. He didn't seem very excited to hear from Clay, and Clay soon discovered why.

Ernest was a rich kid working at being poor. He was busy becoming a junkie. He unrolled a smelly pallet for Clay in one corner and then paid no attention to him at all. Puerto Ricans came and went, all with needles and money. Ernest had even shaved off his beard.

"How's Ira? Tell him I said hello."

"When?"

"When you go back."

"I'm not going back. I'm here to stay."

"Here?" Ernest looked doubtful.

Clay sat outside on the fire escape when it was hot, and it was hot a lot. Beer was fifty cents a quart at the bodega downstairs. Rheingold.

The Puerto Ricans came and went, talking but not of Michelangelo. Ernest knew a little Spanish. They were all into needles.

It was better on the fire escape.

After a few days Ernest was in a better mood. He washed his face in the sink. "I need a walk," he said.

Clay followed him to Washington Square. The Puerto Ricans gave way to beatniks; Clay had never seen so many. He tried to act cool, nodding at a few. Ernest seemed to be in a hurry. They passed though the park and knocked on the door of a townhouse on Twelfth Street, just off Fifth Avenue.

"I want you to meet my cousin," he said. "Her name is Mary Claire but we call her EmCee."

The door swung open and so did another door in Clay's life, or so it seemed to him, not only that day but for a long time afterward. She had long straight blond hair and narrow shoulders and she was holding a paperback book in one hand.

Some girls look good in glasses.

She looked Ernest up and down. "What are you now, Puerto Rican?" she asked scornfully. He was wearing one of his tropical shirts.

"I see you're still a racist," he said.

"I'm not one because you are not a Puerto Rican," she said. "You are not even a black sheep. Just gray."

"Any mail for me?" said Ernest. He brushed past her, into the house.

Clay followed, confused, nervous with delight. The house was filled with books. Her nipples showed through her tank top but she didn't seem to mind.

"This is a friend of Ira's, from Minnesota. You remember Ira?"

"Not actually Minnesota," said Clay. "I'm—"

"Of course I remember Ira," she said. "You met Ira through me, remember?"

"Clay," said Clay. She sailed her book onto a sofa, expertly, and they shook hands. He tried to remember if he had ever shaken hands with a girl before. It didn't seem so. Hers was small and cool.

"EmCee," she said. She examined him over her glasses, as purposeful as a bird. "Come on in, since you are already in. You two want a beer?"

"Sure," said Clay.

"Clay here is a poet," said Ernest. "I thought you might like to meet him. Maybe he'll read you some poems."

Clay decided he didn't like Ernest after all. Neither, apparently, did EmCee. They sat in the back, in the garden, and talked while Ernest called his mother.

"He's asking for money," said EmCee. "He's always hard up."

The back of the house was all glass, and they could see Ernest on the phone, under towers of books.

"You're not really a serious associate of my cousin's, I hope."

"A friend of a friend," said Clay, feeling suddenly ungrateful.

"This is my first time in New York and he's been pretty helpful to me."

"I'll bet." She smiled. "Want another beer?"

"Sure," said Clay. It was a brand he'd never seen before. She had barely touched her own.

He watched her through the glass as she went into the kitchen, ignoring Ernest on the phone. She was almost tall, in loose long slacks. She was pulling on a T-shirt, coming back outside.

"Where's Black Island?" he asked.

"Around," she said, looking down at her T-shirt. "Off the coast. New England. Where are you from, anyway?"

"Kentucky. Western Kentucky, actually."

"Actually again," she said. "Amazing. And what do you want to see while you are in New York?"

"Oh, I'm here to stay. I want to see everything. The Blue Note, the White Horse. You name it."

"Cool," she said. "That could be arranged."

Ernest knocked on the window and waved good-bye. EmCee dismissed him with a wave, like shooing a fly. "My cousin," she said, "is a pain. Looks like you've been dumped."

"I don't mind."

"Drink up. I'll take you to the White Horse."

There were trees on the way. It was a different New York.

The White Horse was a grubby, magical little bar that smelled of poetry and beer, sawdust and Welsh winters. John Coltrane on the jukebox and no Marty Robbins. After a beer or two, Clay recited a poem from memory and EmCee seemed studiously impressed. She was a junior at Barnard, studying anthropology and political science and staying at her father's place on weekends while he was out of town.

"He's out of town a lot," she said. "Especially since my mother died."

"I'm sorry." She nodded. "What does he do?"

"This and that." She said his name and Clay didn't recognize it, but recognized that he should. "He teaches at Columbia. Writes for *The Nation*. Right now he's advising the president."

"Cool," said Clay. "Have you met him?"

"My dad? I'm kidding. You mean the president. Of course not. I am kept safely out of the way. Like Ernest. He works at being the black sheep—it comes to me more easily."

"I see." He kissed her and she let him. The afternoon light was fading. In the White Horse, the bottles and the mirrors gleamed. Behind the bar there were six kinds of Scotch and no bourbon. Clay got two more beers from the bar, and in the mirror he saw behind him the little table between the jukebox and the dirty window, where she waited for him, in her black T-shirt, looking out over the avenue.

He raised a glass to himself in the mirror. "Hello, clowns."

"What's that?"

"Oh, nothing. An incantation."

"I like that." They walked back together, hand in hand. He was explaining his theory of poetry, how it was found and not made, or something like that. She was amused by his accent. "You can come in if you like," she said. "You look like you could use a shower."

"There's no shower at Ernest's," Clay said. "Just a tub in the kitchen."

"He's all style," EmCee said. "There's a shower down the hall on the right. First door."

Indeed. A stack of books by the toilet. Clay looked through them, recognizing none, then undressed and got in. It had a glass door instead of a curtain. The hot water felt good. The glass door slid open.

"I could use a shower too," she said.

SIX

EmCee was at Barnard all week; Clay only saw her on weekends when he lifted the big brass knocker on the townhouse door,
and lifted, with her kind permission, her little knockers under her
T-shirt, friendly in his palms. At first they made love, then talked;
then later, talked and made love. The Puerto Ricans at Ernest's
called him Tex, but EmCee never made fun of his accent, so he
quit worrying about it. "It's different," she said.

It had never been different before.

It was like an affair except there was no home to go home to.
Ernest's was an emptiness, a floor and a refrigerator. There wasn't
even a dresser; Clay stacked his two shirts on the floor by his mattress. Barnard was on the Upper West Side, a long ride on the subway. Clay went up there once just to check it out. The buildings
were like mountains with Broadway slicing through them like the
Ohio, complete with islands. He knew better than to go by the
dorm and look her up. He had his place in her life, and he was
happy with it, for now.

It was a good feeling. He had never been patient before.

*Your father got your postcard. If you had a radio you could
talk to him. I suppose I could too.*

Poems were all over in New York, easy to find but hard to
catch, like pigeons. So Clay polished his old ones, lying flat on
Ernest's sun-washed (only till noon) and stained wood floor. He
wished he had a typewriter. On Sundays, and Saturdays sometimes, he lifted the brass knocker on Twelfth Street and they spent

the day together, in and out of bed, in and out of the garden, in and out of the Village streets.

He knew almost nothing about her, except that she was all books and money and glamour and beautiful besides, and that she wanted to be with him once a week, and she knew even less about him. He started once to tell her about Owensboro, and Harl and the DDI, and Roads and the 4-Way, and even Ruth Ann, until she cut him off with a yawn. "It doesn't matter where you're from," she said. "What matters is where you're at."

"I've heard that before," he said. "Tell me about Black Island." he said. She wore that shirt a lot.

"It's a joke," she said. "A reject from a shop where Lowell used to work." Lowell? "My best friend. He did it on purpose and got fired, but we got to keep the shirts. It's supposed to say *Block* Island."

"Where's that?"

She rolled her eyes and looked at him more closely. "You really don't know, do you? You've heard of New England, I hope. I'll take you there someday."

Clay liked that. *Someday*.

He got a job. Fry cook, a poet's gig, at the Café Wha on Mac-Dougal Street, crowded with tourists, of which he was no longer one. Weeknights, which left his days and weekends free, for Poetry and Enchantment, in that order. Ernest was gone a lot and that was good. He had moved into sales.

I saw your girlfriend at the Southern Kitchen the other day, ringing me up. She asked about you. I didn't know what to tell her so I didn't tell her anything.

There she was, EmCee. Easy to spot in the maniacally, militantly, aggressively colorful crowd; her in her black jeans and black Black Island T-shirt.

With her own small crowd.

"Rebecca, Ginsburg, this is Clay. He's here from Tennessee."

"Kentucky."

"Exactly."

Clay had never met her friends before. He studied them for clues. Rebecca was plump with big tits like Libby and wild curly hair, dressed in a pants suit. Ginsburg ("the Other Ginsburg," he pointed out) wore combat boots and an Army jacket, with a top hat as his concession to the day.

Becca, as she insisted she be called, was at Sarah Lawrence; Ginsburg was at Columbia, which was across the street from Barnard; and Clay was a dropout from Gideon, which was—

"Where's that?" asked Becca.

"Exactly." Clay was learning.

Ginsberg, Allen, the poet—the Real Ginsberg—led the parade in a suit and tie, an electric-yellow suit and yellow plastic tie. A clutch of good-looking boys beside and behind him carried the yellow submarine on their broad shoulders.

THE WAR IS OVER, read EmCee's sign. "Let's see yours," she asked.

Clay's read, AFTER THE FIRST DEATH, THERE IS NO OTHER.

"That makes no sense," said the Other Ginsburg.

"That's the whole point," said Becca. "That's the spirit of the thing."

"It's Dylan Thomas," said EmCee. "You leave my boy alone." She took his hand and they fell into the march.

Clay was totally into the spirit of the thing, all top hats and tambourines. It had been planned in imitation of the West Coast and its Be-Ins, where, it seemed, all cool ideas came from these days. It had expanded to be an antiwar march, and then another war had intervened, directing the march to the United Nations, where the ignominious conclusion to Israel's disastrous Eight-Day War was being negotiated. The sudden burst of hostilities in the Middle East had ended with the Soviet Union's intervention and requirement that Israel pull back to its borders. The US had rattled a saber or two but gone along.

Becca took his other hand. "Is that a dunce cap?" she asked. It was a wizard hat but Clay got rid of it, setting it up at the corner of Forty-second and Fifth like a traffic cone.

"Follow the sub," said the Other Ginsburg. It bobbed above the crowd far ahead.

At the UN there were police, looking cruel and apprehensive. On one side, Jews in their funny little hats leaned into blue barricades, shouting their defiance of the UN, which had ordered Israel back into its borders. On the other, a scattering of Arabs and Palestinians waved hand-lettered, badly spelled signs: ZIONISM IS RACEISM.

The march slowed in the center of the street, the yellow submarine wavering like a compass needle in an electrical storm, now right, now left. The tambourines fell silent. Clay was glad he'd dumped the hat.

Then the sub straightened up and led the marchers past the cops, down the street, away from the UN. Clay was about to follow the ringing tambourines when EmCee's hand pulled him back. She and Becca were following the Other Ginsburg to the sidewalk, where he had spotted friends from Columbia.

They ducked under the barricade and stood with the Jews. Ginsburg was whispering into a shouter's ear. Someone handed Becca a sign: THIS LAND IS OUR LAND TOO. "Woody Guthrie," said Clay. Across the street some of the signs were in Arabic; others were upside down.

"Ginsburg's grandmother lives in Tel Aviv," Becca shouted in Clay's ear.

He grimaced; it hurt. "Which one?"

"Which granny?"

"Which Ginsburg?"

Just then a small Black coterie joined the Arabs across the street. Four men and two women in black leather jackets and berets, standing at attention, holding a banner: POWER TO THE PEOPLE.

"The Black Panthers," said the Other Ginsburg. Clay nodded. He had seen them on the tiny TV at Ernest's. "Black Jew haters!" a shouter shouted.

Clay rolled up his cardboard sign. "Aren't we on the wrong side?" he asked no one in particular.

Your cousin Junior is on his way to Vietnam. Ham says he is about to make Captain. Your pal Bobby Lee is on his way to Vanderbilt according to his mother. And you?

One Sunday morning, EmCee opened the door without asking him in. "My father's home," she said. "Crisis."

Clay wandered back to Washington Square and sat on the edge of the fountain for a while. He bought a hot dog. He bought a paperback off the sidewalk and read all afternoon. It was Heinlein's muddled masterpiece, *Stranger in a Strange Land.*

"Home so early?" said Ernest, when Clay got back to Avenue B. He was boiling something in a spoon with a match. "EmCee find another guy?"

"No," said Clay. *Not that it's any of your fucking business.*

"She will."

The kids had opened a fire hydrant down on the street. They were using a beer can as a nozzle to spray the passing cars. Clay watched them from the fire escape while he worked on his poems. They could always use improving.

Someday came.

The Midwest was green and black, the colors of new corn and good dirt. The South was yellow-green, the color of tobacco and clay. New York was red and black, brick and asphalt, the steel mostly hidden. But New England—

New England was gray. A hundred shades of gray. Clay first saw it from the ferry with EmCee at his side, leaning against the rail, Zelda to his Scott, in her late mother's rabbit coat even though it was almost summer.

Block Island sketched itself in through the mist, all in pencil: all sea and sand and fog and long low cliffs, all hundred shades of gray. Even the sunlight was gray. The air was shivery, and the salt smell was harsh, like the world had just been mopped clean.

It was perfect. Clay had never been to an island before. No one ever set foot on the little mud islands in the Ohio. He was truly elsewhere here.

Lowell was to meet them at the ferry. "He's been my friend forever," EmCee said. "He saved my life. If it weren't for him, I would have never survived high school. If it weren't for him, I would have been . . ."

"What?"

She shrugged. "My father's daughter? I have to warn you, he's gay."

It was Clay's turn to shrug. "I don't mind."

"That's his word for homos."

Lowell picked them up at the pier in an ancient jeep the faded uncolor of Clay's '49 Ford. He wore the same T-shirt: Black Island. He was as tall as EmCee, his shoulders as high and narrow. His hair was as long, and almost as blond, but tied back in a ponytail. They could have been sisters.

"How does one manage to get thrown out of Harvard?" she asked.

"With determination," he said. "Not to mention luck. So this is Clay." In fact he had only been suspended but he had no intention of going back. The jeep was so old it didn't have synchros but Lowell never missed a shift. They sped between stone walls the color of the island itself, which was no color at all.

They drove past a big stone house on a cliff overlooking Long Island Sound. It was closed up with shutters.

"Becca's house," said EmCee.

"Wow."

"Her dad's a big mobster."

"I thought he was a congressman."

Lowell laughed. His grandparents' house was smaller, shabbier, older, and filled with ancient books. "He's *a* Lowell," EmCee said while he fiddled with the locks. "One of *the* Lowells."

"The last but not least," said Lowell, who always overheard everything.

The long yard ended in a cliff of rubble, ancient glacial drift. They sat and watched the ancient sun go down, drinking gin with tonic and lime. The sand was soft but the grass was sharp. There was a single seal on the beach, far below, and then it was gone with the sun.

Lowell knew all the back roads. It only took an hour to tour the island. EmCee had begged off. They parked overlooking another cliff, another lonely seal. "EmCee says you're okay," said Lowell. "That means you are rather special. Do you understand that?"

"I think I do."

"I hope so. Do you mind if I kiss you?"

Clay tried to think of an answer, something cooler than no.

"Well, then, that's okay too," said Lowell, putting the jeep into gear. "No blame. I'm the queer one."

"He makes passes at all my boy friends," said EmCee later that night in one of the ancient bedrooms. "It's a test."

"Did I pass or fail?"

"Both. Come here."

"Steamboat coming round the bend." It was a postcard from Ira: a rocky beach in the foreground, a grand orange bridge in back. "Meanwhile, I'm in an acting group working on a whole new kind of theater."

Gideon was history. Lena was in medical school. Mark was in the Peace Corps. Ira was learning to play the calliope.

Clay wrote back: "I can hear it in New York." But he never sent the card. There was no return address on Ira's. Just San Francisco.

Uncle Ham has hired a new service manager. Remember Round Man? He was a year ahead of you, I think. His stepfather was from Calhoun. He ran the ferry before they built the bridge.

"Mr. Ginsberg."

It was the Real Ginsberg. Clay had almost bumped into him in the doorway of a deli on East Fourth. He was wearing a sport coat and tie, more like a businessman than a poet. Clay was heading "home" to Ernest's from work. It was raining, just a little, doubling all the streetlights.

"Hello?"

"You don't know me," said Clay. "I just wanted to thank you. For everything." He held out a hand, feeling foolish as he did. Did poets shake hands? He could imagine Roads's look of scorn.

"Certainly I know you, young man," said Allen Ginsberg. "And you are very welcome."

Then he placed a nickel in Clay's outstretched hand. IN GOD WE TRUST, it said.

They rode back and forth all night on the ferry till dawn came up like thunder out of Brooklyn across the bay. Clay stood behind EmCee at the rail, Scott to her Zelda, and put the ring into her hand inside the left pocket of her rabbit coat.

"What's this?"

"Just what it looks like." He had bought it on Canal Street for ten dollars. "A diamond as big as the Ritz."

"I can't wear this. I hope it's not real."

"It might be." Clay tried to sound not hurt. "You did men-

tion me as your boyfriend, on Block Island, remember? We were
talking about Lowell."

"I said *boy friend*, not *boyfriend*." But she did turn around to
kiss him. And she put the ring on her right hand. And left it there.

"Voilà," said EmCee. She showed Clay the leaflet that had
gotten her suspended from Barnard. It was a bad mimeo reproduction of the picture from the *Post* and the *Times* and the *Daily
News* of the B-52 that had been shot down over Hanoi.

"Ginsburg too," she said. "Remember Ginsburg?"

"The Other Ginsburg."

"He was already suspended from Columbia. It's an SDS design. We just adapted it."

It was a wing in a rice paddy, with peasants gathered around.
Underneath, in press type, it said, POWER TO THE PEOPLE.

"We ran off a thousand for the Panthers, and they gave us a
couple of hundred which we handed out in front of the school on
Broadway, until they arrested us."

"For leafleting?"

"For theft of services. Which the Dean filed as a complaint
after we gave her a leaflet. The paper and ink, I guess. Can you
believe that?"

"And she suspended you," said Clay.

"She didn't have to. The suspension is automatic when you
are arrested, until the charges are resolved. They love their procedures. I'm the one who handed it to her. She smiled like this
when she took it too."

EmCee smiled.

"So what now? Does your father know?"

"That's where you come in," EmCee said. "Fuck him. Fuck
her. Maybe we should think about getting a place together. You
could still get your mail at Ernest's. Are you up for that?"

SEVEN

Finding a place in New York City is impossible, almost. Unless you have connections.

Clay carried two Vuitton suitcases filled with books down narrow filthy stairs, into the subway at 116th. He carried them up the narrow filthy stairs at Spring Street station. EmCee followed with her folded clothes. "I think I'm going to like it here," she said. She had never been so far downtown before.

"It's a loft," she said as they climbed the stairs at 50 Grand Street. Five dark flights. "Lowell's cousin's place. Lowell has a key."

"And the cousin?"

"He lives in Morocco. Or somewhere like that. He's a painter. He just keeps his stuff here."

It was one large room with paint all over the floor. There was an oil heater in one corner and a mattress in another. A hot plate for a stove next to a tiny refrigerator. Clay opened it and shut it hurriedly. What might once have been a chicken lurked inside.

While EmCee unpacked, Clay looked through the paintings stacked against a wall. They were all huge and hugely colorful, paintings of boys, all nude.

"All boys," said Clay.

"Come here, boy," said EmCee. She was on the mattress, nude as a boy.

"Move over," said Lowell, moving in. Block Island was over and a promised job in Boston hadn't come through. "They could tell I was queer."

"You're not queer," said EmCee. "You're gay."

It was the new word.

"I like *queer* better," said Lowell. "Anybody can be gay. Even our hillbilly there, moping by the window."

"I'm not moping," said Clay. "I'm working on a poem."

"Let me see."

Clay handed him the folder. Lowell leafed through it and handed it back without a word. His stuff was neatly arranged in one corner. One suit, Brooks Brothers, and one book, *Opinions of Oliver Allston.*

"Wish we had a fireplace," EmCee said, hanging her rabbit coat on a nail. They sat in a circle on the floor. There were no chairs yet.

"We have something that burns brighter than that," said Lowell, holding out his hand. Nestled in his palm were three little off-white triangles, huddled together like tiny puppies. That was the first night they took acid.

"Look at this," said EmCee. She handed Clay the *Post.*

The Tet Offensive. "Cool," said Clay. Suddenly they were no longer feeling sorry for a victim. They were on the winning side. Was it possible? The US, which had once seemed so invincible, now seemed vincible.

"*Steamboat comin' 'round the bend,*" he said.

"What does that mean?"

"It's just an old Kentucky saying."

"Well, get serious. Here it says SDS ran off a recruiter in Madison. We could all be part of that."

"Of what?"

"Of a resistance. A serious resistance."

"We are resisting," said Clay. "I've been resisting all my life. You too. Isn't that why we're here?" He meant New York. Downtown.

"I mean for real," EmCee said. "I wish we had a phone." She laid a dollar on the counter. "Excuse me, miss, could you spare me some dimes?"

They were having breakfast at the Tunnel Diner on Sixth Avenue, near Canal.

"Sure thing, honey," said the waitress. "I'm all dimes."

Your father has a new radio. Doesn't seem to help. Dr. Keeley says it's depression, as if we didn't know that. May be hearing too. I can hear it squawk in here.

"Writing captions," said Lowell. He had gotten a job at *Vogue*, or *Vague*, as he called it. He wore his one suit every day.

He got EmCee one as a fashion assistant. He was a Lowell. It was part-time, but it involved a lot of unpaid standing around. She was paid in scarves, as far as Clay could tell. But somehow there was always just money enough. It helped that there was no rent to pay.

"The rich are not like you and me," Clay wrote to Bobby Lee, who was about to graduate early from UK. "They don't need money."

Bobby Lee never wrote back. Clay was starting to feel like his mother.

"I think they're very original," said Becca. She handed Clay back his blue folder. "The poems, I mean. I didn't read the letters." Whenever she was down in the city from Sarah Lawrence she stayed at 50 Grand.

"They're certainly that," said Lowell. "What's this?"

Something had rolled out of the folder. Becca picked it up.

"Allen Ginsberg gave me that," said Clay.

"The Real Ginsberg? A whole nickel?"

Clay told them the story.

"That's a lovely story," said Becca.

"Let me see," said Lowell. He put it into his pocket and then pulled three nickels out. He held them out in his hand.

"Don't be an asshole," said EmCee. She was rolling a joint. She kept starting over. Her joints were terrible.

"Let me do that," said Becca. Her joints were perfect. "You are an asshole, Lowell," she said, licking it. "That was a genuine keepsake."

Lowell was still holding out his hand but no longer grinning.

"No problem," said Clay, taking one of the nickels. He studied it studiously. "This is the one he gave me. It says, IN GOD WE TRUST."

"They all say that," complained EmCee.

"And what's wrong with that?" said Clay, pocketing it.

According to Ham, Junior is in Da Nang, which he calls Dang. Our delinquent friend Harl is also there, or so I hear, though I doubt they run into each other at the Officer's Club. As a matter of fact Harl's stepfather was arrested yesterday, having to do with marijuana, which has replaced moonshine, as no doubt you know.

Lowell was out prowling. He prowled a lot.

The empty loft felt open, receptive, welcoming, like an ear. Clay sat in the open window and watched the rain wash the street below. Cobblestones showed through the asphalt like half-buried memories of another, earlier New York, New York.

Becca had moved in after graduating from Sarah Lawrence. Now all four corners of the loft were filled. Clay rolled a joint and watched for EmCee coming home from the subway. She always walked fast, mistrusting the empty streets. There she was. She looked up and saw him in the window and waved.

There were windmills everywhere.

Becca had never taken acid before. Lowell made it an occasion. He had a way of making everything an occasion. There was even a cake, which they ate with their hands, all four of them: Becca, Clay, EmCee, and Lowell. It was like eating sparklers. EmCee was naked and that seemed appropriate. Lowell too, of course. Even Clay, almost. Becca kept on her panties and bra and that made her seem friendlier. She was smiling at Clay from the windowsill, with the water tanks behind her on the rooftop horizon, and he tried not to notice how big her breasts were. It was all about sparklers anyway. EmCee was smiling at Lowell. That seemed appropriate too.

"I dreamed I dropped acid," said EmCee, looking at Becca, "in my Maidenform bra."

Max's Kansas City, on Park Avenue, was where the fashion people went after their shoots and openings and parties. Clay found EmCee there with Lowell, in a booth filled with laughing people of all sexes.

Lowell and EmCee squeezed over to make room. Everyone else ignored Clay. He rolled a cigarette.

"Don't be a show off," said EmCee.

"They're fifty cents a pack," said Clay. "And unfortunately I'm a fry cook, not a fashion coordinator."

"You two stop it," said Lowell. He handed Clay a menu. "How about a steak? We're on the *Vague* tab."

"I'm not hungry."

"He's a fry cook," said EmCee.

"You two stop it," said Lowell. "Look who's here. Hi, Andy."

"Lowell," said Andy Warhol, looking down. He studied Clay. "Who are these people?"

Your father's cough has not improved. He will not talk to me about it so I have made him an appointment at the new clinic in Evansville through Dr. Keeley. There is nothing here.

φ

The restaurant business in Greenwich Village was nothing if not organized. A man in a brown suit came around once a month for an envelope filled with money. If he didn't get it, the Health Department shut you down.

One night Clay went to work at the Café Wha and found the patrons all leaving. Disappointed surly tourists, all wanting their cover charge ($5) back.

"No refunds," said Benny, at the door. "Come back tomorrow."

"We'll be in Indiana tomorrow," they complained. Or Ohio, or New Jersey.

"What's going on?" Clay asked, taking off his coat in the kitchen. He reached for his apron, but Benny snatched it and waved it at him like a cape at a bull. "No work tonight," he said. "Health Department shut us down."

"No!" Clay tried to hide his smile. He was sick of the Wha anyway.

"Don't worry, I'll straighten it out. Meanwhile everybody come back tomorrow. Business as usual."

"What about tonight?" asked once of the comics who performed for "the hat" and a sandwich. Clay always made him a huge one, too big to carry in one hand. His name was Richard, but Clay called him Dagwood.

"You heard me, Pryor, we're closed tonight," said Benny. "No show, no sandwich. No tickee, no shirtee."

Benny was the boss, a fat Italian from Staten Island with a ring on every finger who looked like he had never missed a meal. Dagwood, on the other hand, was skinny.

Clay loaded on the roast beef, then the cheese, then the lettuce, then more roast beef.

"I'm serious," said Benny. "No show, no sandwich. What the fuck are you doing, Bauer?"

Clay laid on another slice of rye, then some ham, then more cheese. "Tomato?"

"Sure thing," said Dagwood.

"What the fuck are you doing?" Bennie demanded.

"I'm quitting," said Clay, handing the comic the sandwich, then putting on his coat. "Can't you tell?"

It was a lovely spring night in the Village. Clay ran home to get EmCee, whistling all the way. They hardly ever spent an evening together. He thought about calling and then decided to surprise her.

And so he did.

"Clay? Is that you?" she called out as he opened the door. "Ira is here."

"Cool," he said. He thought she meant in town. Then he turned on the light and saw Ira on a mattress with EmCee. She had pulled the sheet up to cover her tiny, familiar, perfect breasts.

"Oh," he said.

Ira was already out of bed, pulling on his jeans. "I'm here with the Mime Troupe," he said. "We're playing Town Hall tomorrow night."

"Ira's an actor now," said EmCee.

"No shit," said Clay.

"Hey, man, wait up," Ira said, catching him on the stairs on the way down to Grand Street. He was carrying his shoes. "She told me you had an understanding. Really, she did."

"Then I guess we do," said Clay.

"I came by to see you," said Ira. "Let me put on my fucking shoes, okay? I'll buy you a beer."

"I'm not in the mood, man."

"So where you going?"

"For a walk."

"I'll walk with you. I'll buy you a beer. We got a lot to talk about. Not that. Everything. It's all happening, man. Everything we dreamed of."

"And much that we didn't."

"Don't be like that."

"Don't be like that," said EmCee when Clay got back, drunk.

"Like fucking what?"

"He was my first boyfriend," EmCee said. "We went to Dalton together." Dalton was an expensive private school on the Upper East Side.

"He saved your life," Clay guessed.

"He stuck up for me," she said. "There's a fondness there, still. Roll me a cigarette. He cleaned me out."

"He's good at that," said Clay.

"Don't look at me like that. It's not about him anyway, Clay. I am *not* your girlfriend."

"I'm not your boyfriend, either, I remember." She was still wearing the ring though. It was on her right hand, unnoticed except by him.

"Not like that. We are not a unit. Not a couple. Not in that same old way. Things are changing fast."

"Is that it?" Clay asked.

"If you're looking for a *girlfriend* I'm sure you can find one back in Owensville. If you want me, the way I am, here I am."

"Owensboro," he said. "Here."

"That's perfect," she said, carefully admiring and then lighting it. "How do you do it?"

"Do what?"

"Come here, damn it."

There were plenty of fry cook jobs in the Village but Clay had grown to hate the smell of food and the sound of folk music. He missed the auto shop smell of concrete, gasoline, chrome and steel and morning coffee. After a few hours of walking he got a job in a taxi garage on Second Avenue, Emily's Auto. There was no Emily, only an enormous Turk named Emil (pronounced "emmel") with a bad temper who put up with Clay "only and only" because he was fast. It was all just repeats of the same endless jobs: points, plugs and brakes, R&R, remove and replace. Engine work was done in another shop in Queens. Transmissions were rebuilt at a shop in Jersey—by elves, the rumor was. Occasionally an elf would be found hiding in a bell housing, and Clay would sneak him out to the street in his hat and let him go. It was a kind of solidarity.

Φ

"I'm just not in the mood," said EmCee.
"You're never in the mood."
"I'm thinking about other things."
"Like what?"
"Like the war."

EIGHT

SINCE THE THING WITH IRA, CLAY HAD HATED COMING HOME. HE found himself knocking at his own door before letting himself in.

"It's all right," said Lowell. "We're just finishing up, as they say."

He was pulling on his pants. His dangling cock looked oiled. His "friend" was also getting dressed: a three-piece suit, nice loafers, even a necktie. It took a while.

He was, it turned out, the editor of *South*, not of the Mason-Dixon line but of Houston Street; his mag was "the hip rage these days," said Lowell. "My friend Clay here, cleverly disguised as a mechanic, is actually an accomplished poet, published in *Plain-song*, right?"

"*Prairie Voices*."

"I'd be glad to take a look at your work," said the friend. "I can't promise anything of course."

"They're not quite ready."

"Sure they are," said Lowell.

"Isn't that your sailboat pal?" asked EmCee.

There he was, on page six of the *Village Voice*: NEW POETS FROM THE SOUTHWEST COMMUNES. Five of them, men and women in leather and odd hats, leaning against a diesel van with an all-seeing eye painted on the side. Roads was the one in the center, taller than them all, leaning over them like a sunflower in a soybean field. He had the same short beard he'd had the first time Clay had seen him, in an open door. "They're reading tonight at Judson Church," said EmCee. "I think you should go and surprise him. It's a fund-raiser for a geodesic commune. Or something."

"*We* should go."

"I have a shoot."

"I'll go with you," said Becca.

They were all ghastly except Roads. He didn't seem at all surprised to see Clay. "Just the man I was looking for," he said.

"Really?"

"I figured you would show up in Gotham sooner or later," Roads said, sitting on the stage, his long legs almost touching the floor. "You should have been reading with us. How goes the poem pursuit?"

"Still chasing them." *You're already talking like him.* "Finding them here and there. Where are you guys staying?"

"With you," said Roads.

Only three showed up at 50 Grand.

Cicero was a "really" a painter who spent his days scouting old friends and collecting money and promises from downtown galleries. Palomina, his "lady," sat on the floor and knitted and scowled. "I'm not really a poet," she said and Clay had to agree. "That was just a fund-raiser. I make jewelry in real life." Roads drank wine from a coffee cup and sat in the window looking out over West Broadway where their borrowed truck was parked, pleased with the surprising lack of crime.

Lowell was in Boston at a funeral. Becca ignored them. Clay waited on them. "What happened with the boat?" he asked casually over his shoulder while he was washing a cup in the sink, even though it had taken him all morning to get up the nerve.

"Boat?"

"You know, the sailboat. The yawl."

"There was no boat," said Roads. "It was a scam. I never really believed it. It was a foundation money hustle or something. Anyway . . ."

Anyway?

"The Southwest is where it's happening. We're building the new world high in the mountains, where the ancient ways still prevail."

"What are you going to do with the old world?" EmCee asked.

"It will do away with itself."

Surprisingly, to Clay at least, EmCee liked Roads. She liked what she called his audacity.

She also liked Cicero's photos. Drop City, where they all lived "with five or twenty others, depending," was a collection of colorful domes made of triangles cut from car tops, scattered like toys in a field in a highway near Almost New Mexico, Colorado. The people all wore funny clothes.

"We're building a new world," said Roads. "Bucky Fuller gave us five hundred dollars."

"It's oddly elegant," EmCee said. "We should do a shoot. I want you to come by *Vogue* and show my boss those pictures."

"Bingo," said Roads.

Lowell, back from Boston, took them to Max's to celebrate the idea. Clay came by after work. Even Andy stopped by their booth to say hello.

"You know you don't belong here," said Roads as they loaded their diesel van to depart for Almost New Mexico. The shoot idea hadn't worked out.

"Nevertheless," said Clay. "Here I am."

Led Zeppelin was already blasting on the state-of-the-art cassette player. Cicero was grinning, tying down the canvases he had reclaimed. The fuel tank was topped off with no. 2. Even without the shoot they had scored big in the big city.

"Take care of my boy," said Roads from behind the wheel. "Come and join us."

"I wouldn't be comfortable in Utopia," said EmCee, waving from the curb.

Roads laughed and started the engine.

"You were born in Utopia," he said. "The trick is to escape."

He then once again escaped.

"Now I get you at last," EmCee said to Clay. They went upstairs and made love. It was to be their next-to-last time.

Red flags everywhere. Horses too. They charged through the crowd, cops swinging clubs from their saddles, while the Weathermen threw ball bearings and marbles under their hooves.

"Who are these Weathermen?" Clay asked.

"We all are!" cried EmCee. She carried a pipe under her mother's rabbit coat. She pulled it out and smashed a window on Fifth Avenue. Then another.

"Run!" shouted someone. More horses.

Clay's feet kept heading for the sidewalks. He tried to pull EmCee with him but she kept pulling him back into the street.

Ira was in back in town, no longer with the San Francisco Mime Troupe. "I told you," he said. "*Steamboat comin' 'round the bend.*" He was with a group of black-clad hippies called The Caravan. They had a suite at the Plaza, paid for by a movie star.

"It's still theater," said Ira. "No stage."

"Shattering the proscenium," said Carolus. "The world is the stage." He was their leader. He was leaving for a meeting with Abbie Hoffman. Ira went along. Clay was not invited.

"It's bullshit," said Clay, after they had gone back to California.

"What is?" asked EmCee. They were alone in their loft, except for Lowell, who was watching *Star Trek* on a TV they had found on the street.

"Ira's idea that you can stay young forever. That life is play." He was still working at Emily's. He still hadn't heard back from *South*. "His calliope thing."

"What calliope thing?"

ɸ

There was a demonstration a week and EmCee went to every one. She was calling in sick a lot. Clay suspected she got checks from her father that no one ever saw.

"Hey, hey, LBJ, how many kids did you kill today?"

Clay tried to keep up with her but she ran too fast. She was running with the Other Ginsburg, who was running with a whole new gang.

He went home alone and watched *Star Trek* with Lowell until Becca came home and made them turn it off.

Can you believe what happened to Elvis? I know you don't care but millions do, and not all of them old ladies like me, either.

Lowell reached into his suit coat and pulled out a little heart-shaped box filled with triangular sky-colored pills. "Window-pane," he said.

"Goody," said EmCee.

They dropped it and hurried down the stairs, five short flights tonight, and hurried to West Broadway and raised their hands. It was like school; soon they were called on by a cab, which took them to Mulberry Street and a little Sicilian joint, Puglia's, the kind the Sicilians never ate at, where they nibbled at sheep's head while the acid flowed over them in waves.

"Isn't that Woody Allen?" Becca whispered. Indeed. There he was, staring into his spaghetti as if looking through seaweed for food. His girlfriend was talking to him. Here it came again, the acid, rising up in waves, and Clay was happily stuck in a tide pool, bowing politely to the other starfish while the seaweed fronds waved excitedly.

Starfish! This tide pool was the very center of the world, New York. "Right?" Clay asked, beaming at Lowell, who understood such things.

"So be it," said Lowell.

Woody Allen looked up and saw them all pretending he

wasn't there, and pretended they weren't, and they hailed a cab on Canal and rode it home like a yellow wave and watched from the roof of 50 Grand the sunrise painting the ancient cedar water tanks with light, as if to set them on fire, an arson star. And some cheered the tanks and some cheered the sun.

They were very young.

They were very merry.

Lowell was injured. A black eye, a gash in his scalp, and blood in his hair. He was limping up the last flight, pushing a man in a dress in front of him.

"This is Dove. Dove, meet Clay, the hillbilly poet." He pushed a young man through the door. He had a black eye also and his crinoline was stiff with drying blood. He was wearing a prom dress.

"A dove of war," said Dove, holding out one hand. "Rhymes with love." They were both drunk.

"He saved my life," said Lowell, who was already applying a wet paper towel to Dove's brow.

"I've heard that before," said Clay.

"Where the hell have you two been?" asked EmCee, applying a wet paper towel to Lowell's scalp.

"Stonewall," Lowell said. It was a bar in the Village where he often prowled; more often, EmCee and Clay both thought, than he let on. "We fought the law—"

"And the law won," Clay finished.

Lowell waved one hand like a semaphore. "No, no, no. We won."

Dove slept over. In the morning, there it was on the news, the boys picking up stones, and bottles too, and flinging them back at the cops, all those boys who threw like girls.

Except of course Lowell, who could drive a jeep without synchros. And throw.

φ

Dove moved in. He had been born in Tel Aviv but had moved to Queens to go to high school, and then to SVA, where he was in the process of flunking out. He showed up at the door with all his stuff in a cardboard box, plus the prom dress, which he wore as often as not, and even more often nothing at all.

"Lady Godiva," muttered EmCee, who didn't approve but didn't disapprove either. It was Lowell's pad, his family's anyway, and her mind seemed to be on other things. Ginsburg, late of Columbia, was around a lot. He and Lowell watched *Star Trek* together.

Dove in his prom dress gave the loft a certain classical air, almost like a ballet set. He even wore it to the demonstrations, tagging along with EmCee, while Clay stayed home with Lowell.

"Hey, hey, LBJ," Dove sang in the shower before prancing out, nude. The shower was a box beside the refrigerator, like a phone booth.

"What are you trying to do?" said Becca scornfully. "Hurt his feelings?" She was more practical, working with McCarthy.

"Desperately!"

"LBJ doesn't have any feelings," said Lowell. But apparently he did, for one night not long after, one warm and almost starry night in March, the perfect exemplar of the city's short, miraculous spring, when they were all five together on Bleecker Street, on their way to hear Lord Buckley at the Village Gate, the streets suddenly filled up with people, pouring out of the bars and delis and apartment buildings, whooping and hollering, horns blowing, lights flashing, even a ceremonial tambourine or two, celebrants dancing in the street, while the traffic crept carefully, almost politely around them.

LBJ had quit.

"Move over," said Ginsburg. It was nine, and his favorite show was on. Clay groaned and made room on the couch they had found on the street and hauled up the stairs, five flights.

Ginsburg was around a lot. Too much, it seemed to Clay.

"This is the wrong channel, man," Ginsburg said. "*Star Trek* is on."

"This is better," said Clay.

"*Star Trek*!" said Dove, squeezing in between them, prom dress and all. "I dig those crazy ears!"

"Don't be such a fairy," said Lowell, joining them.

"This is better," said Clay. "The real thing."

It was all in shades of gray like Block Island. Static, as Collins stepped out of the *Eagle*, onto the grainy surface of the moon, making what he called "one long step for humankind."

"Cool," said Clay.

"One more step for imperialism," said Ginsburg.

Your father is in the hospital, for observation, they say. Junior sent me a card from Australia but is on his way back to Dang, as he calls it. According to him, with Humphrey as president the war will never be won.

EmCee was in Albuquerque, on a shoot. She called collect. She had been promoted to associate fashion coordinator, but she still didn't have an expense account.

"You heard?"

"Of course," said Clay. Martin Luther King had just been shot, in Memphis. It was only five o'clock in Albuquerque.

"It's still light here," said EmCee. "God, I'm afraid of the dark."

"You mean riots?"

"No! Jesus. I mean in general, metaphorically. Is Lowell there?"

"He and Dove are off somewhere. Becca and I have been watching it all on TV. I miss you."

"Me too," she said. As he hung up, Clay wondered , what did that mean?

Meanwhile, night swept across America, East to West. There

were angry, pointless, self-destructive, redeeming uprisings in Detroit, Cleveland, Newark, everywhere but Memphis, where the reality lay too heavily to throw off sparks. Jesse Jackson, who had been wounded by the second shot when he had thrown himself in front of King, addressed the nation on TV to call for calm. "He stood for peace," he said. "Still does."

"He stood for more than peace," said Ginsburg, who showed up looking for EmCee and then stayed to roll a joint. Even Cronkite looked scared.

"White America's chickens are coming home to roost," said Malcolm X from Accra, in Africa, where he spoke at the grave of W. E. B. Du Bois. Denied a US passport, like Robeson, he had left to never, or so he said, return.

Humphrey was president, but it was only temporary. The election was coming up. Clay was still replacing brake shoes at Emily's. EmCee had finally gotten her expense account, and Lowell, who had had one all along, had managed to get Dove a job at Max's as a busboy. And Becca was packing.

"RFK has declared," she said.

"Opportunist," said Lowell.

"Be that as it may," said Becca (it was her favorite saying), "McCarthy is history. I have a job as an intern with RFK's campaign, thanks to dear old Dad. I'm on my way to Iowa. Don't look so blue."

"He's a poet," said Lowell. "They always look blue. It's in their nature."

Perhaps it was true. Clay couldn't remember ever being happy. He was sitting on the windowsill with his blue folder on his lap, unopened, watching EmCee and Ginsburg hurry toward the subway. She still slept on the mattress with Clay; that made it worse. She was wearing her mother's rabbit coat with a pipe tucked up one sleeve. Ginsburg was wearing a fatigue jacket with one pocket full of marbles to throw under the horses' hooves.

Hey, hey, LBJ.

"I'll call," said Becca.

That was the new thing. They had put in a phone.

I like Kennedy, I don't care what they say. I was already in Evansville but I didn't see him. It was too complicated.

"Get me a coffee while you're up," said Ginsburg. He had a sprained ankle. He had fallen on one of the marbles put down to fuck up the horses.

"Cosmic justice," said Lowell.

"Becca called last night," said EmCee. From on her way to California. Clay had talked to her too. "Bobby," as the newspapers called him—or RFK, as he was known to his staff—had just won Iowa and New Hampshire, and now he was going for the big one. If he beat Humphrey in California, he had a chance of getting the nomination in Chicago in August.

"It won't make any difference," said Ginsburg.

"How can you say that?" asked Lowell. "I agree he's an opportunist, but he *is* running against the war. He'll have to at least start winding it down."

"It's the Vietnamese who are winding it down," said EmCee.

"Better we lose it flat," said Ginsburg. "Otherwise people will just be saying he chickened out. They'll be saying if we stayed the course we could have won. There'll be a lot of soul searching and then we'll do it again."

"*They'll* do it again," said EmCee.

"Where are you going?" asked Lowell. Dove was pulling his prom dress on over his head.

"Stonewall! Anybody else?"

"Whoa!" said EmCee.

Clay whoaed.

They were on their way back from a rally at Union Square.

Clay had grudgingly gone along. Ginsburg had stayed behind to confer with his old Columbia buddies. It was a warm spring night, and Grand Street was, as usual, empty. Almost.

"Who was that?" Clay asked. A man had emerged from their door and was walking up toward Sixth Avenue. Even though it was warm, he was wearing a camel's hair coat.

"My father," said EmCee. "That's who."

"Okay," said Clay. "He knows where you live?"

"Apparently."

He disappeared around a corner and they started up the stairs. The phone was ringing at the top. EmCee ran ahead. She was waiting for Clay at the door.

"It's for you," she said. "It's your mother."

NINE

CLAY TOOK THE BUS TO LAGUARDIA FROM GRAND CENTRAL, through Queens. He had never been to Queens before. The plane was an Electra turboprop, Eastern Air Lines, straight through to Evansville, where his cousin Scooter met him in his Thunderbird and drove him down to Owensboro, doing 104 on the long levee between the 4-Way and the Ohio River bridge. His father was dead.

Junior sent flowers. "He would be here but he's on his way to Vietnam," Uncle Ham said.

Clay nodded. It was a funeral. There was a lot of nodding.

"Your father was a good man. Wasn't much at the auto business but he was a good man. He was a radio man, you know. He was the last one off the ship when it went down. Kept the signal out—otherwise they would never have been found. Barely got out. Should have got a medal."

"I know," said Clay. But he had never known.

"He lost something in that war. And one other, bad news, Hosea."

"Hosey?" A world of trouble.

"Died last month. Cancer. Had it for over a year and never told a soul. Never told me. And here, he left you this. Sometimes I think that nigger was my best friend."

It was the Snap-on 3/8 driver, his Cadillac.

There was the burial, then a reception at Uncle Ham's big house with country ham, the first Clay had tasted in several years. Beaten biscuits too.

"What happens to the radio?" Clay asked.

"My name is Jimmy, I'll take what you gimme," said his mother. She seemed more angry than sad.

"I didn't mean it like that."

"It's yours if you want it," said Clay's mother. "Otherwise it stays in the garage."

"How did you get my number?"

"There are ways."

After it was all over Clay borrowed Uncle Ham's Lincoln and went for a long drive. The DDI was dead. The old schools were dark and empty. Even the creeks were dry.

At ten of ten he stopped at The Southern Kitchen.

At 10:05 Ruth Ann came out, locking up behind her. She wore a white blouse and a blue skirt. It was like a uniform.

"I heard," she said. She was so sorry. "Thought you might be coming around. Whose car?"

They parked in the old spot, out on Panther Creek. She took off the white blouse and folded it. "It has to last two days," she said. They shared a cigarette, just like in the old days.

Old, old days.

"I'll bet you like New York," she said. "I'll bet you have a girlfriend."

"Not exactly," said Clay. "Not necessarily."

"I'll bet. You'll be going back, I know. You don't belong here."

"I'll bet you have a boyfriend." He hoped not, he realized.

"Not for now." She was the best kisser, just like in the old days. The bugs were still loud.

After, they sat on the hood and waited for Old No Show. "I'll bet you are against the war," she said. "Those demonstrations."

"I've been to a few."

"I hope Bobby wins," she said. Everybody was calling him Bobby. He had already won Iowa and Washington. He was about to win California.

"I have a friend who's working for Kennedy," said Clay. "She's out there with him now in California. She's on his staff. She says—"

"Let's head back," said Ruth Ann. "We're almost out of cigarettes."

Even though they weren't.

Clay was smoking the last Winston in the Evansville airport, the next morning, when he passed a newsstand and saw the headline.

"Shit!"

RFK SHOT!

In the back of the head.

"I was there, beside him, almost," said Becca. She had somehow beaten Clay back to New York. "About ten feet behind him. We were all following him out toward the microphone, to make the announcement. I would have been part of the crowd in the background. You would have seen me there."

"Show him the blouse," said EmCee.

She showed Clay the blouse, still on its hanger with the blood dark on the sleeve. It was black, like a shadow.

"Shit," said Clay.

Becca took it back, still on its hanger. She had remained standing while everyone else hit the floor. Now it was over and she was in New York, at 50 Grand, looking both shattered and brave. She was wearing another blouse just like it, without the blood.

The shadow.

"Shit," said Clay, again.

"They're not going to allow it," the Other Ginsburg said. "It's time we got the message, that peace is not part of their repertory."

"I never heard the shot. It was just like a banging and there's lots of banging—it was a big hotel. Everybody hit the floor. It was like a kid's game and I wondered for just a moment why nobody had told me we were playing."

"It *is* a kid's game," said Ginsburg. "It's time we got serious."

"Just shut up," said EmCee.

"So where is he now?" asked Lowell. He and Dove were on the couch, holding hands.

"Nobody knows. That's the thing. We all got turned loose. He never regained consciousness at the hospital. Then they took him away somewhere, the family and who knows who else. The CIA or the Kennedy mafia. Maybe he's dead and they're just not telling anybody."

"Where are you going?" asked EmCee.

"To work," said Clay. It was almost ten and he had to be at the garage. He rolled a joint and put it in his pocket. "People are still hailing cabs. The old world still spins."

"He said thanks but no," Lowell said, handing Clay his poems back.

"Leave them on the table. They're just xeroxes." He didn't want to touch them.

"Too many rights problems, for one thing. Using song lyrics can get you into trouble. The last thing *South* needs is trouble. They're about to go under anyway."

They were in a coffee shop on Sixth Avenue, sitting in a booth by the plate glass window. Clay opened his blue folder and looked in. His originals were the ones he loved. They had been worked over so many times that they were shiny along the edges, even where they were not supposed to shine.

"And that was it? That's all he said?"

"Look, the guy's a pig," said Lowell. "I knew him from prep school. We used to call him Shoes."

"I thought titles weren't copyrighted."

"That's literature. This is ASCAP, or something like that. Anyway. That was his main problem."

"Main problem? What was his other problem?"

"Look, Clay—"

"Just tell me."

"He said they weren't about anything."

"Dig," said Ginsburg. "Pigs."

"Huh?"

"They're watching this place. Down there."

Clay looked out the window. There was a late model Chevrolet at the corner of West Broadway and Grand.

"There's no one in it," he said.

"Yes, there is."

It was hard to argue with Ginsburg, almost impossible in fact. He and EmCee were going over a list of phone numbers, calling people. They kept changing their voices.

Lowell was out somewhere with Dove. Becca was still in Rhode Island for Easter.

Clay watched out the window. After while a man got out of the car and walked off without looking up, or back, or around.

Then the car drove off.

"I'm tired of doing brakes," Clay said.

"So?" Emil didn't look up from his dispatch log.

"So maybe I can troubleshoot." That was the only other job. There was no regular engine maintenance, only oil changes, and that was more boring than brakes.

"Luther troubleshoots. Elmo does transmissions. You do brakes. If you don't want to do brakes, you can always get another job. Maybe work for the Supreme Court or something."

"Fuck you," said Clay.

"I didn't hear that," said Emil. "Why don't you take a walk around the block and smoke a joint and chill out."

Clay took a walk around the block and smoked a joint. He tried to call EmCee but she wasn't home. She was almost never home.

He went back to work. Cabs are hard on brakes.

φ

"It's just for a few days," EmCee said. She was packing her clothes. Everything but the rabbit coat. "Weeks, maybe. Daddy wants me to keep an eye on the Twelfth Street place while he's in Europe. We're on better terms."

Clay was off Monday. On Tuesday he and Becca went to see *Bonnie and Clyde*. On Wednesday he went to Union Square, to see the shattered stub where the police memorial had been. On Thursday he and Dove went to see *Bonnie and Clyde*. Lowell had already seen it. On Friday he went to the Modern with a card that Dove had lifted from a drawer at SVA.

On Saturday he did something else. On Sunday he gave in and went to the house on Twelfth Street and lifted the knocker.

It felt just like old times. He had even brushed his hair.

He let the knocker fall, twice, and there she was, in her Black Island T-shirt, glad to see him again, at last, just like always, just like before.

Only it wasn't like that at all. It was the Other Ginsburg. He looked like he hadn't slept in days. He was smoking a cigarette, which supposedly wasn't allowed in the house.

"Clay," he said. "What are you doing here?"

"What do you think?" He could hear Dylan in the background, the other Dylan: "Like a Rolling Stone."

"We're awfully busy right now."

It didn't sound like it. "Just tell EmCee I'm here, okay?"

"She knows that," Ginsburg said. "She's in a meeting. She told me to tell you she'll see you soon."

And the door was closed.

TEN

IT WAS IN ALL THE PAPERS. PICTURES. LIKE A KICK IN THE STOMACH.

"Don't go," said Lowell. "I went this morning. There's nothing left. There were cops and firemen everywhere."

Clay went anyway. He only got as far as the Fifth Avenue end of Twelfth Street. He could see the big hole in the middle of the block where the townhouse had been. Only the steps were left.

No knocker, no door, no nothing.

"No go," said the cop. He was one of many. "Crime scene."

"I live here. On the block."

"Let's see some ID."

Clay was having trouble breathing. It was as if the air had grown too heavy to process. It smelled of ash and smoke.

Another cop was approaching. Clay walked away, fast.

"Maybe she wasn't there," he said.

Lowell was packing, throwing his stuff and Dove's stuff into the same bag, crying. Clay couldn't cry. He had tried twice on Thompson Street but there were too many people around. "Maybe she wasn't there," he said again.

"She was there," said Lowell. "We have to get out of here." He started to cry again, then quit just as suddenly. Dove was standing by the window, waiting to be told what to do.

There was a *Times* on the couch. WEATHERMAN BOMB FACTORY above the fold was almost confusing. *Bomb* can be either a noun or a verb, depending, and if *man* got an *E* or you added an *S*, you could almost change everything.

Everything.

"Clay! We have to split, man," said Lowell. "The feebs have already been around." *Feebs* was what Ginsburg, the Other Ginsburg, called the FBI. He was dead too.

"I didn't open the door," said Dove, looking proud of himself. Clay wanted to hit him.

"Listen up, Clay, we have to go. They will be poking around here especially. You'll get questioned, subpoenaed even. Things are getting real, real fast."

Real? Clay was numb. The numbness seemed real. He sat in the window and watched the street, as empty, as quiet as ever. Far below he saw Lowell and Dove, hurrying north, toward Houston Street. Then they were gone. Then he was alone.

"I wish we had a fireplace," he said aloud, just to hear his voice. She had blown herself up. She was no more. It was better to think of it that way. There was no other way to think of it.

Steps but no door.

EmCee's rabbit coat was still there, hung on a nail. Inappropriate for a Weather recruit, Clay supposed. He went over and put his arm in the sleeve, the empty sleeve. The coat was empty, like a house darkened, and he pulled his arm out and wiped his eyes, careful of the fur.

Even when she was breaking windows, EmCee was careful of the fur.

The next morning he went downstairs and walked up to Houston Street for food, some bagels and a box of cereal. Two men watched him from a parked car. He forgot milk. He even forgot cigarettes. It seemed so odd, the way the world went on, chatting and making change as if the very heart of it had not been destroyed, demolished. He started downtown, then stopped halfway down Thompson Street. He didn't want to go home.

He wanted only to go home.

The car was still there. It was a gray 1966 Chevrolet, parked at the corner of Grand and West Broadway. Two guys were sitting in it, smoking cigarettes. One was Black.

Couldn't they afford new cars? Or at least something less conspicuously regulation? Ignoring them defiantly, Clay went upstairs. It seemed like the least he could do.

Opening the door, he smelled smoke. He entered carefully. Becca was in the bathroom burning papers and flushing the ashes down the toilet. "Where have you been?" he asked.

"Staying with a friend. We're not supposed to be here."

"Who says?"

"We can't be connected with this place, Clay. You can't either. Who knows what they were up to. I'm just making sure there's nothing left around, then I'm out of here."

"Where?" He had nowhere to go.

"That remains to be seen. Do you have any matches? I'm out and I'm almost done."

There was a book in the rabbit coat. Max's Kansas City. He waited till he caught his breath before taking them to her in the bathroom.

"Do you have any cigarettes? I went out to get them, then forgot. There are two cops watching this place, I think. In that Chevy."

"I saw them. Look in my purse. Bring me one."

Shermans. Becca only smoked the best. Clay lit two and gave her the pink one. His was pale blue. They sat and smoked in silence.

"I don't know what to do," Clay said.

She stood up and looked out the window. "They're still there."

"There's a way out over the rooftops. I scouted it once. None of those stairways are locked."

"They saw me come in, they might as well see me leave." Becca was washing her hands. She dried them, uncharacteristically, on her skirt. "You have to leave too," she said from the doorway. "The feebs will be here any minute with a warrant, or a subpoena, or who knows what. You definitely don't want to be talking to them."

No shit. "I should stay. One of us should stay. I mean what if . . ."

"She's dead, Clay. Gone. The townhouse took them all. Read the paper. All they found was one finger with that ring on it. The ring you gave her, the big diamond."

"Where are you going?"

Now Becca was crying. "She was my friend too. I knew her longer than you. You're not the suffering martyr here."

She tossed him the box of Shermans and she was gone.

Threw it at him.

That night Clay dreamed EmCee was in the other room. He couldn't see her but he knew she was there. "Let me get that," she was saying. "Let me." She wasn't talking to him.

He woke up. The phone was ringing. He grabbed it. "Hello?"

There was nobody there. Slowly but suddenly he remembered where he was. What had happened. The loft had never looked emptier. Even Dove's prom dress was gone. Only the rabbit coat was left.

He looked out the window. The Chevrolet was still there. Had they been there all night or did they have shifts?

The blue folder was on the windowsill, where he had left it a lifetime ago. He left his mother's letters alone and took out the poems and burned them, one by one by one, dropping the ashes into the toilet. It was time to go.

He was flushing the toilet when he heard the footsteps on the stair.

It was a tall man in a camel's hair coat.

"You are Clay," he said.

Clay said nothing. Weren't they supposed to show a badge?

Clay stood in the door, blocking it.

"You've been in my house," the man said. "I know she trusted you. I don't know if she's alive or dead. I don't know if you know."

"I don't," said Clay although he did.

"I want you to give her this if you see her."

It was her father. He handed Clay an envelope, white, business-size.

"That's all. Thank you. Good day."

The return address said "The White House, 1600 Pennsylvania Avenue." The envelope wasn't sealed. There was five hundred dollars in it, all in twenties, five times five.

What does one leave? What does one take? Only the Shermans, the blue folder, the white envelope, and his Emily's Taxi jacket for those long winter nights that were sure to come. After turning out all the lights, just like LBJ, Clay left over the rooftops. It was time to hit the road.

ELEVEN

CLAY HAD FORGOTTEN HOW AGGRESSIVELY ORDINARY AND UNRE-markable the modern South was. Redbrick churches and redbrick schools. It was suffocating. It was Nashville. The address was a two-story frame house the color of smog ten blocks from Vanderbilt, divided into four tiny apartments. A library file card cut to fit the mailbox read "Robert E. Lee Bragg III." A Honda motorcycle with a Confederate flag decal on the tank leaned against the porch, a 350 Scrambler, missing a seat.

Clay sat on the steps to wait.

It was almost dark when a boat of a car that Clay recognized as Bobby Lee's father's old Olds pulled up, the back seat filled with library books.

He helped Bobby Lee carry them inside. The apartment was a dump, but a neat dump. There were four beers in the refrigerator but no food.

"I eat out," said Bobby Lee. He was working on his PhD: the Fugitives. He didn't ask why Clay had left New York. He figured he knew.

They sat on the porch and drank the beer and Clay told him anyway. The bugs were loud. He was back down South. They all said the same thing over and over.

"Jesus," said Bobby Lee. "I read about that—it was in the papers, even here—but I had no idea you were involved."

"I wasn't involved."

"It was her house. She was your girlfriend."

"Not exactly."

"Still."

Still. That night he slept on the couch while EmCee looked on in silence from the shadows of his dream. She had followed him from New York, not surprisingly. She wore a fatigue coat like Ginsburg's, only hers was fur.

She was trying to hand him a ring. He didn't want to take it.

When he woke up, Bobby Lee was gone and there was a note on the kitchen table: "Back at noon. There's a river here."

There was a saucer filled with change on the counter by the toaster. Clay found a pay phone around the corner and called his mother.

"Where are you calling from?" she asked. "Your phone is disconnected. The FBI called here."

The FBI?

"They wanted to know where you are. I told them New York. What are you doing? They just said they wanted to talk to you. What about? Where are you?"

"In New York," Clay said. "On a pay phone. I was a witness to a mugging."

"The FBI doesn't investigate muggings."

"It was a mailbox, Mother, a mailman. I'm out of quarters, I'll have to call you back."

"Wait. You can always reverse the charges."

Breakfast in Nashville was more expensive than in New York. That was weird. In New York, at the Tunnel Diner on Sixth Avenue, Clay got eggs, toast, and hash browns for 89 cents with coffee thrown in. Here it was two dollars and the coffee was extra.

The FBI had called. That complicated things. No, it made them simpler.

There wasn't enough change left to call California so Clay used one of Lowell's magic numbers.

"Where you calling from?" Ira asked. First thing.

"New York." Who knew who was listening? "I need your help. I guess you heard about EmCee."

"Oh, God, man. Of course. First-fucking-hand."

"What do you mean?"

"Lowell was here, with some other fag. He said the pigs are

all over 50 Grand, and sure enough, a day later the brown shoes show up here. I thought they were looking for him but it was me they wanted to talk to. I can't believe what happened."

"What happened?"

"You know what happened. *The best are full of passionate intensity.* We're doing things communally here. We can't get involved in all that Weather shit."

"Me neither," said Clay.

"Well, they showed me your picture and Lowell's too. They had a picture of me and EmCee from high school! I can't believe what happened to EmCee."

"Is Lowell still there?"

"He split for Canada, I think." He said it again: "Canada, I'm pretty sure. Or maybe Mexico. Meanwhile, my lawyer says I can't be talking to anybody from back East."

"Lawyer?"

But Ira had hung up. Who knew who was listening?

"They were radicals in their own way," said Bobby Lee. He was talking about his PhD thesis. They were perched on a log by the Cumberland, shooting bottles.

"Homesick Southerners, you mean," said Clay.

"They had a vision," said Bobby Lee.

"A vision of a past that never was. For an idealized version of a racist order."

Two more shots, one each. Then Bobby Lee reloaded while Clay opened two more beers.

"That's one version, I guess," said Bobby Lee. "The rhetorical Marxist version. I'm taking a more literary view of the whole enterprise." He threw his empty in, fired, missed. He passed the pistol, a .22 that looked like a cowboy .45, to Clay, who nailed it, two-handed.

"Armed and dangerous," said Bobby Lee. "Fugitives. First Harl and now you."

"Harl?"

"Haven't you heard? He's AWOL."

"I thought he was in Vietnam."

Two more shots, one each. "He was but he got wounded. Not too bad, but they sent him to Germany, then home to DC for rehab, I guess. Purple Heart. Anyway, according to his sister, Donna, he split. I've been seeing her, you know."

"I remember her," said Clay, remembering the little pink arc. "Just barely."

"She remembers you. She's in nursing school at Western Kentucky, in Bowling Green. I see her on weekends. I'm picking her up at the bus station tomorrow."

"Tell her hello for me," said Clay. "I'll be on the road again."

"*On the road again,*" said Bobby Lee, singing and reloading. He handed the loaded gun to Clay. "Fugitives."

"I'm *not* a fugitive. They just want to talk to me, and I just don't want to talk to them. That's all."

"That's enough, these days. You could stay here awhile. I'm supposed to have a roommate but he split, stiffed me on the rent. That's his Honda on the porch."

"Too close to home. I have a friend in California. He's expecting me." He threw another empty in.

Clay had never lied to Bobby Lee before. He was, oddly, pleased at how easy it was.

Meanwhile, the bottle was getting away.

He aimed, fired, missed. The Cumberland lacked the grandeur of the Ohio. It was warm and muddy like the Green in Calhoun. No trace of the mountains that had given it birth.

"Fugitives," said Bobby Lee the next morning, at the edge of town. "Do you need money?"

He gave him a twenty anyway and Clay unfolded it as the Olds made a wide U-turn and headed back into Nashville. It looked just like the one the football players had given him what sometimes seemed like several lifetimes ago. Ira too. He stuck out his thumb.

The rides gave out in Memphis. Everybody was Black. It felt

like the Deep South, so Clay pulled two of EmCee's twenties from the White House envelope and bought a Greyhound ticket to Oklahoma City.

He was afraid of the Deep South.

He could always replace them.

There is a line they call the Dry Line. It's the ninety-eighth meridian, where the Midwestern prairies stretch out into high plains; where the fences give out, the long loose grasses grow short and tough, the scrub-filled creekbeds dry out to dusty draws, and the broad Earth begins to beautifully undress.

"The West!" shouted Clay aloud, to himself, alone—roaring through the star-crowded night on the back of a flatbed truck, a two-ton International; struggling to light a cigarette just like Sal Paradise, in the wind. He was let off under the Milky Way, lighted like a sign, and when he woke up he saw dry bluffs to the north, treeless, and to the west, what looked like a line of low clouds, until two more rides took him close enough to see that it was the Front Range of the Rockies, still hung with snow.

They rose like a wall at the end of the plains. A north-south interstate ran along their foot, either dividing the world into highs and lows or stringing its parts together; it was hard to tell.

All Clay had was an address near Aquinas on Route 24, the old north-south highway, two miles south and west of Exit 9. Aquinas was just a stockyard and a post office, closed.

Drop City was a ruin. It was on the highway, between an ancient closed-down gas station and a pasture populated by bored goats. Two small domes, each the size of a house trailer that had been rolled up into a ball and then partially smashed. Blackened spars, trash, litter. A wheelless Corvair on concrete blocks, the engine gone, one door hanging open. America's air-cooled experiment, Nadered.

This was hardly the new dawn of humankind. There wasn't even any traffic. A red pickup rolled slowly by and that was all.

But surely it had looked better once. The domes were banged together out of old car tops; they had been many-colored once.

Clay banged on one, then peered through a low triangular opening, once a door. The inside smelled of ashes and old mattresses. Books were scattered across the peeling plywood floor: *Stranger in a Strange Land* was one; *Building Your Cabin in the Woods* was another. It seemed an odd selection for a collection of domes at the edge of the plains.

One empty triangle looked out on the highway. The red pickup was turning around.

Clay backed out of the dome and watched as the truck rolled back and rolled to a stop at the highway's edge. It was an ancient Chevrolet Apache, maybe a '56. That was reassuring. A cowboy complete with hat sat in it, both hands on the wheel.

He didn't look like a cop.

The cowboy beckoned with one hand and Clay went to the truck, picking his way through the trash.

"Looking for Roads?" He was rolling a cigarette, one-handed. Clay was impressed.

"As a matter of fact, yes. What happened here?"

"Burned them out," the cowboy said. "Folks around here don't take to hippies." He nodded toward the two houses facing the highway with their eyes closed. "Your friend Roads is okay though." His name he said was Johnny. Just Johnny. He licked his cigarette to seal it, then used it as a pointer. "Roads and his folks moved up into the valley."

He pointed toward a blue notch in the Front Range, a few miles to the south.

"I can give you a ride, part way at least. I wouldn't stay here, I was you, know what I mean. Throw your stuff in the back. That all your stuff?"

A shopping bag with a cardboard handle. Bendel's, NY.

"That's it," said Clay.

Route 24 followed the interstate south, like a poor relation. They turned off the highway onto an asphalt county road, which followed an almost-dry riverbed through the notch into a narrow valley surrounded by steep hills and even steeper mountains. Shangri-la, thought Clay. The mountains looked impossible. The cowboy, Johnny, wore a stained gray felt genuine Stetson, which he took off every thirty seconds or so to scratch his bald head.

He talked the whole way: about how to make coffee; what wood was best for heat, for cash, for convenience; how to wash clothes cowboy-style by putting them in a drum in the back of a pickup with soap and water and "letting the road wash 'em."

There was such a drum in the back of the Apache.

"The little woman takes hers to town of course." His wife's name was Brenda. They turned off the county road onto a gravel road that wound up into the hills. The truck kept popping out of second. The gravel gave out at a mailbox in front of a neat little manufactured home, like a trailer without wheels (like Ruth Ann's house, Clay thought). A horse peered out of a new pole barn behind it. A dirt road led on up the hill, through low trees toward a big rock that looked like a bad tooth.

"Roads's up there," Johnny said. "Roads and his Rockers. I'd take you but it's *Huntley-Brinkley* time." He had a color TV.

Clay walked up the steep two-rut dirt road between low piñons that looked rootless, like 2/3–scale cartoon trees. He rounded a turn into a meadow and saw a small settlement on the edge of a deep arroyo: two VW buses, and a wall tent, and a ratty-looking hogan built of slab and Celotex. Several hippies, all guys, were sitting around a campfire stirring a pot with a long spoon. One waved.

Clay was approaching them when the blanket door of the hogan opened and a tall man with short hair and a long beard came out. He was older then the others, in his thirties at least, carrying a rifle crooked in his arm, like a trapper: a Winchester .30-30, the cowboy model.

He wore greasy leather pants. Was he one of the people Clay had met in New York? They all looked the same.

"Looking for something?"

"Hello." Clay set down his Bendel's bag. "Is Roads around?"

"Not exactly." He used his hand to point, wiping it first on his leather pants. "He's on up the hill, at the Rockers."

"Rockers?"

"Other side of that big rock." He rolled a cigarette badly: fat in the middle, sharp on the ends. Clay gave him a light. "Good man, Roads."

A girl came out of the hogan and clung to his side. She looked about fourteen. She wore a long scarf like a sari and men's underpants, and that was all.

"It's just a half mile. Unless you wanted to stay here. Everybody's welcome here."

"Thanks," said Clay, picking up his bag. "Roads's expecting me though."

"Roads's always expecting somebody. He's a good man. Tell him Yosemite Sam said so."

It was almost dark. The road got steeper. Clay trudged on around a three-story rock that would have justified a state park in Kentucky, and saw lights. They seemed far away at first until he adjusted his perspective. Then there it was, as if it had just landed from outer space, lighted dimly from inside: a huge dome, thirty feet high, covered with plywood, with a long arc of windows near the top. It looked like something from Arthur C. Clarke, a space station that had fluttered and fallen to earth like a leaf. Dim as it was, the light helped as Clay picked his way over scattered boards, between two trucks, a pickup and a van. A wide board stairway led up to an arc-shaped deck, all of new-smelling wood.

"*Klaatu barada nikto,*" he muttered.

There was a heavy triangular door. Clay studied it, trying to figure out where to knock, when it swung open on its own, opening outward like a supermarket EXIT ONLY entered by mistake. Long-haired people, three women and four men, one very short and one very tall, all turned to look at him. There was the sweet smell of pot. And the tall one was Roads, standing and holding the rope that opened the door, gray-haired but beardless like a boy.

"Just the man I was looking for," he said, long in the arms, outstretched.

TWELVE

COFFEE WAS BOILED IN A TALL POT, COWBOY STYLE, THEN SLAMMED on the stove to sink the grounds, then carried it out to the big crescent-shaped porch of the dome, with cups and a Bugler can.

It was morning. Roads poured. "We bought this canyon from Johnny. He still runs a few cattle up above, and has a water line running through."

"PVC," said Annie. "A bunch of leaks strung together."

"He bought a color TV with the money," said Roads.

"And a horse."

"Shoulda bought a truck," said Clay.

The dome seemed even bigger in the daylight. Half covered with mismatched shingles, it loomed behind them as they sat looking over the valley with the Bugler can and the coffeepot between them. Clay felt he had slept for a century and awakened in another world.

"That one straight across the Valley is called Fu Manchu," said Roads. "You'll see why when you see its long moustache when the snow comes; those two across the valley are the Huaja-tollas, the Breasts of God. The one on the left, the north, is twelve thousand something." He saved the biggest for last: Blanca, which brooded over them all at the end of the valley. "There you see," Roads said, "the southernmost glacier in the USA."

Shangri-la. "They all look familiar," said Clay. "It's almost like I've seen them before."

"You have," said Annie.

"What?"

"In the movies."

"She's from Hollywood," said Roads. He went inside to make pancakes. Annie followed. She wore bib coveralls that barely covered her full breasts. Clay was sorry to see her go.

He rolled another cigarette, overlooking a meadow filled with junk: board ends, trash, rolled roofing. The Rocks looked very different in the daylight, less science fictional and more provisional, a perch on a high mountainside. Scattered vehicles clustered around the dome like filings around a magnet: a maroon International pickup with a camper on the back; a VW bus painted with red and orange hearts, with an engine on the ground behind it, like scat; an old Chevy delivery van with WONDER BREAD in faded red and yellow paint on the side; and an even older Ford pickup, gray as fog, on blocks.

The rest of the Rockers were waking up, slowly, like a little scattered city coming to life. Most didn't sleep in the dome.

Gantz and his lady were climbing out of the camper at the edge of the elfin piñon trees. He wore leather pants and a leather vest. She wore a long dress that dragged the ground. A metal door slammed. It was Plain Bob and Plain Jane emerging from the VW bus where they slept. Wearing a blanket like a tent, she squatted to pee; he stood over her, squinting toward the morning sun. His long beard and her long hair glowed copper in the morning sun; they were as alike as two pennies. The dome door groaned open and Little Richard, the short man, came out shaking two gourd rattles at the morning sun, singing, sort of, in monotonous Indian tones while the door groaned shut behind him and Clay reached for the Bugler can.

That was everyone, it seemed.

The geodesic dome is the lightest of structures for its size, also the strongest, not to mention the cheapest, as well as the easiest to build. Once built, it reverses itself. It's all roof, and hard to cover. There isn't a right angle to be found. Windows and doors must be custom made, like false teeth.

"Easy to build but hard to finish," said Plain Bob. He was working on the door with Gantz. It was easy to open but hard to close.

"Like communes," said Annie.

"Or poems," said Roads. "You still chasing poems?"

"They all got away," said Clay. "Guess I did too. Turns out I'm better with cars."

"How about trucks?" asked Plain Bob.

The International with the camper was almost new. Gantz had gotten it for finishing law school in Boulder. He had added the camper and the girlfriend, in that order, according to Annie. The wonder truck (for so it was called) pertained to Roads in much the way a dog pertains to its owner; it was more about affinity than property. It was the Rockers' principal vehicle. The VW bus, or honeymoon van, was used as a bedroom by Plain Bob and Plain Jane. It had dropped a valve climbing Johnny's road and been demoted from transportation to architecture.

The Ford pickup was what interested Clay.

"Johnny says it was here when he bought the place," said Plain Bob. "Roads says that's impossible since Johnny bought the place in '46, right after the war, according to the deed."

It was a '49 with no tailgate and no plates. The front was up on blocks—stumps, rather. The rear axle was flat on the ground.

"Anyway, who knows," said Plain Bob. "It was probably here when the Pilgrims arrived back in 1492."

Clay reached behind the grille and unlatched the hood. It felt oddly intimate, like reaching under a dress. He was reluctant to lift the hood with Plain Bob watching.

"Are there any tools?" he asked.

"Under the dome." Plain Bob ran off to get them.

Clay opened the hood and saw, for the first time in several years, the simple lines of a flathead six, as clean as a cast-iron skillet. The battery was gone of course, and two of the spark plugs, but everything else was there: radiator, generator, starter, distributor. Even the plug wires were all in place.

"What do you think?" Plain Bob was back with a shoebox. He set it on the fender. There was nothing in it but pliers and screwdrivers, plus one 8-inch adjustable wrench. No sockets, and his Cadillac was useless without them.

Clay lifted off the air cleaner and looked down the throat of the carburetor, expecting the worst, but this wasn't Kentucky: there was no spit-and-clay wasps' nest nestled inside.

"What do you think?"

"Honey," said Clay, "I think you in a world of trouble."

There were three communes in the valley, two on the mountainside and one down by the county road. Libra, the oldest, the mother of them all, was only four miles from the Rocks, but it was a seven-mile drive: down past Johnny's to the county road, then three miles west, then two miles up another dirt road, but a better one, to a scattering of low trees across a gentle shoulder of the fierce, rocky Sangres, which loomed above.

Libra was house-proud, a small collection of artful dwellings, two of them domes, two others jewel-like octagons of railroad ties and old tires, all experimental, all under perpetual construction, tin cans and plaster. All mostly unseen. Librans lived in close seclusion, no house in sight of another but all in easy walking distance of the twenty-five-foot orange-and-silver-dome in the center.

Clay parked by the dome, alighting on the one level spot, like a visitor from another planet.

Klaatu barada nikto.

The door groaned open (all dome doors groan) and Clay followed Annie in to be introduced. "I'm showing him around," she said.

The dome, half the size of the Rockers', was Libra's common workspace, lighted by an arc of windows.

"I remember you," said Palomina, barely looking up from her loom, a weaver now, apparently. She extended a hand though. Cicero was more hospitable. In New York he had looked country; here he looked like a displaced New Yorker: a chubby little man with an English accent, too old to be a hippie. "You barely caught me," he said. "I'm supposed to be in New York."

"According to who?" muttered Palomina.

"Whom," said another Libran, Louisa, who was stretching canvas on a frame. Another, Denver, sat on the floor making jewelry out of seashells. He wore coveralls that looked like they were made out of mattress ticking.

Annie stood in the open door, rolling a cigarette out of Libra's Bugler can. Hellos done, Clay joined her, while Cicero located the chainsaw they had come to fetch.

"It probably needs sharpening," he said. It was a 22-inch McCulloch, bright as a school bus. He followed them outside and dropped it into the bed of the truck. "Isn't this Johnny's old truck? How'd you get it running?"

"Filed the points," said Clay. "Just needed a little encouragement."

"Denver was my old man," said Annie, as they headed down toward the county road. "Back before Drop City. Now he's with Lucille, the chick with the giant ass."

"I thought her name was Louisa."

"Seashells in New Mexico," said Annie. "Imagine!"

"I thought we were in Colorado."

"Almost New Mexico. We are right on the line. Do you always grind the gears like that when you drive?"

"The synchros are gone."

"Is that why it's steaming like that?"

"A separate problem," said Clay. It was easier shifting up than down. There were no plates on the Ford, but they only had to cover a mile or so on the county road.

"Cicero and Roads started Libra after Drop City," said Annie. "The dome was supposedly communal but nobody wanted to live in it. Nobody wanted to pool money. Then they wanted couples only, to minimize the he-ing and she-ing. That's when Roads left and started up the Rocks. That's Triple A up ahead. The big house with the bus out front and the barn out back."

"That is some bus," said Clay.

"It oughta be," said Annie. It had been painted by Peter Max himself, Clay found out later, and was said to be worth thousands, hundreds less every week as the paint faded in the high desert sun.

"Merry! How come you have a black eye?"

"We were playing a gig at Denver Community College night before last. Somebody tried to tear our banner down, and there was a fight."

"Stop the War?"

"Yeah, it started a war. And who's this?"

Annie explained. "I'm showing him around," she said.

The Activist Artists of America, or Triple A, lived in and around a big old frame house right on the county road. It had once, according to Merry, been a boardinghouse for Italian coal miners who were trucked to the Ludlow mines every day by the Rockefellers. That was in the twenties. The big kitchen still smelled like garlic. The Triple A women wore long dresses and the men wore tight jeans. There was a pack of kids which, according to Annie, no one had ever counted, and which flowed from room to room and from outside to in like colorful loud water. Their parents seemed weary of them, or perhaps just weary. It was noon but they were still having breakfast.

Clay and Annie sat in the sun on the back porch next to a big freezer that snored like a bear while Merry, the "Merry Dane," made espresso on his machine, which no one else was allowed to touch. He was a rich kid from Copenhagen who, according to Annie, had bought the place for six grand. He had also bought the bus. He was also the lead singer in the band.

While Annie and Merry sampled the herb Roads had sent down to swap for eggs, Clay took the chainsaw out to the barn for Rotella, Triple A's bass player and bus mechanic, to sharpen.

"It's all in the wrist," she said, "like a fiddle. Who had this thing last, Libra? What have they been cutting, rocks? And who in the world are you?"

Clay told her, approximately. She was a compact little woman with bright squinty eyes, a dead cigar, and a matched set of SK tools, hung with nails on the rough wood walls, gleaming in the darkness behind her.

He showed her his Cadillac. "Snap-on," she said approvingly. "That'll dress up a box." Not that he had one. She gave him enough spare sockets to almost make a set.

The Ford had quit steaming. Clay opened the hood and topped it off for the return trip. "It's losing water somewhere," he said. "It's not the radiator. It's not the hoses, either."

Rotella slid underneath on a flattened cardboard box, a hill-billy creeper. "It's the water pump," she said. "You've got yourself a weeper."

Rotella, according to Annie, was a Navy brat from San Diego. Cicero ran an art gallery in New York by phone and had acquired a British accent by mail order. The Merry Dane was not only merry but positively gay. Little Richard was a Bible college dropout from Oklahoma, born again into the Peyote Church. "That's what all those rattles are for," she said. "Plain Bob and Plain Jane are from Drop City. They tried Taos but it didn't work out. They fight a lot."

"What about Gantz?"

"Gantz is just a tourist. He'll be gone as soon as he passes his bar exam."

The weeper wasn't steaming, yet, and they were halfway up Johnny's road. Clay was encouraged. "So what about this bunch?" he asked. They were passing the little settlement on the arroyo. Clay counted six, all guys, poking their fire with long sticks as if it were an animal they were tormenting.

Yosemite stood in the door of his Celotex hogan with one arm around his girl. He tipped his leather hat.

Clay waved. Annie didn't.

"They shit in the arroyo," she said. "Roads calls them loose change, fallen out of the pockets of the suburbs. They're not building anything. Roads says they'll be gone with the first snow."

"And what do you say?"

"I say they shit in the arroyo."

The next morning, Roads gave Clay two eggs with his pancakes. Everybody else got one. Then he held out his hand. Two tabs of acid were nestled in his palm.

"You missed the solstice peyote meeting," he said. "This will get you up to speed. Take and eat."

Clay took and ate.

"Now let's you and me go for a walk."

A path behind the dome led up the mountain, through the rocks, between tiny trees. The acid was lighting up the back of Clay's throat, just barely. They emerged from the piñons into the upper meadow and already the dry buffalo grass looked green. Dancy.

"I suspect you're on the run," Roads said.

"Not exactly." Clay had told Roads what had happened in New York, most of it anyway. He had left out the FBI.

"But that's okay. You were on the run when I met you. You were just a teenager but you were already on the run."

"I was?"

"So what are you going to do now?"

"I'm doing it, I guess. Following you. Up the mountain."

"Good for you."

The path followed Johnny's pipeline right up the middle of the meadow. It was not so much a path as a trail, connecting the raw spots where the buried pipeline had been dug up and repaired, and the green spots where the plants fed on the seep in the summer. The plants were big. Soon it would be time to haul them inside, according to Roads. He crushed a bud between his fingers and held it up to Clay's nose. It was a rich smell, like ripe tobacco, like green wax.

"Like money," Clay said.

Roads shook his head. "Like wealth, not money. We give it away to the world," he said. "The world gives back."

"The world." Clay nodded. The world nodded back, up and down. The acid was definitely coming on.

"Come on, let's walk."

The pipeline gave out at a stock tank fed by a dripping half-inch pipe that emerged from a low rock ledge. Beyond the ledge the woods were made up of thick ponderosa instead of cedar and piñon. Roads was undressing. Clay rolled a cigarette and watched as Roads got in, shivering comically as his butt hit the cold water.

"Aren't you sitting in our drinking water?"

"If it was a creek it would be the same. Get in."

Clay stripped down and stepped in.

"Sit down."

Clay sat down. The water made room. Over the edge of the stock tank Clay could see all the way through the pass to the long reach of the plains, impossibly flat and impossibly empty.

He ran his hands along the horizon, smoothing it further. "I can see all the way to Kansas," he said.

Roads laughed. "That means you're not in Kansas any more. Let me ask you a question, a serious question."

"Okay."

"Do you want to spend your life tearing down the old world? Or do you want to spend your life living in the new one?"

"Let me think about it," Clay said. Even though he knew, or thought he knew, the answer.

"So?" said Annie.

"So . . . what?" asked Clay.

"Isn't it time you put your money in The Can?"

"That's the rule," said Little Richard.

Annie was braiding his hair while he glued feathers onto a rattle. It looked like an assembly line.

There were two coffee cans on the back of the cook stove. One held grease and the other, The Can, held money: two crisp twenties and a few dingy ones.

Clay dropped in the three bills and change he had left from Bobby Lee's twenty: $3.57.

The White House envelope with EmCee's money, short only forty dollars, was rolled up in the bottom of his sleeping bag.

He left it there.

Every morning started with a bang. Roads made cowboy coffee, banging the pot to settle the grounds. Annie straightened the wide, low bed she shared with Little Richard. Plain Bob, who was afraid of heights, sorted the shingles. Clay and Plain Jane nailed them up, swinging around the dome on long ropes like rappelling mountaineers. Each round had to be cut, or folded, or bent, punished and mutilated to fit around the long curve of flat surfaces. It was like dressing a planet. From the top of the dome Clay could see a thin slice of the Great Plains through the valley's narrow opening, fading off to the east, wonderfully featureless, like memory.

Little Richard marched off to the upper meadow with rattles and a hoe, to tend Roads's plants. Annie opened a letter from her mother and shook the money into The Can. Gantz tried to tune his twelve-string, an endless task, while his lady dropped acid and wandered through the piñons like a ghost, searching for something, her clothing perhaps, while Plain Jane nailed the last round of shingles into place.

"That's it," she said, good with a hammer.

Clay followed her down. They arrived on the deck of the dome in two long leaps, like victorious acrobats. Plain Bob gave her a kiss.

"Hooray. Now all we have to do is insulate," said Roads, just back from the outhouse.

"Hooray!" said Annie, in the doorway, adjusting the bib of her coveralls.

"Color TV!" said Johnny, who happened to be visiting. He stopped by once or twice a week at least, supposedly to check his

water line and have a cup of coffee, but mainly to enjoy the side
view of Annie's magnificent breasts.

Color TV was also the name of his horse.

"It's air-cooled," said Rotella, when Clay told her about the
VW forty-horse that sat on the ground behind Plain Bob and Plain
Jane's honeymoon bus, half covered with a tarp. "They're like
Dixie Cups."

She showed him four broken ones in the Triple A barn, all in
a pile. "Bring yours down and we'll put one together."

Why not? The shingles were done, and there was always
something happening at Triple A: someone on acid, someone trying out a new song, someone rolling in or rolling out, a constant
stream of visitors. Plus Triple A had electricity. On the radio there
were riots in Paris and Warsaw and New York: students, according to Merry, who cheered them on. Plus they had a *Times* from
their last gig in Denver. Martin Luther King was sitting up in his
bed at Toronto's McGill Hospital, showing the bandage over his
heart. He disapproved of the marbles that had been rolled under
the NYPD horses' hooves, almost crippling one. He had been invited to speak at the Democratic National Convention. He still
had a dream.

That night Clay dreamed of EmCee for the first time since
Nashville. She had followed him.

"We have to insulate," said Plain Bob. "Winter will be on us
soon."

"Soon?" Summer in Shangri-la seemed endless.

"We get our first snow in September, sometimes. We can't
nail up bags, they'll just pull down. Plus they cost money."

"Maybe I'll hear from Mother today," said Annie, pulling on
the flannel shirt she always wore over her coveralls when she went
to town.

Clay rode in with her, eighteen miles on the county road.

They took the wonder truck, the only Rocker vehicle with plates.

Colorado City was hardly a city. The Rockers called it Burg. It was just a cinder block courthouse, a post office, and a jail surrounded by rundown houses and cottonwoods, plus a Safeway and a car parts store a mile east of town on the edge of the Great Plains, at the interstate interchange. All the streets but two—Old Route 24 and the county road, which ended at the interstate—were dirt.

"It never rains here," said Annie. First stop was the post office: nothing from Hollywood, which was their only reliable source of cash. Next stop was Lopez Auto Parts to order a water pump for the weeper.

"Hard to find stuff for those old flatheads," said the counterman, a dour Chicano. He wanted a two-dollar deposit. That left only four dollars and twenty-seven cents for gas, groceries, and Bugler, but Annie didn't seem worried.

"Time to see the Nice Lady," she said.

Next stop was the courthouse. Clay waited in the wonder truck. Annie came out, grinning, holding up a booklet of food stamps. "Girl money!" she said, fanning them out like a poker hand. They bought groceries at the Safeway, then filled up and bought Bugler at the Lopez Mini Mart, the last stop, where tobacco and gasoline were considered food.

Triple A, the band, had one Black player, Indigo, the drummer. He and Merry and Rotella were sitting on old tires, having coffee in the doorway of the practice barn, when Clay drove up in the weeper, barely steaming.

"I brought that forty-horse down, like you suggested," he said.

He pulled up a tire and sat down and reached for the Bugler can. Indigo got up and left.

"It's your accent," said Merry.

"It's no big deal," said Clay.

"He just went to take a shit," said Rotella.

"Can you blame him?" said Merry. "Isn't the South going to rise again?"

"Kentucky's not really the South," said Rotella. "Except for Fort Campbell maybe."

"Owensboro is right on the river," said Clay. "That's the Mason-Dixon line."

"Kentucky had a star in the Confederate flag," said Merry, who had studied American history at the Sorbonne. "Though it never successfully seceded."

"I had a Confederate great-grandfather. If it had, he would have been governor."

"Would you have seceded?"

"I like to think I would have been an abolitionist."

"Or maybe a Weatherman," said Merry.

"Don't even say that. Where did you get that idea?"

"I'll bet he had a sweet Southern girlfriend," Rotella said. "Or two or three."

"Just one."

"The pause that refreshes," said Indigo, sitting down next to Clay. "Roll me one of those cracker fags, bro."

"Something's coming up the road," said Annie. She had not only the best tits and the best home address (Beverly Hills), but the best ears too.

Plain Bob pulled on the rope to open the door.

"Oh shit," said Clay.

A white Ford Bronco was rounding the Rock, with SANGRE DE CRISTO COUNTY SHERIFF painted on the door in law enforcement blue.

"It's just Lopez," said Plain Jane. "Not to worry."

Roads was pulling on the striped pants the Oklas had given him. "They're for peyote meetings," said Annie. "And for meetings with authorities."

Lopez wore a huge hat, white, and a huge gun, blue-black. Roads tossed a plastic bag into the back of the Bronco, the last of last year's herb, and he and Lopez shared a ready-made, sitting on the add-on running board.

"Lopez and Roads have an arrangement," said Plain Bob.

"Roads is allowed to grow dope for the hippies as long as he doesn't sell it to the Chicano teens."

"That's sort of cool," said Clay. "Looking after his own."

"Sort of," said Annie. "Lopez sells to them."

"Right on!" said Merry in what Rotella called his tie-dyed mix of accents: Viking overlaid with Parisian slang plus Carolina Black. A diplomatic brat, Merry had been raised partly in Paris and partly in DC, spending summers reading cowboy novels at his grandmother's place in Jutland.

"Right on what?" asked Clay who had come in for coffee after sifting through Rotella's pile of forty-horse corpses.

There was a radio over the stove in Triple A's kitchen. Merry turned it up.

Weather had blown up a Chicago police station in a "bloody act of pointless violence" designed to disrupt the preparations for the Democratic National Convention. They had emptied the place with a phone call first. Almost.

"The cops assassinated two Black Panthers last week," said Merry. "Shot through the door and killed them in their beds."

"At least this time they emptied the place out first."

"Almost. Here. This one's for Rotella." She liked her coffee half cream.

The stove was an Ashley, recommended by the *Whole Earth Catalog*, the hippie *Good Housekeeping*, vented with a thirty-foot stovepipe assembled piece by piece, secured with sheet metal screws and lifted straight up and into and through a hole in one of the dome's top triangles.

That took four people and five tries.

"Color TV," said Johnny, who had stopped for coffee and stayed to watch the show. "Where's our Annie today?"

"Pueblo," said Roads. "She and Plain Bob are looking to score some insulation."

"Looks better without it," said Johnny, picking up his hat and putting down his coffee cup. Above him, the inside of the dome was beautifully naked, plywood triangles between 4x4 struts.

"He seemed disappointed," said Clay, watching him ride off.

"Cowboys are always disappointed," said Roads. "It's the cowboy way."

Clay was at Triple A to help Rotella do the brakes on the bus. Each wheel was as big as a millstone, each shoe as big as a small dog curled up on a rug.

Her SK wrenches had a nice cold shiny feel. The story was, Bill Graham had bought them for the band as a going-away present.

After they finished, they tried out the bus on the county road. Rotella let Clay drive. "Why are you downshifting?" she asked.

Clay gave her a curious look. "To slow down?"

"Think of it as wear," Rotella said. "You can distribute the wear among the cylinder walls, the piston pins, the transmission gears, the thrust bearings, the planetaries, the mains, the wheel bearings, the inserts, the clutch—or you can dump it all on the brake shoes and use them up and throw them away like Kotex.

"Do the math."

Annie was back from Burg with Bugler, coffee, nails, sugar, and mail. She shook the change from her mother's hundred into The Can and handed Clay an envelope.

"Go ahead, take it," she said. "It's for you."

It was from his own mother. It had been forwarded from San Francisco.

Saw your trashy tramp last night. I was downtown and she asked about you. Junior writes from somewhere in Germany. He's a First Lieutenant now.

φ

How did she find Ira? Clay wondered. How did Ira find me? He slipped the letter into the blue folder at the bottom of his sleeping bag and went out on the deck to join the others.

"Call themselves One Way," Annie was saying. "They look just like hippies. We stopped in to check them out on the way back from the city. They're living in VW buses and tepees but they're not exactly hippies. They smile a lot but they don't say much. The women all look pregnant."

"How long have they been here?"

"They weren't there last week. They're set up on that little patch of gravel under the edge of the mesita, just after you cross the river. They actually bought the place. Overpaid for it, of course."

"Who told you all this?" Roads asked.

"The Nice Lady."

Plain Bob was for sending the new arrivals a bag of herb as a welcome gift.

Plain Jane was against it. "They're born-agains!"

"Aren't we all born-agains?" Roads suggested. He phrased it like a reminder.

"I think we're talking about Christians," said Clay.

"So, aren't we are all Christians?" Little Richard asked, genuinely confused.

Annie was rolling a cigarette for Plain Jane. She looked up, shocked. "I'm a Jew."

"Me too," said Clay.

Roads cooked the meat, and gathered it too, spotlighting deer and then dispatching them with slugs from a double-barreled Mossberg 12 gauge that he kept out of sight under a pile of coats in the dome. That was at night, once a week or so. Little Richard usually went with him, working his rattles like deer calls.

Clay went along with them only once. It was like church.

There were prayers setting out, prayers when the big eyes were spotted, prayers with the noise, and prayers with the blood.

"Thank you, Brother Deer," said Roads as they pulled the warm body into the bed of the weeper.

Once was enough.

"They're called trims," said Rotella.

They were snow-white Styrofoam planks, in various odd widths and lengths, but all one-inch thick. They had been donated by a sympathetic box manufacturer in Pueblo, "a cool guy," according to Plain Bob, who was convinced they could be used to insulate the dome.

Clay wasn't so sure. But there they were, piled on the wide back seat of the Triple A bus.

He and Rotella gathered them up in stacks of eight or ten and maneuvered them down the long aisle and around the short, sharp corner out the door: hard to do without breaking them. They stacked like planks in the bed of the weeper, as light as soap bubbles, like a platonic ideal of lumber. The leaf springs didn't even know they were there.

"Better lay something over them," said Rotella. "They'll float away at the first bump you hit on Johnny's drive."

They sat in the sun on the steps of the Big House. Merry brought coffee out. Clay rolled cigarettes; Rotella lit her cigar, then let it go out. It was always the same cigar.

"Plain Bob will be glad to see those," said Merry. "He's been waiting weeks. I told him we would do our best. We don't usually stop in Pueblo."

"They're called trims," said Rotella.

"Plain Bob's gone," said Clay. "I think he's at Libra. He and Plain Jane had one of their fights."

"Imagine that," said Merry. "And who might this be?"

A VW bus was pulling into the lot, shaking softly like a dog after a run. On the sides it said, MCCARTHY FOR PREZ. On the front, between the headlights, it said, CHICAGO OR BUST.

"'Or bust' on a forty-horse?" said Rotella. "That's tempting fate."

The wide side doors swung open and two people got out of the back.

"This our world is looking merrier every day," said Merry. "A girl in a prom dress."

Clay was already on his feet. "That's no girl!" he said.

THIRTEEN

"THAT ONE STRAIGHT ACROSS THE VALLEY IS CALLED FU MANCHU," said Clay. "You'll see why when you see its long moustache when the snow comes. Those two out at the edge of the plains are the Huajatollas, Indian for 'the Breasts of God,' right?"

"Indian? That's a language?" protested Lowell.

"Okla, then," said Clay. "That's what Roads calls Indians." He had saved the biggest for last: Blanca, which brooded over them all at the end of the valley. "That scoop of snow near the top is ice," he said. "The southernmost glacier in the USA."

"Looks cold," said Dove, following Annie into the dome for more coffee. He had ditched the prom dress for jeans and a T-shirt.

"It was good for getting rides," said Lowell. "Though problematic at times."

Clay could imagine that. They had bid their ride good-bye and spent the night in the dome, on the floor next to his sleeping bag. Now here they were, Lowell especially, in the morning sun.

"You're beaming," said Lowell.

"I'm glad to see you," said Clay. "It's good to see you. It sort of stitches my life together. How'd you find me?"

"There are ways. We were just looking to fade into the Southwest communes. California was getting *très* weird, and it was time to go."

After San Francisco, Dove and Lowell had headed down to Los Angeles, where a long-lost Lowell cousin had put them up for a week and even introduced them to the Hollywood gay scene, "which is too queer even for me," said Lowell.

"I can't believe Ira was so weird."

"Ira has his reasons," said Lowell. "The FBI was nosing

around. They even gave him a subpoena. He showed it to me. He's trying to put a caravan together to connect all the communes up and down the coast. He's afraid the heat from the townhouse will mess up the scene."

"He wants the Hells Angels to join," said Dove.

"I told him that was crazy but Ira never listens to me," said Lowell. "Never did."

"A subpoena? Ira had nothing to do with the townhouse."

"Neither did we, remember? Apparently, the feebs are checking out everyone who was in and out of 50 Grand. They even have subpoenas drawn up for the rest of us. Even Dove."

"'Even Dove'? What's this 'even Dove' shit?"

"You want one, honey? Then keep your mouth shut. All we have to do is lay low awhile. From what I hear, it's mostly procedure, and they have other fish to fry."

"Meanwhile I'm glad you're here," said Clay. "We're all invisible here."

"Are we now? Maybe. Maybe we should park ourselves at Triple A or Libra. I'm not so sure Roads wants us here."

"I want to check out Libra," said Dove. "Roads says that's where the artists all end up."

The door groaned open and Little Richard came out, shaking his rattles at the sun.

"Chicago looms," said Merry. "Could be a game changer."

"The game was changed when JFK was shot," said Clay.

"Not to mention King," muttered Indigo.

"We played a benefit for McCarthy last week," said Rotella. "In Colorado Springs. He actually likes rock."

"No, he doesn't," said Indigo. "He's pretending."

"Is that so bad?" said Clay.

According to Roads, it would start to snow in September at the higher elevations. The snow line would move down week by week, "like pulling on a T-shirt," and hit the Rocks by mid-October at the earliest, mid-November at the latest, and the dome wasn't insulated yet. One big round space, easy to heat and even easier for the world outside to cool.

Plain Bob was back from Libra, where he had gone to sulk for a week. Clay sat on the deck watching him and Plain Jane glue the Styrofoam together into six-foot squares, then cut the squares into triangles with a hot wire looped between two poles of a twelve-volt battery, "borrowed" under protest from Gantz's truck.

Denver arrived from Libra to watch; this was a new and untried technology. Lowell was with him. He and Dove were living in Libra's community dome, sleeping on a feather mattress under Palomina's loom.

"We're not official yet," he told Clay. "There has to be a meeting when Cicero gets back from New York. Then we pick a spot for our house."

"House!"

"Dove likes it at Libra. He's learning to weave. Palomina has made him her slave. Roll me one of those."

By the end of the day there were thirty-four triangles in three configurations, in three separate stacks beside the weeper, ready to be fitted and glued to the plywood triangles inside the dome.

Lowell and Clay tried one on the bottom round. A perfect fit.

"It'll take a better glue to go higher, where they all start facing down," said Denver. "Unless you can turn the gravity down in here."

"What's this white stuff?" asked Johnny, who had just arrived from the upper meadow on his morose-looking horse. Roads and Little Richard were right behind him, returning from tending the herbs.

"Installation," said Little Richard.

"Color TV," said Johnny, tipping his hat and mounting up, since Annie had taken the wonder truck to Burg.

Rotella called them Dixie Cups. Clay was in the Triple A barn, sifting through her stash of forty-horse crankcases, when a familiar figure appeared in the doorway.

A Lowell. Clay was beaming again. They went outside and sat in the sun. Lowell had walked all the way from Libra, where there was nothing for him to do, he explained, since Palomina was working Dove like a Mexican peon, and they couldn't start their house until The Meeting was held, and The Meeting couldn't be held until Cicero was back from New York, where he had gone to work his gallery for the late-summer rush and, according to Palomina, fuck his other, supposedly secret girlfriend, the little Smith College bitch who opened and closed the gallery every day and then just sat there doing her nails all day because no one ever came in.

"Smith girls don't do their nails," said Lowell. "But Palomina won't listen to me. What's up at the Rocks?"

"Nothing to do at the Rocks either," said Clay. "We're waiting on some hide glue that Plain Bob has ordered."

"What about Chicago?" said Merry, joining them. "You guys should be in Chicago. Me too."

"That clown show?"

"Maybe you're right, maybe we should," said Clay. "Wonder if Becca will be there."

"Chicago? No way. She was all about RFK and that's over."

"What about Weather?" Merry asked. He approved of Weather.

"Weather is gone," said Lowell. "Dissolved into the Black Panthers or something, or so I hear—the honky auxiliary. They never recovered from the townhouse. Probably the same for the Kennedy people. They never recovered either."

Merry went into the Big House to get coffee.

"EmCee would be there," said Clay. They never talked about EmCee when anyone else was around.

"No shit," said Lowell. "She liked fighting in the street."

Clay remembered following EmCee, watching her disappear around the corner, just out of sight, just like in his dreams. "A fur coat and a lead pipe. It was like Clue. It was like a game. And then . . ."

"And then it wasn't a game anymore," Lowell finished.

Merry was back, three cups in two hands, beaming as well.

The foam triangles went up slowly, lighting the dome with their no-color as they went. The bottom row of triangles made the inside of the dome beautiful, all white inside, like an egg with struts laid into the shell.

"Let it snow," said Plain Jane. She was on the ladder, starting on the second round, holding the triangles in place with a broomstick while the glue got tacky enough to hold. The higher she went, the longer it took.

"We're going to need a scaffold," said Roads.

"We're going to need a better glue," said Plain Bob.

Little Richard and Clay were holding the wobbly ladder, looking up Plain Jane's long dress. She never wore underpants.

"What you need is a girlfriend," said Annie.

"What? I have one," said Little Richard.

"I was talking to Clay."

"You look like you lost someone."

"Huh?"

"The way you watch the highway," said Tulip—or was it Julep? She was one of Triple A's many visitors, traveling with a friend to Chicago, which was filling up with demonstrators protesting the inevitable choice of Humphrey at the Democratic National Convention.

"It's not a highway," said Clay. "Just a county road."

Their VW bus had coasted in, sputtering. Rotella was on her knees behind it, muttering.

"I was supposed to meet my boyfriend—he's there with McCarthy," said Julep—or was it Tulip? "Now I'll never make it in time."

"McCarthy doesn't have a chance," said Indigo. "So what's the point?

"My sort of boyfriend," she said to Clay.

"The point is to make a point," said Merry, who liked all the ruckus; who was European; who was a Dane but a Parisian Dane. His father had been an attaché. His uncle, who was with the embassy in DC, had gotten him into the US on an open-ended student visa when he dropped out of the Sorbonne.

"Wobble in the distributor," said Rotella. "I can probably find one in that pile but you'll have to stay the night."

"I'll look on it as an adventure," Julep—or was it Tulip?— said to Clay.

It was Julep—a made-up name of course. She was from Pennsylvania—or was it Ohio? She wore long braids and no bra and combat boots. Clay suspected her "Clean for Gene" boyfriend wore a tie.

"I might as well stay the night," he said to Merry.

Merry shrugged—or was that a wink? Guests slept in the loft of the practice barn, above Rotella's shop. Julep put her underpants with her socks in her combat boots so they wouldn't get hay in them.

She waited until after, when Clay was rolling her a cigarette, before she asked him if he had a girlfriend.

"Once upon a time," he said. Already it seemed like a fairy tale: the White Horse, the rabbit coat, the ring on the ferry.

Had they been together for a long, long time? "Not as long as you and me. You and me both grew up on the same street with no sidewalks, and both went to the same little brand-new school, and both our fathers bought a new car every other year, and both our mothers made cake from a box and ironed in front of the TV."

But she was already asleep.

She slept late; adventurers often do. Clay headed for the Big House for coffee. Merry met him on the porch, carrying a little plastic portable radio. "Listen up, America," he said, turning it up.

"Omigod!" said Clay.

Lowell came out, pulling on his pants, hopping from leg to leg. "I didn't know you were still here," said Clay.

"Just hanging out. Just like you. Are you heading for the Rocks?"

"I think I had better."

"I'm going with you."

They hurriedly put some water into the weeper. Merry followed them out to the truck, holding up the portable radio. "Take it or otherwise no one will believe it."

Clay shook his head. Roads had a thing about radios.

They were halfway up Johnny's road before Clay realized that he hadn't said good-bye to Julep.

Farewell, actually.

"Listen up, Rockers!" Lowell said as the dome door swung open, for once without a groan.

FOURTEEN

"LISTEN TO WHAT?"

"Kennedy has just been nominated for president. By the Democrats. In Chicago."

Kennedy? "Teddy?"

"Bobby. Robert. RFK. This morning. It's on the radio. Everybody thought he was dead or worse; he hasn't been seen since he was shot, but there they are, about to nominate Humphrey, trying to ignore the fighting in the streets, when in he walks with a bandage around his head, and before the day is over—yesterday, August 8, 1968—he is the fucking Democratic nominee. Humphrey is out."

"That means McCarthy is out," Annie said, disappointed as well as amazed.

"It was on the radio," said Clay. "At Triple A."

"You should have brought a radio," said Roads.

Johnny had the only color TV in the valley. He had bought it and a lemon-colored leather Barcalounger with the money from the Rockers. He was at a cattle sale in Aquinas, but his wife, Brenda, like any ranch wife, was glad to see company coming.

Even a truck full of hippies.

They crowded together on her plastic-covered couch like bees or puppies. Dove and Palomina arrived from Libra and sat on the floor. They had heard it on the radio.

Only Roads dared to sit in Johnny's Barcalounger. Brenda brought them all tea.

On TV it was the same clips, over and over: the fighting in the streets, the shouting and fighting in the great hall. Then there he was, with an entourage of grim-faced, expensively suited Irish thugs, with a bandage around his head, walking down the aisle and up onto the podium, as if it all been planned.

"As I'm sure it was," said Lowell.

"Sssshhhh," said Annie.

California was first, then Massachusetts; then the other states fell like LBJ's dread dominos. It was chaos. Kennedy signs appeared as if by magic, all printed to look improvised, and Daley was torn between his cops outside, who were in full cry, since one had been killed by a sniper even as he was gleefully nightsticking a girl on TV, and the Irish mafia inside, calling in their chits. . . . Meanwhile Humphrey's minions stalked out in protest but Humphrey stayed, perhaps hoping for the VP nomination, but that was not to be.

McCarthy's people looked dazed. So did Annie.

"I guess that means McCarthy's out," said Dove.

"He was never in," said Lowell. "He was an entertainment."

"Sssshhhh!" said Annie.

"Before I accept this honor you have offered me," RFK said, holding on to the podium with one hand as if still weak, dressed in a suit without a tie, and with an all-but-bloody bandage wrapped around his head, "this very great honor . . ."

And a silence fell over the hall, and over Johnny's living room as well.

"I want you to understand that I intend to end this war. This evil, brutal, tragic war that has torn our country apart."

Cheers in the hall, and Johnny's living room as well.

"And the war at home, the war against the young and the poor and the disenfranchised. We live in an awful, hopeful time. A time for healing and a time for new beginnings. I myself have been granted a new beginning . . ."

Cheers, mixed with hellos. Clay turned and saw that Johnny was back from Aquinas. He leaned in the doorway, rolling a cigarette one-handed.

"And it is my hope, with your help, to lead our beloved country to a new beginning too. I cannot do this alone. I need your help, and your understanding. I need strong souls. To that end, and with that promise, I wish to introduce, for your approval—and I need and expect it—my running mate, a man you all know well . . ."

The cameras closed in on Humphrey standing to the right and a little behind RFK, then mercifully pulled away as his face fell in on itself and Martin Luther King walked in from the wings, where he had been waiting—

"Jesus fucking Christ," said Lowell.

"Sssshhhh," said Annie.

—and took RFK's hand, and both were raised as a hush as loud as a cheer swept over the room.

The applause, polite at first, then swelling.

"Jesus fucking Christ," said Johnny.

There was a car at Triple A, a pink Cadillac, a '59.

"Whose is that?" asked Clay.

"See the stringy dude on the porch, rolling a joint, sitting beside the yellow dog?" asked Merry.

"He looks familiar," said Clay.

"He should," said Rotella from under the bus. She was replacing a U-joint. Clay had driven down in the weeper to help. Merry had come out of the kitchen to watch. The stereo was blasting in the Big House (which was not so very big). Kids were running in and out, so the music came in spurts, punctuated by the screen door, like a ride cymbal.

"Guess who I literally almost bumped into on the porch?" said Plain Bob, on his way to the practice barn with two cups of morning coffee. He and Plain Jane were staying in the loft. They had been asked to leave the Rocks after one of their fights.

"Gram Parsons," said Rotella, from under the bus.

"Of course!" said Clay.

"Only don't call him that," said Merry. "He's in the cognito, so to speak. We opened for the Flying Burrito Brothers at Denver State last week. We found him asleep in his car, parked behind our bus. He said he'd been kicked out of the band; they said he quit. Or was it to other way around? Anyway, he says he's starting a new life. Wants us to call him Rimshot."

"Rimjob it is, then," said Plain Bob, heading off. Plain Jane was waiting impatiently in the barn door, nude.

"Rim*shot*," said Rotella. "Hand me that 7/16 combination."

"Wants to play drums," said Merry. "Sick of singing, being out front, which is all right with me."

"As long as he doesn't want to play bass," said Rotella.

"Suits me," said Indigo, who was on his way to the practice barn, fingering a strat. "I'm not really a drummer anyway."

"Neither is he," said Merry.

"What's his dog's name?" asked Clay.

"Listen to these guys, jockeying for position," said Rotella. "Clay, come under here and take a look at this."

One of the too-small 7/16 bolts was rounded off. "Honey, you in a world of trouble," he said.

"Don't 'honey' me," Rotella muttered. "We're going to need a six-point socket, and loan me your Cadillac."

"I thought you were going to build at Libra."

"We were," said Lowell.

"We had the spot picked out," said Dove.

"But they finally had their Meeting. We can stay as long as we like, but we can't build."

"No single men," said Dove.

"But you're not single men," said Annie. "You're a couple."

"That's what we told them," said Lowell.

"Cicero is back," said Roads. He was cleaning the shotgun with a rag soaked in ATF. He had killed a deer the night before.

"You belong here," said Annie. "I knew it all along. Throw your money in The Can."

"We don't have any money."

"Then throw that in," said Roads.

Φ

"King looks amazingly like Humphrey," Lowell said. "He looked a little embarrassed when he got the nomination."

"Elmer Fudd," said Clay.

"Martin Luther Coon," said Little Richard. They were having supper, a mess of sticky rice cut with venison, on the deck of the dome, watching the sun set over the Sangres. "A nigger President."

"Vice President," said Clay.

"And exactly what the fuck do you mean by that? Which I find insulting," said Lowell.

"You're not a nigger," Little Richard pointed out.

"Me too," said Clay.

"Little Richard is just pointing out what everyone else is going to say," said Annie. "Out there."

"Little Richard can speak for himself," said Lowell.

"I think he just did," said Roads.

"Ooga booga," said Little Richard, shaking his rattle.

Two days later he was gone. "What about free speech?" Annie asked.

"It's overrated," said Roads.

"Voilà," said Dove. The French went with the prom dress; they were of a piece. It was ceremonial.

"Voilà indeed," said Lowell. "I can look up your dress."

"Bien." Dove had decided to take up where Plain Jane and Plain Bob had left off, and put up the triangles. He was standing on tiptoes on a shaky twelve-foot scaffold, trying to fit a triangle over his head.

Clay and Lowell were trying to hold the scaffold steady, without much success.

"We need more glue," said Dove, peering down like Michelangelo. "Staples are too short. Nails are too thick. They split the plywood, plus they conduct heat."

"I'll see what I can do," said Annie. She was rattling the keys to the wonder truck, on her way to town. "Meanwhile, you need to triangulate that thing."

When she returned it was two feet taller: a fourteen-foot three-legged tower made of leftover two-by-fours, angle-braced on three sides and topped by a triangular platform of miscut 3/4–inch plywood.

Clay helped her carry in the supplies and Lowell put them away in Roads's kitchen: Bugler, sugar, cornmeal, rice, yellow cheese, Crisco, Spam, and Oreos.

"And glue?" Dove asked, peering down, brushing the sawdust off his prom dress.

"The glue will have to wait. Mother's letter didn't come. We're down to girl money." She looked up, darkly. "And that thing still looks shaky."

"He likes shaky," said Lowell.

"You oughta know," said Dove. "It's very romantic up here. Come up and see."

Smoothing his prom dress under him, he lay down on his stomach and leaned over the side, extending an arm down toward Lowell, who shook his head.

"You come down," said Lowell.

"I looked for Becca," said Clay. He and Lowell were alone on the moon-shaped deck of the dome, rolling cigarettes out of the same Bugler can.

"Where? On the TV?"

"Do you think she was in Chicago?" he asked. "Is there a subpoena out for her?"

"I don't think so. Her old man's a bit of a fixer."

"Wonder if she's back on board the Kennedy campaign. Now that there's a Kennedy campaign again."

Kennedy was leading in the polls. "Polls don't mean anything," said Lowell. "This country will never elect a progressive president."

"This country is against the war," said Clay. "And I thought you didn't consider RFK a progressive anyway."

"Even if he was. And this country will never elect a Black vice president."

"That is a sticker," said Clay.

"Litter of pigs," said Clay.

He and Roads were driving back from Triple A, where they had just delivered a deer haunch into the freezer, which muttered and sighed on the porch like a hibernating bear, even though it was only September.

Yosemite stepped out of his Celotex hogan. He waved solemnly with his .30-30, lifting it like a coupstick, Indian-brave style. His squaw beside him, her tiny breasts bare.

Roads waved back.

Near the edge of the arroyo, blanketed figures sat around a fire. Clay counted four. One of them raised a stick in greeting; something smoked on it—meat? Roads waved back.

Clay didn't. "Wasn't that Little Richard?"

"Ooga booga," said Roads.

"They shit in the arroyo," said Clay, shifting down for the last long pull up to the Rocks. The weeper was already steaming: the water pump going from bad to worse.

"Everybody shits in the arroyo," said Roads. "That's what arroyos are for. The Earth provides a home for us all. Anyway, it's Johnny's arroyo, not ours."

"Johnny just likes to ride by and look at that little girl's titties."

"And don't we all?" said Roads.

Everything suited him. Sometimes Clay found it annoying.

"Look like we have company," Roads said.

"Huh?"

"Aren't those motorcycle tracks?"

Little diamonds in the dust, like a snake's trail. Clay shifted down for the last turn around the Rock.

A motorcycle was parked by the steps to the dome with a sleeping bag and duffel on the back.

"I know that bike," said Clay. It was a 350 Honda Scrambler, with high pipes and a Confederate flag decal on the tank. Had Bobby Lee dropped out of Vanderbilt?

Annie and Lowell were sitting on the deck with a man in a black beard and a fatigue jacket like the Other Ginsburg had once worn. But it wasn't him for sure, and it wasn't Bobby Lee either.

It was Harl.

FIFTEEN

"I THOUGHT YOU WERE IN GERMANY."

"I was in Vietnam. Then Germany. Then DC."

Harl showed Clay his bad arm. He couldn't lift it over his shoulder. The fingers barely worked.

"What happened?"

"You don't want to know. Roll me one of those."

Clay and Harl were sitting on the moon-shaped deck of the dome. Everybody else was inside. "Want me to light it?"

"I'm not a fucking cripple." Harl pulled out a Zippo. "I just can't roll cigarettes."

"Well, that's good, I guess. Purple Heart?"

"Not exactly." He tossed Clay the Zippo. It was engraved: DA NANG '68.

Harl had been wounded by friendly fire in Da Nang. He had been evacuated to Germany, then to Walter Reed for rehab. "I was supposed to get a Purple Heart. A Colonel delivers them, pins it on you in the ward. Then they send you back. Three of us split the night before the ceremony. It's like your ticket back, no shit."

"So you're AWOL?"

"I wish. Worse than that. Since we were active duty and still technically in-country, it's desertion. Or so I understand."

"Yikes. Does Roads know?"

"Roads knows," said Roads, from the doorway behind them. He sat down between them and rolled a cigarette from the Bugler can. "We needn't say another word about it, and probably shouldn't."

"Suits me," said Harl.

"You two always made quite the pair. One without illusions,

and the other all illusions. Opposites in a way. You two belong together."

"So which is which?"

"That's my secret," said Roads.

"I did at first," Lowell said. "I dreamed about her every night. She was my best friend. My only friend for several years."

"She always said you saved her life."

"Well, she can't say that anymore. Why do you ask?"

"I dreamed about her last night," Clay said. "For the first time in a while. She and her father were standing in the doorway of that little deli on Thompson Street, the one where I met Allen Ginsberg and he gave me the nickel. She was holding an animal. I knew what it was in the dream but I don't anymore."

"You dream about the old man too? You never met the old man."

"Actually, I did," said Clay. He told Lowell the whole story: the knock at the door, the White House envelope filled with twenties. "I keep it in the bottom of my sleeping bag," he said.

"You never put it in The Can?"

"It was never mine to put in The Can."

It snowed.

This time as far down the mountain as the stock tank at the top of the upper meadow, at the edge of the National Forest, where the Rockers gathered their wood.

"It's time," said Roads. Harl had replaced Little Richard as his helper; they cut the plants with a machete. hauled them down in armloads from the upper meadow, and hung them under the dome to dry. It made for a wonderful smell. Clay was reminded of the tobacco barn in Calhoun. "Tobacco you have to strip though."

"What's that?" asked Plain Jane.

"Pull the leaves," said Harl. "Grade them, tie them together in hands. Big ugly sticky leaves."

"Big beautiful sticky leaves," said Clay. "Burley and dark both. I helped out one year on my grandmother's place. A share-cropper grew it, and he paid folks a dollar an hour to help. Even the landlady's grandson. We'd all stand around a table out in the barn and people would tell stories. It was November and it was cold."

"What kind of stories?" Annie asked.

"Hillbillies know lots of stories," said Harl. "Problem is, they are all about hillbillies."

In October Ham died. Annie brought the news from Burg in a letter, forwarded from California.

I need you here for this.

Clay shook the envelope and three twenties fell out.

Annie picked them up and put them in The Can.

Clay plucked them back out. He showed Annie the letter. She handed Clay The Can.

There was only $18.20 in Hollywood money. Clay left it there.

He waited until he was sure no one was looking and pulled three more twenties from the envelope in the bottom of his sleeping bag; that left twenty, or $400.

He searched the ome for clean socks.

"*Vaya con Dios,* my friend," mourned Dove from above.

Clay got a ride to Denver in the Triple A bus, and to Evansville in a Lockheed Electra. He was expecting his mother but she had sent Bobby Lee to pick him up in a new Mercury with dealer plates. They drove east on 60, then turned south at the 4-Way.

"Wonder what's on that jukebox these days?"

"Marty Robbins and Dinah Washington," said Bobby Lee. "Speaking of which, do you have a mailing address for Harl?"

"For Harl?"

"Donna and I are getting married. Harl needs to know."

"Congratulations," said Clay. "But isn't he AWOL or something?"

"I thought all you fugitives stuck together."

"That would be stupid."

"The wedding's not till March next year—I have to finish my orals and my dissertation first. But Donna got the invitations printed up already. You know how she is."

"Actually I don't. I hardly knew her."

"She always maintained you had a crush on her."

"I don't know where she got that idea."

"We even invited her good-for-nothing father."

They were leaving Indiana, crossing the two-lane bridge over the muddy Mason-Dixon line: the Ohio River. "Speaking of fugitives," Clay said, to change the subject. "This is the bridge Bill Monroe crossed on his way to Chicago to invent bluegrass. He was one of your cultural fugitives. Is he going to be in your doctoral thesis?"

Owensboro looked the same. Low buildings on a high bank like leavings from a flood.

"It's rather a different bunch," said Bobby Lee. "Welcome home. I'll drop you at your mother's."

Junior wore a captain's bars. He stood at attention by his father's coffin until the ceremony was over, then got swiftly, expertly drunk.

"I was always little sister to him," said Clay's mother. She looked older, dressed for church. "Now he's gone and so is your father, Clay. So are you. And I'm an old lady. Pour us another, Scooter."

"Yes, ma'am."

Kentucky Tavern, Bottled in Bond, four years old. According

to Scooter's father, the Kentucky Supreme Court judge, bourbon stopped improving after six years, and four was almost enough.

"Fifty's not old, Lou Emma," said Scooter. He winked at Clay; he knew better. He was in law school at Vanderbilt, having put it off as long as possible.

"A little old lady," she said.

They were sitting on the screened-in front porch of Ham's big house. October nights in Kentucky are still warm. The reception was over and the guests were gone. The house was littered with best plates and best silver, left around on every level surface. Hosea's oldest daughter, Edna, was cleaning up. She knew where everything went.

Like her old man, Clay thought.

"I have to get back to Nashville," Scooter said. He rang the keys to his Thunderbird like a bell. His father had left for Louisville right after the graveside ceremony.

"Sleep here," said Clay's mother. She lay down on the wicker couch and closed her eyes, as if to demonstrate.

Clay walked Scooter to his Thunderbird. It was a classic, a '57.

"Summer of Love," said Scooter. "I love it that you didn't cut your hair."

"That was the summer of '67. Are you sure you can drive?"

As if to prove it, Scooter turned the key. The T-Bird started with a low, expensive glasspac roar. Hardly ten years old, it looked like a relic from another era, turquoise and white, as it disappeared into the night.

"Good old Scooter," said Junior, when Clay got back to the porch. "It's always a pleasure to see him go. Sit down and I'll tell you a secret. Sit down, soldier."

Oh no, thought Clay. Junior was pretty drunk too. So, for all that, was he.

"My father's the one who should have gone to law school, not Uncle Clayton. Daddy should have been the judge. In those days they couldn't afford it though, so his big brother went and he became a Ford dealer. He was a disappointed man."

"Ford-Lincoln-Mercury," said Clay's mother from the couch. "He was more a big brother to me than Clayton ever was. Marry that Yankee, he said. Get the hell out of here."

"My father was a disappointed man," said Clay.

"If you don't like my peaches," said Clay's mother, "don't you shake my tree."

"I should have gone to West Point," said Junior. "You should have gone to Vanderbilt. Let's go sit on the steps and let your mother go to sleep."

As he got up to follow, Clay saw himself in the window glass, wearing a suit and tie, the same suit and tie he had worn to his father's funeral. It was in fact his father's suit and tie.

He took two Kents from his mother's pack and sat on the steps beside Junior.

"I never wanted to go to Vanderbilt. I was a fugitive from Vanderbilt."

He tore the filter off one and lit it.

"My name is Jimmy," said Clay's mother, from the wicker couch. "I'll take what you gimme."

"I'll drink to that," said Junior. He studied Clay through his empty glass, holding it like a telescope. "You were always a better shot than me."

"Bet I'm not now. You're an officer."

"Officers don't shoot," said Junior. "Though I did get a Marksman medal." He pointed it out on his breast. "Daddy was proud of that. I'm glad he was proud of something I did. He didn't know shit about the Army. Everybody gets a fucking Marksman medal."

Clay stumbled off to pee in the bushes. He didn't like where this was going.

"You should join the Army!" Junior called out after him. "Get a Marksman medal. Get a Purple Heart!"

"Clay doesn't even have a job," muttered Clay's mother from the wicker couch.

"He's building a new world!" said Junior. "Aren't you? Zip up your pants, soldier."

Clay zipped up his pants. He poured another drink and set the bottle down on the porch steps between him and Junior.

"Isn't that what you all are doing? Building a new world. That's what it said in *Life* magazine. There was a whole story on you guys, the hippies, the Love Train Generation. You didn't see it?"

"I missed it."

"The new world. Some of it looked old-fashioned though. The tepees and stuff."

"There aren't all that many tepees," said Clay. He tried to change the subject. "Are you still in Vietnam?"

"DC. They wouldn't have flown me home from 'Nam. Daddy wouldn't have wanted them to. I did 'Nam. 'Nam and then 'Nam.

"They sent you twice?"

"I volunteered." Junior laughed. "Wanted to make captain. Don't get me wrong. I love the Army, I'm not complaining. Didn't you like it just a little? Didn't you like ROTC?"

"Actually I did," said Clay.

"There's my ride," said Edna, Ice's mother. "Your mother is asleep on the couch, Clay. I pulled a blanket over her."

"I hope you put out her cigarette," said Junior.

"Thank you, Edna."

She was pulling on her coat. It had once belonged to Clay's mother. "Your father was a good man, Junior. He was always good to me and my family."

"Thank you, ma'am."

She stepped between them, out the door and down the steps and out the driveway, to the Olds idling silently under a tree in front of the house. Clay hadn't heard it drive up. Colored people never honked in white neighborhoods. Not even Ice.

"But it has turned to shit," said Junior as soon as he heard the Olds drive away. "It's all draftees, colored. They don't care. I have good colored friends, don't get me wrong, noncoms. They are the best, but these draftees are for shit. And if Kennedy wins we will never win this war."

"He's not elected yet," Clay pointed out.

"Then the colored will win. They'll get their way. The draftees will run the Army then. Maybe it'll be better. Hell, don't get me wrong. But it won't."

"If you don't like my peaches," Clay's mother called out from the wicker couch, behind them on the screened-in porch, "then don't you shake my tree. Either of you boys have a match?"

"I have a Zippo," said Junior. He fumbled for it, tossed it to Clay. It was engraved: DA NANG '68.

"For you," said Merry. He handed Clay a campaign postcard: *RFK for a New America*. On the front it showed three people: a smiling white woman, a scowling Black teen, and a determined-looking *bracero* holding up a HUELGA sign.

On the back it said, "Hampton Inn. Here till Mon. Be that as it may."

"Where'd you get this?"

Clay had hitched into Denver from the airport, hoping to catch a ride back down to the valley with Triple A, which was playing an All-For-Bobby benefit at Mile High State.

"You have a lady friend," said Rotella.

"I think she thought you were with the band," said Merry.

"She was smoking these long pink cigarettes," said Rimshot. "Pink and baby blue. I thought I was back at the Chelsea Hotel."

Clay found Becca at the Marriott, in a room set up as a mobile campaign headquarters. A Black girl was on the phone. Becca opened the door.

"Clay!" she said. "Should you be here?"

"It was your idea."

"So it was." She kissed him back, then led him downstairs to the bar, just off the lobby. It was empty.

"We're ahead in the polls."

"Good for you. But Nixon's full of surprises."

"So are we."

There were only four stools; they took two of them. Becca wore a lavender pants suit and a Gucci scarf.

"So you were there."

"I was there," Becca said. A cowboy in chaps looked on from a mural behind the bar. "And now I'm here."

"I looked for you on the TV."

"I was not in the streets. Daddy got me on as an alternate delegate with Rhode Island. Didn't you know, I'm Italian. Daddy's a big Democrat, the kind no one says no to. I was a Humphrey delegate. I still don't know if any of them knew what was coming."

She set the Shermans on the bar between them.

"I suspect some did though. The rest of us were stunned. The speaker, some in-between Democrat but a Californian, stopped in the middle of his speech, contriving, I now think, to look stunned. We're all like, what's this? Then everybody's turning around and there he is, not only alive but walking down the center aisle . . ."

Clay had seen that part, he told her. Everyone in America had, over and over: the familiar unfamiliar figure appearing at the back of the convention hall, walking down the wide center aisle between the rowdy but now silent delegations, in silence, surrounded by his security guards.

"Like a bride," he said.

"Like a groom," she said.

Walking slowly, step-by-step down the aisle of the Democratic National Convention. Walking straight up to take the podium from the silenced speaker—"who had pretty clearly been in on the maneuver as well," Becca said. "And when he spoke, he spoke like one who had been in the fire and survived, and who knew what had to be done, and was willing, now, finally, to do it. It was thrilling, even though it was all trickery. It was right."

Kennedy was nominated by acclaim. One go-around. The chaos outside had penetrated in, like smoke. People couldn't stay off their feet. A few journalists specializing in the tragic filmed Humphrey slinking off, shamed, dishonored, remaindered.

"Another casualty of war," said Becca. "Bartender? Unless you're in a hurry to get back to Utopia," she added, turning back to Clay.

Clay was in no hurry. They ordered burgers and the bartender set them up at the end of the bar. Clay hadn't eaten out in months, since he had been on the road. The beer was cold.

And the Shermans, with their gold-and-green filters.

"You're still on the expense account? I hope."

"Unofficial," Becca said. "From Dad. To keep me off the streets."

"So you never saw the fighting in the streets."

"Only after it was over. Daley had called off the cops. It was like Motown, dancing in the streets. Bonfires in Hamilton Park. The cops were nowhere to be seen. The Panthers were out in uniform."

"And Weather?"

"Weather is history, Clay. The story is they dissolved into the Panthers, the ones that were underground, and the rest went home."

"Talk about Motown," said Clay. On the TV men and women in long coats were dancing in the street, in Russia, not Chicago. The bartender turned up the sound. The Red Army had refused to move into Hungary. They had taken over their troop train and returned to Leningrad.

Their wives were meeting them at the Finland Station with cakes and babies.

"Do you ever dream about her?" Becca asked. "I do sometimes."

She paid the bill with a credit card and he followed her upstairs. He kissed her in the elevator. She kissed him back.

She slipped off her shoes outside the door.

"You can stay the night if you like," she said. "The girls have the room next door. We have to be in Salt Lake City tomorrow night."

"I'm riding back with the band tomorrow. I'm not with them, you know. I'm just staying at a place nearby."

"In Utopia."

"Not exactly."

"Well, then. Be that as it may."

She took off her blouse and pants and hung them, carefully, in the doorless closet. She pulled on a T-shirt over her bra and panties. She moved the stacks of papers off the bed and turned off the light and slipped under the covers.

Clay joined her.

There was just enough light from the big sign out the window to see her eyes, open, only inches from his own.

"You look the same," she said. "How'd you manage that?"

"Sometimes—" he began.

Becca shook her head to shut him up. Placed her finger on his lips. Then placed his hands, one and then the other, on her breasts, one and then the other.

SIXTEEN

"I saw your sister," said Clay.

"You didn't tell her I was here."

"Of course not."

"More glue," said Dove from above. Harl passed it up, hanging the little bucket from a long forked stick. The glue had to be mixed in small batches and cost $9.95 a quart, according to Annie, whose Hollywood money had finally arrived.

"But only fifty dollars," she said. "I think my mother has a new boyfriend." The letter had come from Mazatlan.

"It's made from wild horses," Dove called down. His scaffold was almost twenty feet high. He lathered on the glue with a paint stirrer, then held the triangle in place with a broom until it held. His crinoline, already stiff, was stiffer still with glue.

"He won't take off the prom dress," said Lowell. "He's become a madman."

"He's found his calling," said Roads. "Winter is coming."

Gantz was gone, with his lady, back to Denver to take his bar exam. Plain Bob and Plain Jane had moved to Taos, to make a new start.

Harl passed up the triangles, each matched to its destination. They were so light they all but floated up.

"I saw Becca."

"So I hear. I have friends at Triple A."

"So I hear."

Clay and Lowell were on the deck of the dome; they only talked about New York when they were alone.

"So how does she look? What did you talk about?"

"Everything but everything. You. Me. New York. EmCee. I didn't mention that you were here. I didn't really mention here. She didn't think there were any subpoenas out for her."

"Or if there were, they went away," said Lowell. "Connections."

"You ought to know about connections."

"Different sort. How does she look?"

"As ever," said Clay. "Well fed. Well dressed. Fits right in. All those Kennedy people look like the Clean for Genes."

"Let's hope they are more successful. I hear you spent the night. How did that go?"

"None of your business."

"Everything's my business," said Lowell. "You, Clay, of all people should know that by now."

"Something's coming," said Annie.

It was Rimshot's pink Caddy, slipping and sliding through the light new snow, with a smiling Dane at the wheel.

It was Merry, with a *New York Times.*

It was spring in the south of the planet. Robben Island, South Africa's Devil's Island, had been attacked at dawn by masked commandos in speedboats: three sleek twenty-seven-foot "cigarettes," approaching from both the north and west. Whispering in French and shouting in Russian, the commandos had overpowered the guards and loaded all the prisoners onto a waiting submarine while two Tupolev Badgers circled at a thousand meters, providing unnecessary air cover.

One Boer and one Coloured guard played hero. Both were killed in the ensuing gun battle on the stony west beach; one Cuban "adviser" and two Congolese commandos were wounded, and one speedboat was disabled. When it was IDed as a Baikal the South African government had issued a formal complaint to the United Nations, backed by Israel and the US.

Meanwhile, Nelson Mandela and several of his comrades

were welcomed in Kinshasa by the Congolese president, Patrice Lumumba.

"There's your new world, said Lowell. "The Russians are Bolsheviks again. Since the coup."

"Of course they deny they are even involved," said Merry.

"Of course," said Lowell. "Everyone always denies they are involved in everything."

"You both oughta know," said Dove, glaring down at Lowell and Merry.

"Help! People are crazy here."

Back from Burg, Annie passed the note around. It had arrived in the mail. Clay tuned the wonder truck. It ate plugs.

Lowell rode with Roads down to New Buffalo, the ur-commune in Arroyo Hondo, near Taos. When they returned the next day with Plain Bob and Plain Jane, who had been asked to leave after one of their fights, Dove's tower was twenty-four feet high.

"Cool!" said Plain Jane. "What's that smell?"

"Wild horses," said Dove. He looked over the edge, peering down like Michelangelo from his aerie. "So you're back. How'd you like New Buffalo?"

"People are crazy there," said Plain Bob.

"It's just another utopia," said Lowell.

"Mud is first among their sacraments," said Roads, setting his boots by the door.

"It's all adobe," said Lowell, at dinner. "Far from geodesic. They make their own bricks out of mud and shit and straw. They eat beans and government cheese. A goat jumped onto the kitchen table while we were having dinner. It's very patriarchal."

"Patriarchal?"

"A billy goat."

Nothing beats Bugler. Clay rolled two, then asked, "So what's it like?"

"What?"

"Sleeping with Annie."

"None of your business."

"I just wondered."

"It's titty heaven," said Harl. "If you have to know."

"They're shitting in the arroyo. They're stealing Johnny's water. They're cutting thousand-year-old piñon for firewood."

That was Annie. The Rockers used only down wood, mostly pine.

"The world shits in the arroyo," said Roads. "You just don't like those kids."

"Kids!" said Clay. "That Yosemite is thirty-five if he's a day."

"They're squatters," said Lowell.

"We're all squatters," said Roads. "But I'll tell you what . . ."

"What?"

Instead of answering he pulled on his coat and pulled the door open and took off walking: not on Johnny's road, down through the meadow, but on the shortcut that led through the ledges and the piñons around the back side of the Rock.

An hour later he was back. "They'll be gone by the end of the week."

"What did you tell them?"

"I told them that the Earth doesn't belong to us, we belong to the Earth. I told them that when winter comes the snow will pile up deeper and deeper until May or maybe even June."

"That's not true. This isn't fucking Minnesota."

"I told them it never snows down near Taos."

"That's not true either."

"Then I told them there were two girls for every guy at New Buffalo. Then it started to snow."

There was a party at Triple A. It lasted all night and into the morning. Rimshot played drums and Plain Bob played harmonica.

"Where'd he learned to play like that?" Harl asked.

Merry put acid in the punch. Roads danced with Palomina for the first time in years. Dove wore his prom dress, glue and all. Little Richard showed up, then left. Clay caught Merry and Lowell kissing on the porch while the freezer rumbled behind them like a hibernating bear. RFK was ahead in the polls.

The sun was just appearing over the mountain when the Rockers headed home in the weeper. "Looks like it snowed up here," said Clay.

"Just a skirmish," said Roads. He and Annie rode jammed in the cab with Clay. The rest of the Rockers were stacked in the bed of the truck like cordwood, under an imitation buffalo robe.

"A lot of good your lecture did," said Annie.

Yosemite was standing outside his Celotex hogan with his teenage "lady" by his side. The rest were gone. Their fire was out; they hadn't even left tracks, or if they had they were covered by the snow, the second of the year.

Only an inch, it was already melting away into the bright morning air.

Yosemite waved. Roads waved back.

"He's the one I hated," said Annie.

"You kids want some more tea?" Brenda asked.

She loved company.

Johnny was in his leather Barcalounger, silent tonight. Clay and Annie were on the floor; Lowell was on the plastic-covered couch with Brenda. Dove had stayed behind with Roads.

"No, thank you."

"RFK could still win it," said Lowell. Nixon's whirlwind tour of the South in a military helicopter had cut into Kennedy's lead.

By six thirty New York was in. An hour later, Illinois was in. By nine p.m. Mountain Time, Huntley and Brinkley had called it: RFK by a hair. Humphrey looked dazed. Nixon, glowering, was preparing to concede when Johnny got up from his chair and unplugged the TV.

"A nigger hair," he said. "A nigger president."

"Vice president," Annie offered. It seemed like time to go.

"I can make some more tea," said Brenda. Johnny opened the door.

"Trouble," said Lowell as they piled into the waiting weeper. "I smell trouble."

"It was not exactly a landslide," said Clay.

"He will end the war," said Annie.

"Or start one," said Roads, when he heard the news.

"I'm not sure I believe in utopias," said Harl.

"Me neither," said Clay.

"So who does?" asked Roads. "Your boy Bobby?" He was cooking breakfast. Clay and Lowell had taken acid the night before. The cast-iron skillet gleamed, a window into night from day.

"You," said Lowell. "Isn't that the whole idea?"

"You guys have it ass-backwards," said Roads. "Utopia is what we're getting away from. You were born in Utopia." Roads boiled his own syrup from brown sugar and water, reversing the process. "Postwar America, the suburbs—what is all that but a utopian vision, dreamed up during endless nights in foxholes and steerages around the world?"

"I believe we've heard this before," said Annie.

"You were born and raised in Utopia. That's what the suburbs are. The utopian dream of the men in the war, dreamed through cigarette smoke in the bottom of crummy troop ships, tossing on an endless sea, created like cotton candy out of the fabric of young men's horny dreams: a car in every garage, a woman in every house, a couple of kids, a tree in the yard, all just alike of course—these were Army dreams, and these were not the most imaginative of men."

"I was a TVA baby," said Clay. "TVA was kind of a utopian vision, I guess. My father came to Kentucky to build the dams."

"The New Deal," said Roads. "There's a utopia for you, and look where it led."

"Vietnam," said Harl.

"Lawn mowers," said Roads. "An air-conditioner in every window. Look closer to home."

Like an experienced fry cook, he worked with a cigarette in his mouth, using both hands. "Dismantling Utopia is what we are doing. Letting the grass grow. Setting the kids free."

"We were always free," said Clay. "All the yards ran together. We played out after dark."

"Then you grew up." It was the old Roads: the teacher.

"I thought you said it was a waste of time to destroy the old world when what we should do is build the new."

"Did I say that? Sounds right."

"But it's a contradiction."

"And that's so bad?" Roads grinned.

"Guess who I saw in Burg?" said Annie. "Little Richard. He's staying at One Way. That born-again bunch at the edge of town."

"Serves him right," said Harl.

"Did you bring glue?" The last two rounds of triangles at the top of the dome still awaited insulation.

"No letter from home. All I had was girl money. This is all I could get." One bag of groceries plus Bugler.

Clay didn't even bother to ask about his water pump, still on order at Lopez Auto Parts. The weeper wasn't so bad when the weather was cold, and it was getting colder.

"Did he convert?" Plain Bob asked. "I converted once."

"I didn't ask. He was always a Christian, I think. He kept a Bible in that box of stuff."

"All those peyote types are Christians," said Roads. "They don't read the Bible but they like to thump it; they pass it around the peyote circle sometimes like a drum."

"I thought it was an Indian thing."

"Same thing," said Roads. "You'll see."

The big peyote meeting was planned for the solstice in December.

"It'll just make Dove crazier," Lowell said. "You'll see."

"This just in!"

It was Merry with the *New York Times* from Denver.

Mutiny in Vietnam. Da Nang locked down. The enlisted men were bucking the line. The war over as far as they were concerned. The Black Panther Party (of Vietnam!) was negotiating, in masks.

"There's your new world," said Lowell.

"They should wait for the inauguration at least," said Annie. She liked procedures.

"Easy for you to say," said Lowell. "Who wants to be the last guy killed in the wrong war? Any volunteers?"

"Some of those guys are pretty badass," said Harl, rubbing his bad arm.

It was a dark and stormy night.

There was a knock at the door.

Clay was reading by a kerosene lamp: *Dune*, about a planet without water. He was beginning to get back into science fiction, almost, after all these years. Plus it was from Chilton, a publisher of automotive flat-rate manuals. Rotella had loaned it to him.

There it was again. The door to the dome was a counterweighted triangle that had been designed by Plain Bob to keep out wind and rain, but never people. There was no lock or latch. Nobody ever knocked. That would have been too weird, like knocking at a supermarket or an office building.

There it was again.

Clay steepled his book and looked around the dome. Harl and Roads were playing Scrabble. Lowell and Annie were looking through an old issue of *Vogue* with a kerosene lamp between them. Dove was up in his tower, sulking. Nobody else had heard.

There it was again.

Clay got up and swung the door open. It was Yosemite's girl.

She had walked up the canyon, almost a mile, with a black eye. In moccasins.

Annie made her some tea. Roads made her some spaghetti. Harl threw a log into the Ashley. The girl sat by it and shivered. She was wearing a Brando-style motorcycle jacket, way too big, over nothing at all but a pair of men's jockey shorts and the moccasins, soaked with old snow. Annie wrapped her in a blanket. She wouldn't say anything, but when Annie asked, "Did he hit you?" she looked up at her and nodded.

Annie stuck a finger in the girl's open mouth, as if she were a horse. She had a loose tooth.

"She's staying here," Annie said.

Lowell shook his head. "She's underage. Do we really want to inherit Yosemite's trouble?"

Annie shot him a sharp look and folded her arms. The girl just sat there.

"What's your name?" Clay asked. "Where are you from? How old are you?"

Harl just looked on, rubbing his bad arm. Someday he's going to rub it away, Clay thought.

"Want some pancakes?" asked Roads.

"Please," said the girl.

And that was her name, from then on.

SEVENTEEN

"THEY'RE LIKE DIXIE CUPS," SAID ROTELLA. "USE THEM AND THEN throw them away."

She and Clay were sifting through pistons and jugs for the honeymoon bus's forty-horse when a strange truck pulled into the Triple A drive. Truly strange, not just unfamiliar. It was an old Chevy with an A-frame plywood camper on the back, painted black and white like a pirate flag: a skull and the words OAKLAND HELLS ANGELS.

"Uh-oh," said Rotella.

"It's okay," said Clay. "I know these people."

It was Ira, leaping from the driver's seat all smiles, wearing a leather vest. He walked in a ceremonial circle around Clay before breaking off and hugging him almost off his feet. He was, as always, bigger than his size.

"Just the man I was looking for," said Clay.

"A diplomatic visit," Ira said. "Making connections."

A skinny girl looked on from the cab of the truck with narrow hillbilly eyes. Ira opened the door and made her get out. She had tattoos and a grumble.

"Alameda. My lady."

She leaned against him, eyeing Clay mistrustfully.

At the back of the truck, the door of the camper opened. A big black-bearded man got out and pissed against the left rear wheel. He was bald except for a long pigtail; shirtless, even in the cold, except for a Hells Angels vest; expressionless except for a scowl. He zipped up his jeans and got back in the camper.

"His name's Hawk," said Ira. "He's an Indian. Doesn't talk much."

"Nice enough truck," said Rotella.

"He's not really an Indian," said Alameda.

"Can't beat the old 235," Ira said.

"We are all of us not really all sorts of things," said Merry, the diplomat, bringing coffee from the house and introducing himself.

"I've heard about you," Ira told him. It wasn't true (or was it?) but Ira wanted everyone to shine. He shone brightest of all, taller by almost a head with his long hair tied up with a pirate scarf.

Clay couldn't have been more proud. "You're coming up to see the dome," he said. It was a question, an invitation, a suggestion, a plea.

"Of course. We're only here for the night or two, then down to Taos and back to Califor-nye-ay. This is a diplomatic visit."

Ira looked the diplomat, with his beribboned ponytail and new tattoos. He and Alameda had one that matched: an American flag with a skull and crossbones instead of stars. Hers was on top of her left breast.

Merry made more coffee while Rotella gave them a tour of the barn. Clay followed happily.

"Nice shop!" said Ira. "SK. Nice tools."

And Rotella too was his.

"Calliope," said Ira, as they rounded the Rock and the dome loomed into view.

Clay was beaming again. He introduced Harl as his oldest friend. And Roads, of course.

"Of course," Ira said. "Your name looms large in his legend."

Lowell was the big surprise. Should they pretend they had never met? It seemed pointless, then impossible. Ira and Lowell circled each other, then embraced, then circled some more, all evening. They were more like rivals than friends, Clay realized; it was an even closer bond. Roads made spaghetti. Annie was charmed, she was sure. Please glowed from her blanket by the stove; she was pregnant, though no one knew it yet, not even her.

Plain Jane and Plain Bob, back but no longer speaking, offered their bed in the honeymoon bus to the visitors. At midnight Ira and Alameda came in both scowling and slept on opposite sides of the stove.

The next morning Ira woke Clay while everyone else was sleeping. They pulled on their coats and walked through the upper meadow, up to the stock tank at the edge of the National Forest.

"It's not me," said Ira. "Nothing makes her happy."

Lowell joined them, out of breath. "What happened to that subpoena?" he asked.

"Nothing," said Ira. "I got a lawyer and they dropped it. They had one for you too. I don't know about what's-his-name or Clay."

"Dove," said Clay. "We've been avoiding them."

"Maybe they gave up," said Ira. "Nice view though."

"I'm not so sure we should bunch up," said Lowell.

"If you're talking about me, don't worry. I'm heading for New Mexico and then back to California. We have stuff doing. Nice view though. Roll me one of those."

"Make me a favor and get that asshole out of here," said Merry. Hawk had spent the night in the Triple A parking lot. Now he was sitting on the running board of the Chevy, unloading a revolver.

Two boys were watching. Two mothers jerked them away.

"What did he do?" Ira asked innocently, almost. He and Clay had just driven down in the weeper, with Alameda scowling between them.

"He took a shot at Rimshot's dog."

"He missed, I hope. He generally misses."

"As you see." The dog, a yellow lab, was on the porch, unharmed, peering out from between its master's legs.

"Isn't that Gram Parsons?"

"Oh, I don't think so," said Merry.

Alameda got into the camper and slammed the door. Hawk pissed against the left rear tire and got in the front seat, passenger side, staring straight ahead. It was time to go.

"You'll be back," said Clay. "I always imagined us doing all this together."

"We are, you'll see," said Ira. "And anyway, you're the one who left, remember?"

Clay had never thought of it that way before. "Does that mean I owe you twenty bucks?"

Ira opened the door of the truck and got behind the wheel. He adjusted the bone-and-feather totem that hung from the rearview mirror. The starter groaned, then clicked, then fell silent.

Rimshot gave them a jump from the Caddy.

Clay and Merry watched them drive away.

"For you," said Annie, back from Burg.

There were two in one envelope, one for Clay and one for Harl: wedding invitations.

"This is fucked," Harl said. "I can't believe you told them I am here."

"I didn't."

"Somebody did."

"It's a weird guess. It's a Hail Mary."

"They all think I'm just a draft dodger or something. I'm a deserter. I'm the one they shoot."

"It's not till March," said Clay. "There'll be an amnesty by then."

"Or a war," said Lowell.

"There's already a war."

"What kind of amnesty?" asked Annie.

"A general settling of peace and love over the world, like snow," said Roads. "Did the Hollywood money come?"

φ

Your cousin Junior is back in the Nam, as he calls it. Meanwhile, have you heard Bobby Lee is getting married, to your friend Harl's sister? I heard it from his mother who is afraid it will endanger his Vanderbilt fellowship, since Harl is now a deserter, I hear.

"You see?" said Harl, reading over Clay's shoulder.

"She's the first girl I ever thought was pretty," said Clay.

"Your mother?"

"Your sister."

"It's a horse. And another. Somebody's on one, leading the other. And it's guess-who."

It was snowing outside.

"Johnny?"

"It's not Johnny." Annie closed the door. If it had had a lock, she would have locked it.

It was Yosemite. Moments later the big triangular door opened and there he was, his beard and hair all dusted with snow, the first real snow of the year.

Please ran to Annie's bed and hid under the covers.

"Told you," said Dove, from the scaffold, where he was gluing up insulation, nearing the top.

"Leave the gun outside," said Roads, from the kitchen platform.

Yosemite ignored him. He was carrying the Winchester in one hand. He set the butt on the floor, parade rest, with a loud thump. "I've come to get my woman," he said.

"Shit," said Clay.

Yosemite ignored him. He pointed at the girl, Please, wrapped in Annie's Navajo blanket. "You," he said. "Get your stuff and let's go."

She didn't move. She seemed, in fact, to get smaller, if that were possible.

"She doesn't have any stuff," said Annie.

"Get the fuck out of here," Dove said from high above. "She doesn't want to go with you."

"You little fairy," said Yosemite without looking up. "Shut the fuck up."

"She's staying here," said Annie. "Where it's warm."

"You shut up."

"Make me."

Roads set down his spatula and turned off the stove. He wiped out the skillet with his special rag that was never washed, then folded it more carefully than usual. Then he stepped down off the kitchen platform and walked over to the "mess-up," where the coats and boots and tools were kept.

Dove looked down from the scaffold. Lowell, who was sitting on a milk carton by the woodstove, put his book face down on his lap: *Fanshen*.

Clay held his breath.

"Come on, woman. I brought you a horse."

"She's not a woman, she's a girl," said Annie.

Roads reached behind the coats and brought out the Mossberg 12 gauge.

"I don't want any trouble," said Yosemite.

Roads opened a box of deer slugs and cracked the Mossberg. Each barrel took one slug. He closed it with a loud crack.

Yosemite just watched. The Rockers all just watched.

"I think you should go," said Roads, his back still turned.

"Not without my woman," said Yosemite.

Roads turned to face him. "Go!" he shouted. He waved the shotgun like a broom. Clay had never heard him shout before. It was hugely loud in the dome.

He felt a cold wind on his face and realized his eyes were shut. He opened them; the door of the dome swung open. Yosemite was gone. Clay went and shut the door while Roads leaned the shotgun, still loaded, against the stove and went back to his pancakes.

"Where'd he get the horses?" Lowell asked.

"Must have borrowed them from Johnny," said Annie. "Didn't you recognize Color TV?"

Please looked out from under the blanket.

"She's pregnant," said Annie.

"It's an Tu-95, a Tupolev Bear," said Harl.

"How do you know?"

"I was in the Civil Air Patrol, with your pal Emil."

"I never knew that."

"There's a lot you never knew. Plus, it's in the caption."

So it was. It was a big four-engine turboprop with steeply swept wings. The photo had been taken from inside a C-130, filled with troops, heading home from 'Nam. It was on the front page of the *Times*.

The Soviet planes were tracking the Americans as they left. They would pick them up a hundred miles out of Da Nang and follow them to within a hundred miles of California, then peel off and head home to Sakhalin, where their maintenance crews shivered and waited, tossing their cigarette butts into the old snow.

The Tu-95 with counter-rotating props was the fastest propeller-driven aircraft in the world.

"They couldn't keep up with a B-52," Harl said. "But they can easily keep up with the C-130. They cruise at four hundred forty-five miles per hour."

"So what are they doing?" Annie asked. "What do they want?"

"Gloating," said Merry.

"They want what we all want," said Lowell.

Clay had always hated Thanksgiving. It reminded him too much of the long table in Calhoun, loaded with cousins from Louisville he didn't know and liked less. His stern grandmother, glaring at his mother for talking too much and his father for talking too little. Junior trying to please his dad. Scooter sneaking cigarettes out to the barn, whiskey too, daring them all.

Roads had different memories: "It's an Okla holiday." He changed slugs for birdshot and killed three wild turkeys, in the daytime, not at night, since they quite sensibly ran from headlights even though they were supposed to be dumber than deer. Maybe they were too dumb to listen to Roads's prayers, Clay thought. Please and Harl dressed them (he was teaching her things), Annie and Dove polished the silver (which didn't take long), and the wonder truck, not to be outdone, delivered the invitations.

Triple A sent regrets, via Merry. There was a series of "Peace Thanksgiving" demos planned for the day—one in Denver, one in Chicago, one in DC, and one in LA. Triple A was the house band in Denver, to set up behind the speaker's platform in the city park renamed La Raza Plaza.

"Would you rather be tearing down the old world or building the new?" Roads asked.

"Both," said Merry, who had heard this riff before. "This demonstration is very strategic. The troops are starting to mutiny. Demonstrations across the whole country and not just in New York will encourage them.

"We can use the old world for parts," said Lowell. He had decided to go to Denver with them.

"Better not get busted," said Clay.

Dove glared down from above.

Libra arrived first, at noon. Cicero was still in New York, but Palomina brought salads, Denver brought cowboy bread, made without eggs or milk, and Louisa brought cranberry sauce and a tambourine. Clay drove Triple A's stay-at-homes (mostly mothers) up in the weeper. When he rounded the Rock, leaking steam, he saw a maroon International with a camper on the back.

Gantz was back. Little Richard was with him.

"Who invited him?"

"Me," said Roads. He had also invited Johnny and Brenda

but no one expected them to show. All was forgiven, for the day at least. Little Richard kissed Annie on the cheek and all but shook hands with Harl.

Roads carved, then said the prayer, blowing smoke in four directions, tobacco, then herb. The turkeys were alarmingly lean.

"With any luck, we'll eat better next year," Gantz said. He was hoping to flunk his bar exam so he could become a farmer. He had even grown a beard. His lady was back in Denver having Thanksgiving with her family. A Triple A baby started to cry. Annie grabbed it up and started to dance. There was no music with Triple A gone so Gantz got his twelve-string out of his truck. Roads made him put it back. Louisa played the tambourine. Little Richard sat on the raised kitchen floor and played his little drums, showering blessings on them all, a runty pope.

It was long after dark when Merry and Lowell arrived in Rimshot's pink Caddy, which only Lowell, they all agreed later, could have coaxed up around the Rock in six inches of new snow.

"It never happened," Merry said. There was no rally. "We were stopped by a roadblock, just outside Denver."

"National Guard," said Lowell.

"Toy soldiers," said Merry.

Humphrey had declared a National Emergency. A Tupolev Bear had been shot down just off the California coast, and a Tomcat had gone down with it. It wasn't quite war, but the interstates were restricted.

"A National Emergency," said Harl, alarmed. "What the hell does that mean?"

"It's a war," said Little Richard.

"Who invited him?" Lowell asked. Merry stayed the night and Dove's tower shook with silent sobs.

It won't be much of a Christmas this year. Half the leaves are still on the trees. My brother, your uncle, left me half of the dealership, which I am sharing with your cousin Junior, who was

*home on leave last week, just for two days. He's back in the states
as he calls it, stationed in California.*

He has an eye infection.

The revolution in Mexico was being blamed on Nicaragua
and even Cuba. "As if Mexico had no revolutionary tradition of
its own," said Lowell, disgustedly, folding his *Times*.

Merry delivered them faithfully, one or two or even three a
week. It was his excuse for coming up Johnny's road. He usually
parked the pink Caddy at the arroyo and walked the rest of the
way.

The picture on the front page showed the crowds in Mexico City, marching under banners with pictures of Ortega and
Che. There was a smaller picture of Che holding his own
Argentine flag. Governor Reagan was welcoming the refugees
into California.

"I thought he hated Mexicans," said Harl.

"These are rich Mexicans," said Lowell. "They all have
cars."

"Not any more," said Annie, turning the page. They were
streaming across the border into San Diego on foot, leaving their
confiscated Caddys behind. Bored soldiers were stamping their
hands. Reagan had pulled out the border patrol and put in the
California National Guard.

"How can he do that?" Harl asked. "Is that part of the Emergency?"

"He can do what he pleases," said Lowell. "He's a movie
star."

"B-list," said Annie.

Meanwhile, the Mexicans in the US, mostly illegal, were cel-
ebrating.

They were marching in Denver and LA, demanding that the
UN recognize their new government. They were packing their
bags, selling their shitty jalopies, quitting their crummy jobs,
ready to head home as soon as the interstates were open.

"*Sí, se puede,*" said Roads. He was cleaning his skillet with his rag. Soap never touched it.

"What does that mean?"

"Just what it sounds like. Means everything is going to be okay."

The solstice came and went. No peyote. Roads returned from New Buffalo, back roads all the way, with the bad news on Christmas Eve.

"The Oklas never showed. I guess they like the interstates. I'll try again after the New Year."

The good news was that Humphrey's Christmas bombing was a bust as well. Two B-52s shot down and the rest turned back by Soviet MiG-21s.

"Fishbeds," said Harl.

"Season's greetings," said Lowell. "Even Santa can't get through."

Merry brought the *Times* on Christmas Day with more good news. A riot at Fort Bragg, a standoff at Fort Campbell, a "die-in" at Dix.

The troops were refusing to board the planes for Vietnam. Most of them, anyway.

"There's no water!" It was Harl's turn to do the dishes.

The line was cut off.

"So that's what he was up to," said Clay. Johnny had ridden past the dome that morning without waving or stopping. No coffee. No titties. No cowboy talk.

"We can settle this peacefully," said Roads. He combed his hair and put on clean pants with colorful braid.

"I'm going too," said Clay. He had always liked Johnny. Brenda was in the front yard, hanging the dingy clothes that had been "cowboy washed" on her plastic picket fence.

"Johnny's in the barn," she said. "I'm sorry he's turned so mean. Would you boys like some tea?"

"Rain check," said Roads.

Johnny was rubbing down the quarter horse he called Color TV while another horse looked on.

"It's my water," he said.

"Nobody ever doubted that," said Roads. "We were sharing as friends."

"There's friends and there's friends," said Johnny. "It's my line and my water. My country too. Remember that."

"Let's have a cigarette and talk this over," said Roads, pulling out the beaded pouch the Oklas had made for him. Clay stayed silent, stepping back to watch, staying out of it. Color TV did the same, silent as ever. Such big soft eyes!

"I'm trying to quit," said Johnny, abruptly turning his back. "You two'd best be on your merry way."

"I guess," said Clay, as they drove back up the road, "it's the chickens. Coming home to roost."

"*Sí, se puede,*" said Roads. "We can haul from the creek."

Annie had already thought of that. The dishes were done. She and Harl made a good team.

"Happy New Year," muttered Dove, climbing down. He even broke a grin. The last round of insulation was in place and the dome inside was as white as the snow outside, all the way to the top. Everyone applauded, especially Plain Bob and Plain Jane, who had moved inside from the honeymoon van.

Especially Harl, who had been worrying about the woodpile. Especially Annie, who had very reluctantly spent last month's Hollywood money on glue.

"Wild horses," said Lowell, folding up last week's *Times*, which Merry had brought from Denver. The Emergency was still on, but their bus had a sticker good for in-state travel. RFK, the president-elect, was promising to lift it after the inauguration; his veep-elect was demanding an investigation of the Christmas Mutiny in Da Nang, where the US had fired on its own troops. Marches in Oakland and Chicago commemorated the fallen, most of whom were Black. There was a smaller march in Denver but no one even considered going.

Gasoline was $3.99 a gallon.

The shah of Iran was on his way to Washington, having been refused asylum by the French and the British. The royal family of Saudi Arabia was expected to be the next to fall. They already had several homes in Georgetown and a horse farm in Virginia, where last year's derby winner grazed and dreamed at stud.

Roads was in Taos, hoping for peyote.

Dove even sneaked a look at the paper, which he usually ignored. He was worried about his grandmother, he said, who had just bought a condo in Tel Aviv, even as the Arab nations were demanding a seat for Palestine in the General Assembly.

The tobacco was getting lower in the Bugler can and the snow lower on the mountainsides.

Junior's eye is no better. His resignation was accepted but delayed. Your old friend Round Man is running the shop but sales are down. Gas prices don't help.

"Luckily, she never asks me to come home," said Clay.

"Would you?" asked Harl.

"Probably. I would have to."

"Wonder truck!" said Annie. And moments later there it was, rounding the Rock in low, slipping and sliding in old snow like a salmon making its way upstream.

Roads emerged, looking like a band leader in new ribbon jeans, a gift from the Oklas, it turned out. Roads held up a brown paper bag.

"Good news," he said.

EIGHTEEN

THE RENAMED AND RESCHEDULED NEW YEAR'S MEETING WAS HELD at Libra, on a level patch of ground near the community dome. Palomina wanted to hold it inside the dome, because of the cold, but Roads just shook his head. Peyote required a fire, and a fire required a tepee.

The tepee was in the back of the weeper, a pile of canvas under a long bundle of peeled aspen poles, looking to Clay like a small collapsed universe.

Cicero, back from New York for the holidays, helped Roads and Clay set up the tepee, while Harl and Denver cut and stacked cedar for the fire. The rest of the Rockers arrived at dusk in the wonder truck with Annie at the wheel. Little Richard came from Burg with Gantz, who was still awaiting the results of his bar exam.

"Who invited him?" Lowell asked.

Rimshot and his Caddy were in LA, so Triple A made it as far as they could in their bus, then walked the rest of the way, dressed in varied finery. Merry wore a tie-dyed tux.

"Who invited him?" Dove grumbled as he pulled on his prom dress over his long johns.

Clay wore his Emily's Taxi jacket. Inside the tepee, Roads set out his rattles, his beaded tobacco pouch, his corn silk papers, his ceremonial pipes. He nodded to Little Richard, who struck a match, who lit the fire.

The sun sank over the Sangres to the west, setting the last high clouds aglow.

"It's time," said Roads.

Plain Bob, who was afraid of high places, joined Palomina in the dome: Ground Control. The rest filed one by one out of the darkening universe into the smaller cone-shaped one and sat in a circle around their tiny new sun.

"Take and eat," said Roads.

The new revolutionary government in Mexico had clamped down on drugs, including peyote, and there were only eleven buttons, but Roads had boiled them all down into a thick, nasty green tea. He drank, then passed it in a mason jar.

They prayed, they sang, they drank. They puked and prayed and sang and drank again. Little Richard passed his drums to Indigo, who made the fire dance. Roads rolled a giant cigarette and sent smoke in four directions. Clay, who never sang, sang. Dove sat between Merry and Lowell and said a prayer for his grandmother Rachel, who had just bought a condo in Tel Aviv. Roads said a prayer for the Oklas, a prayer of thanks. Please sat between Harl and Annie, who said a prayer for her unborn baby, who opened her eyes wide in Please's womb, yet another universe. Gantz went to sleep. Clay looked up and saw a star, two stars, tangled in the tent poles, universes in universes, nested together like Russian dolls.

It was midnight before the Old Ones came, riding in on horselike swirls of smoke, according to Roads, who alone could see them all at once. Clay only caught glimpses: there was Crazy Horse, looking like Lincoln, followed by leathery men in stained hats, and one in uniform (Roads said later that it was Lopez's nephew who was killed in 'Nam earlier that year); there was Jesus in white like a snowbank with kind eyes; then even EmCee, barefoot, carrying her shoes, passing through the fire so quickly that Clay caught only the shadow of her hand, missing a finger. Then she was gone. The worlds overlapped here, but they didn't touch, not even at the top of the tepee, open to one star at a time.

Then even the stars were gone.

"*Se presente,*" said Roads, addressing the sun. He had pulled the tent flap open and there she was: Dawn, her dingy robes stained by the centuries but washed clean every day, growing brighter.

Stretch. Yawn. Pee. One by one they all stumbled out as the

fire went out. Ground Control welcomed them on the wide step of the Libra dome with cold fresh water and toasted blue corn-meal and strips of venison, much prayed over and hard to chew. Clay's legs were stiff but his heart was full.

Even Lowell's experienced eyes were shining as he peed, his eyes fixed on Blanca's lone glacier, shining in the new sun.

"So," he said.

According to the National Guard, charged with enforcing the Emergency, interstate travel meant travel on the interstate system, not travel between states, which was unenforceable anyway. Three categories were allowed: COMmercial, RELigous, and ADMinistrative.

Rotella showed Clay the sticker on the windshield of the bus. It was an American flag the size of a postcard, with a COM instead of stars.

"I guess we're hauling entertainment," she said.

"I applied for RELigious," said Merry. "I told them we were delivering spiritual advice."

The band was back at work, and Clay was catching a ride to Denver. He had gotten the postcard after their first gig: a date, a motel, and the words "Be that as it may."

It was a good time to get away.

"Will you get to go to the inauguration?"

"If it happens," Becca said. RFK had challenged not the Emergency but the delay of the inauguration. His challenge had been denied by a lower court, but the Supreme Court was in special session to hear it.

"And if it doesn't?"

Becca shrugged and lit a Sherman. It was a nicer hotel, a Holiday Inn, with a six-stooled bar. Becca looked like a lawyer in a dark-blue skirt and trim jacket; Clay told her so.

"That's the idea," she said. "I'm official now, working with the transition team. Officially I'm settling poll complaints, coordinating with the locals in all the big states. Bureaucratic stuff, not very exciting, but I get an expense account and I get to stay in nicer hotels than before. As you see."

"And unofficially?"

"What makes you think there's an unofficially?"

"Because you said 'officially.'"

"Clay, a lot of people have been rounded up. Under the Emergency and before too. And are still being held. We're not even sure where. Most of them are not on the books. A lot of it has been done by the National Guard, on these highway stops, which means they are not in the justice system."

"I had no idea."

"That's because you don't pay attention. Isn't that what the communes are all about? Not paying attention?"

"We read the *Times*."

"It's all off the books, not reported. It's illegal for the newspapers to report it under the Emergency, and the underground papers that pick it up are being shut down. Nobody even knows who they are or where they are . . . supposedly."

"Which is where you come in?"

"Me and some others," said Becca. "As soon as RFK is inaugurated there will be an amnesty. In the meantime, as you can imagine, RFK has certain allies in the Justice Department and in the military as well. It's difficult and all very hush-hush. I'm getting the printouts from, let's say, different sources in the Justice Department. I'm not showing you this."

She unrolled one, a xerox, and showed him a name with a fingertip.

"Ginsburg," he said. "The world is full of Ginsburgs."

"Ginsburg, Alter? Alter is not a Jewish name. Maybe a Jewish joke."

"Ginsburg had no sense of humor."

"Look at the next name, right under it."

Clay didn't like this. He found a Sherman in the box and managed to pick it out, managed to light it.

DOE, MARY C.

"They were picked up at the same time, apparently, by the National Guard on the Pennsylvania turnpike. They were both logged in at a high school gym styled as a refugee center in Maryland. I'm not saying it means anything. It means these were important enough or interesting enough to be turned over to another agency."

"What agency?"

"That we don't know. That's what I'm trying to trace. Not just with those two. Most of the ones that we are tracking are ex-SDS, Weather, Panthers. Not just random people."

"I don't get it," said Clay. "Are you saying you think EmCee's still alive? Or are you just trying to spook me?"

"Of course not. Sometimes I'm wondering if somebody's trying to spook *me*. I don't know half the people I'm dealing with, and I don't know what they know. Or what they want me to know that they know. Everything is all tangled up. Bartender?"

She ordered two more beers. It was too late to eat. The kitchen was closed.

"It's like fucking Argentina," said Clay. "Are you in touch with anybody, you know, Weather? They're supposedly gone with the wind."

Becca returned the printout to her purse, a neat little Vuitton. It closed it with a click.

"I just wanted to talk to somebody. Anyway. Now you know what I know. Which is that I don't even know what I know."

There is a famous Remington painting of an "Indian" in war regalia, on a bluff staring at the horizon. Someone had added a cowboy and a Mexican to the reproduction over the bar. It was like the Hopper where James Dean and Marilyn Monroe are in the diner, staring at Bogart. Only not a joke.

In her room, they both exhaled. It even had a balcony, which overlooked an empty midnight parking lot. Becca came out in the T-shirt she wore for a nightgown.

"You're so quiet," Becca said. "What are you thinking?"

"What do you think I'm thinking?"

They slept that night with EmCee between them, like a sword.

"Beware their ceremonies," said Roads.

"I wouldn't miss this one," said Lowell. Even Dove was going. Johnny's was out of course. They all piled into the wonder truck and headed down the hill toward Triple A. Rimshot had returned from Christmas in Laurel Canyon with a new nineteen-inch color Philco in the back of his pink Caddy.

Plain Jane came along. Harl as well. The snow was reduced to patches—the January thaw—so Clay drove the wonder truck, which was good in the mud. Annie and Please sat in the front with Clay. Only Roads himself stayed behind.

"Beware their ceremonies," he called out after them.

"Surprise," said Merry, but the Rockers had already heard about the new TV. The picture was fuzzy but colorful. "Like youth," said Rotella, who was pretending not to watch from the doorway.

Cicero and Palomina arrived from Libra, with Denver. Plain Bob had saved a seat beside him on the floor for Plain Jane. Merry made popcorn. It was snowing just a little, either in DC or inside the tube, and now outside as well.

Meanwhile the celebrities were filing silently into the stands, their arguments all over for now.

"It's MLK that makes it interesting. RFK wouldn't have gotten away with a Black running mate if he hadn't been shot."

"He wouldn't have wanted to!"

"He's more radical than if he had just won the vote."

"It's all just business as usual."

"It's about the war, folks!"

"It wouldn't be about the war if he hadn't been shot."

"Bullshit, he came in because of the war."

"He came in to cool out the antiwar movement. He was never intended to win."

"He didn't want to himself."

"None of this would mean shit if the Vietnamese weren't winning."

"They wouldn't be winning if the Russians weren't helping. And the Russians wouldn't be helping it if it hadn't been for the coup."

"Shhhhhh!"

Ginsberg was reading a poem. The Real, the main, the magic nickel Ginsberg. "Turn up the sound," said Clay. Merry complied happily, the Host.

It was a dull poem, an inaugural poem. It went on too long. Ginsberg looked like a professor in his dark suit and goofy tie. "Always the showman," said Lowell.

"You know him?" someone asked.

"Clay met him," said Lowell. "He's the poet."

"It was raining," said Clay, who loved to tell the story. It changed a little every time, but the essence was always the same. "I went home and burned my poems," he said. "One by one."

The room slowly filled up with bodies and voices and smoke. Even the kids came in, sensing as kids do that something was about to happen.

"There's King." He stood with RFK, behind him and to the left, appropriately enough.

"Look at Humphrey, that piglet."

"He's pretending."

"He could do worse."

"Shhhh."

The judges—the justices, they were called—stood arranged in their robes, like chessmen. The ladies stood beside their men. Snow in the TV and swirling outside, but not so colorful.

Merry scurried in and out of the kitchen, topping off coffee from a dented pot. Cigarettes were rolled, joints were passed. There was no room to move. Maybe we're all Americans after all, Clay thought. Americans in colorful clothes with colorful futures. Americans in farmhouses just like this, coast to coast, watching the country coming together on TV, where everything real and important happened.

Merry adjusted the rabbit ears. A Black choir from Harlem—or was it Tuskegee?—was singing. They stopped and the Chief Justice stepped forward. A nearby kid wailed.

"Shhhhh."

On the TV there was a prayer. Then the traditional Bible; then the oath, also traditional.

Then the traditional gunshot.

NINETEEN

CLAY WAS SLEEPING ALONE. THEN HE WASN'T. HE WOKE UP WITH THE feeling that someone was in bed with him, had joined him on tiptoe. It wasn't a dream but a feeling, and a line from a Thomas Wyatt poem, one of those that Ira had memorized, floated into his head: "*With naked foot, stalking in my chamber* . . ."

As a matter of fact, he had a hard-on.

He sat up, and a moon-white slab the size of a tabletop slipped off his bed and fell to the floor, as light as a leaf, without a sound.

Dove's foam triangles were coming down. Another piece gleamed like a snowbank by the door; another leaned against the woodstove, which was, thankfully, almost out. The Ashley kept time like an hourglass, and Clay could tell by the dim glow through the isinglass insert in the door that it was long after midnight.

He had been sleeping in the plank double bed Plain Bob and Plain Jane had left behind. It was too cold in the honeymoon bus, even with two sleeping bags, one tucked into the other. Looking up, he could see another triangle hanging, one end pointing down.

It gave, it fell, it floated down. The pieces Dove had so carefully and laboriously glued into place were peeling loose just when they were most needed, in the deep dead of winter, February, when the wind stripped the blanket of snow off the dome.

He could see plywood. Another fell.

They fell like huge snowflakes, reluctantly, in long slow stages. One lit near Annie snoring on the wide bed she shared with Harl. Another nestled next to Please curled up on her pallet by the coats; another was dropping toward Lowell on the other side of the Ashley.

Like snowflakes, they were all alike. It was disastrous but beautiful in its way. Looking up into the cathedral darkness of the dome, Clay thought of waking Dove high on his platform to watch his work, his slow and lovely show, but he wouldn't appreciate it, he knew. So he watched silently, as alone, and for the moment as glad to be alone, as a snowman in his paperweight.

"Roll me one of those."

"I thought you quit."

Clay and Dove were driving north on the interstate. There was almost no traffic, even though the Emergency had been lifted. It was easy enough to set the Bugler can on his lap and drive with his elbows.

"I did. Then everything started coming to pieces, remember?" They were driving to Pueblo in the wonder truck, the only Rocker vehicle with plates, looking for a new and better glue. The high plains to the east were white with snow. Clay found their blankness more interesting than the mountains to the left, which were calendar ordinary. The long roll to the east suggested horizons, one after another. Pages to turn.

They even had Hollywood money. Annie's letter had arrived.

The owner of the box company called Dove Bob. We all look alike to him, Clay realized. It was kind of reassuring. "It's the foam giving away," he said, "not the glue. You need something that sticks it without dissolving it."

"Like?"

He shrugged. "We'll have to experiment." The *we* was encouraging. His name was Jimmy. Behind him on the wall of his messy office was a picture of Jimi at Woodstock.

He made three calls and sent Dove to three different distributors, for three different glues. "It's samples, not consumer stuff," he said. "You're to tell them it's for me."

They were done before noon. The glue—one tube, one pot, and one canister—was complimentary, so they celebrated with lunch at the Arkansas Eagle, a little Mexican joint named after the river, not the faraway state, near the old steel mills the Japs had put out of business.

The TV was on, up over the bar. Talking heads, all white, in black-and-white. The Commission of Inquiry was inquiring. The issues were many. Had the oath actually been given? Had RFK's hand actually been on the Bible? Was the Bible the King James? Clay wondered. What was the succession? It was like looking for a short in old, bad wiring; or an open.

The lunch crowd came in and the bartender reached up and turned off the sound. More Spanish was spoken than English, but the Spanish that was spoken was more English than Spanish. "What'll you boys *qué quieren?*"

Green chili and "red ones," beers mixed with tomato juice.

Marty Robbins was on the jukebox and the news was on the TV. No sound, just tear gas and white crosses, a rerun of last week's "riot" when the National Guard had turned back the mourners who had insisted on following RFK's casket in through the hallowed gates. When they were beaten back, MLK had joined them, turning his back on the ceremony at the graveside. There was his sorrowful face, then Humphrey's.

"They do look a lot alike," said Clay.

"*Dos* more," said Dove. Holding up two fingers.

Dove and Clay watched in silence as the Eternal Flame on RFK's brother's grave was relighted after the crowd was dispersed.

"Arlington," Dove said finally. "My grandfather is buried there."

"Your grandmother's husband? The one in Israel?"

"She was married twice. Her first husband wasn't Jewish, or maybe he was. He fought in the Pacific. I say 'fought.' He was killed at Pearl Harbor. He looked up is probably all. She was just nineteen."

"My father was in the Pacific. He was a radioman."

"What ship?"

"He never said. I never asked. But I saw a hat in the closet once. It was the *Indianapolis*, I think."

"Turn it up," said a steel-cowboy.

"Turn it off," said another.

"We'll do another red one," said Clay.

The Commission of Inquiry was going to release its findings very soon; meanwhile Humphrey was still president and, as president, regretted the fact that some had exploited the occasion of a nation's farewell to a fallen leader to advance their own agendas, while MLK reminded both Huntley and Brinkley that the fallen leader himself would have followed his followers, and that he personally had done so out of respect and not opposition to the interim president.

No, Humphrey said, not interim president—*president*. Until the Commission finished its Inquiry.

LBJ was asked for comment and expressed his faith in the system. Nixon had no comment.

"It's like a rodeo," said a man in a John Deere hat.

"You never been to no rodeo," said another.

"We should be heading home," said Clay, leaving a five on the bar.

A storm was blowing in from the plains, and that was ominous. The ones that came in from the east were the worst.

"Roll me one of those," said Dove. "What's that up ahead?"

Blue lights, stinging through the blowing snow.

"It was no big deal," said Dove. He was in his prom dress, high above, hammering eagerly, extending the scaffold so he could replace the fallen triangles.

"Seems like a deal enough to me," said Lowell. "I thought the Emergency was over. State cops or Army?"

"National Guard," said Clay. "They were looking for Mexicans. Apparently Mexicans can enter the country illegally but they can't leave."

"They pretty much just waved us through," Dove called down. "They didn't even sniff my glue."

"Glue is overrated," said Harl. Duco had been big in the

hospital in Stuttgart, even bigger at Walter Reed.

Dove even added a ladder. Merry was away on his annual trip to Copenhagen to visit his mother, who was related in some undetermined way to the queen, not of Denmark but of Norway, and Dove, filled with forgiveness, was trying to lure Lowell up to his lofty bed.

"I think ladders are romantic," said Annie. "Think of Romeo and Juliet."

"I'm no Romeo," said Lowell. "I don't like heights."

Rimshot was back with a new guitar, a Les Paul Plain Top—and Alameda.

She had looked him up in LA, Rotella explained, or maybe Vegas. Long drives are hard on romance. They were no longer speaking.

Rimshot and the kids were watching cartoons in the Big House. They complained when Clay switched to the news.

There had been a full-scale riot at Da Nang. The men didn't want to go out on patrol, or stand watch, or even salute their officers. The VC responded by lobbing mortar shells into the base, killing four, maiming two. Or so it seemed, until it was discovered that the mortar shells had come from a renegade group of officers, Jefferson's Cousins.

"The Army is coming apart," said Clay. He was thinking of his own cousin, Junior.

"Go, Speed Racer," said Rimshot.

It was an experiment. Dove labeled the top twelve triangles after the Beatles—John, George, and Pete—four of each, depending on which of the three glues he used. He was leaving out Paul, he explained, because of his statements about the war. The process was quicker this time, since the scaffold was steadier then before. The ladder provided triangulation, Annie explained.

The last two went up on Lincoln's birthday. H. Rap Brown

was shot that day by a sniper in Oakland. A man named Booth was arrested, then released.

The snow was deep, driving the deer down from the mountain. Harl's arm was bothering him in the cold, so Roads took Dove on his midnight hunts, when the deer waited for him by the highway, their big eyes shining in the headlights. He always said a prayer, then took his shot, then muttered a prayerful thanks or, if he missed, an Okla curse.

He made it sound like a wedding, Dove said, or maybe a divorce. Plain Bob and Plain Jane dressed them out in back of the dome, on a ledge at the edge of the trees, where the stones, and now the snow, were spattered with blood. They filled two plastic coolers with wrapped fresh meat, then cut the rest into strips to hang outside to dry.

Lowell and Clay took the coolers down to Triple A in the weeper, slipping and sliding in chains. Humphrey was on Rimshot's color TV, announcing that he was going to start bringing the troops home "in honor of my fallen colleague and his great crusade." He looked a little green; the colors came and went.

"Like he has a choice," said Lowell. "A Soviet nuclear sub has been tracking the *Valley Forge* since the assassination, not doing anything, just holding off the stern a few points to starboard."

"Starboard?"

"He's from Block Island," Clay explained to Rotella.

TWENTY

The Rockers hunkered down. Harl split wood. Annie found her Scrabble set. Dove's three glues were holding and the dome was warm. Please was twice her own small size.

Meanwhile, Humphrey moved back into the White House while the issue of what the courts called rendition (*succession* seeming too royal) was being decided. MLK protested through his lawyers that residency would influence the Court's decision. He was in a suite at the Watergate.

Meanwhile, the troops were being ferried home to Oakland in cruise ships on lease from Carnival, since many of the C-130s had been sabotaged by the very troops that were clamoring to get home. *Rolling Stone* featured a picture of shirtless crowds of men cheering Peter, Paul and Mary, who had responded to an emergency call from the USO.

Meanwhile, exhausted from falling, the snow lay still.

Even the wonder truck got stuck, halfway up the road. Annie and Harl carried groceries up on foot, only two bags. The Hollywood money hadn't come. Clay and Lowell walked down to fetch the wonder truck, carrying a set of chains, and decided that since they were halfway there, they might as well drive on down to Triple A to see what was up, if anything.

Surprise: Merry was back. He was watching *Speed Racer* with Rimshot and the kids. The wheels spun but the cars never went anywhere. He made room for Lowell on the ruined sofa, and Clay went out to the barn to find Rotella.

He found her putting a sticker onto the windshield of the

Triple A bus: an American flag the size of a postcard, with IE/2 in the field where the stars should have been.

"You have to get a new one every month," she said. "It's the new deal under the Interim Emergency."

"Some new deal," said Clay. "At least put it on upside down."

"To protest? To protest what? You don't have to get on the interstate and go to Denver every week. We do." She smoothed out the bubbles with her hand. "Plus you don't need a sticker on the county road. Plus there's no charge; they're free."

"Welcome to the land of the free," said Lowell from the big square doorway. He and Merry were holding hands, which they never did when Dove was around.

"It's just the deal," said Merry. "You get it from the National Guard in Burg."

"There's no National Guard in Burg!"

"There is now," said Rotella. "They've set up a trailer on the courthouse lawn."

Pete came down first, during supper, like entertainment. Another Pete fell later that night and a George early the next morning, as Harl was stirring the stove to life. Dove was not amused. He put on his prom dress and tried to nail them back up, but Roads protested, Annie too. That way lay leaks.

Dove stacked them under the dome, discouraged.

"Wait till the big snow comes," said Roads. "The snow will keep us warm."

"He speaks in parables," said Lowell.

"You oughta know," muttered Dove. He had heard that Merry was back.

John came down that night, all at once.

Your cousin, now Major Junior, has applied for an early release so that he can come home and help with the dealership.

He may lose his eye. Round Man can't sell cars. Meanwhile, your
pal Bobby Lee is getting married next month, his trailer tramp.

"Things are getting weird all over," Merry said. "I got detained at Idlewild. I had to call my Uncle Hans at the embassy in
Washington. Otherwise I would have been put back on the plane,
coach no less." Merry only flew once a year and only flew First
Class.

"Poor you," said Annie. "I'll make some more coffee."

"I'm already on it," said Roads.

Harl and Plain Bob brought in more wood.

"I saw Woody Allen at Puglia's. I saw Cicero at his gallery.
They stopped construction on the World Trade Center; there's just
a big hole downtown. And there are demonstrations every day at
the United Nations."

"That's nothing new," said Clay as Roads banged the coffeepot to settle the grounds, cowboy style.

"It's cold in here," said Merry; he was looking up.

Dove was glaring down, disconsolate.

Pete was the last to go. The top of the dome was naked, plywood the color of an old Flesh crayon, but Roads was right: the
snow piled on top kept the heat in. Harl's woodpile was holding.

Dove hung up his prom dress, still stiff with glue, and played
Scrabble with Plain Jane, who wasn't speaking to Plain Bob. Their
silent games were deafening.

Lowell was reading *Dune*, skipping whole paragraphs. Annie
was teaching Please to knit. Clay fished through his blue folder
and found the wedding invitation.

It was a good time to get away.

"She's your sister."

"I can't hitchhike," said Harl. "I have a bad arm." It was his idea of a joke. It was the Army he was worried about.

"I'm not about to hitchhike," said Clay. The Can was almost empty, so he slipped three more twenties out of EmCee's White House envelope, which was in the blue folder with his mother's letters. That left seventeen, or $340. He caught a ride to Denver with Triple A.

There were National Guard soldiers at the Greyhound station, mostly leaning against the walls. They were not allowed to sit. They were supposedly looking for Mexicans trying to sneak back over the border without the exit stamp that proved they had paid their bills, and for AWOL soldiers, who had been redesignated deserters under the Extended Emergency (EE), but no one was checking papers. They just looked. Now that the war was over, the country was at war. Clay had to show an ID to get a bus ticket, and then again to get on the bus to Evansville, Indiana. Kentucky wasn't on the route.

Clay's seatmate was a fifty-year-old vet with a pint of brandy and a grudge against the Panthers, who had shot the president so that their nigger could take over. He offered Clay a taste but Clay declined.

He amused himself by going from seat to seat in the bus, talking with the other passengers, who blamed the CIA, the Army, the Kennedys, the Jews, the "protesters," the Catholics, and of course the Cubans, who had just been admitted to the Security Council over US protests. Each then offered him a drink: brandy, tequila, fortified wine, bourbon, rye, scotch, etc.

All this in his imagination, while he stayed in his seat and pretended to sleep.

"Junior is here?"

"Major Junior," muttered Clay's mother. She was in her bathrobe; Junior's hat was on the sofa in the tiny living room. The leather on the bill, Clay noticed, wasn't really leather. It was shinier, as if that made up for being less real. "He's at Old Hickory."

"He's staying here?"

"No reason Junior can't stay here, in your old room, when he's in town. Blood is thicker than water."

"I sold Dad's house," said Junior, coming in the front door with a soggy box of barbecue. He wore a gauze bandage over one eye. There was a purple heart drawn on it with Magic Marker. "I couldn't stand it there, with him gone."

"You couldn't stand it there with him there," Clay's mother said.

"Everything is thicker than water," said Junior. "Dig in."

They scooted chairs around the kitchen table. This was the house where Clay had been raised, and there was no dining room. Just two small bedrooms, one bath, the tiny living room, and a one-car garage off the kitchen.

The barbecue was mutton, a western Kentucky specialty. The buns were Wonder bread. The chips were Lay's. The bourbon was Kentucky Tavern, the Bewley brand. Clay slipped a Kent out of his mother's pack on the table.

"My name is Jimmy, I'll take what you gimme," she said, sliding him a book of matches.

"Who's getting married, anyway?" Junior asked.

Clay told him, leaving out the part about Harl. Who knew who knew what? But Junior didn't seem to know or care about AWOLs or even deserters. He wasn't on leave from 'Nam. There was no more 'Nam.

"I've been in Oakland," he said. "It's a mess. It's all doubled up. Da Nang was coming to pieces so they are bringing the troops home too fast."

"Or too slow," said Clay.

"Five thousand at a time on cruise ships? They trashed the *Hawaiian Princess*. You should have seen it. It was disgusting. Plus, all these guys think that since the war is over they should all go home."

"And they shouldn't?"

"They're still in the Army. There's no *esprit*. No morale. Half the Army is colored, and that's okay, but they're all draftees. I think we'd be better off to let them go. I even told them as much, but I also have my orders. The whole Army is on extended service until the court case is decided, anyway. Stop-loss. Nobody gets out. Not even me."

"Junior's trying," said Clay's mother.

"I thought you liked the Army."

"It's still a bureaucracy. All the promotions are on hold. I should have been a major by now."

"I thought you already were."

"That's your mother, thinking ahead." Junior raised has glass. "The Bewley way."

"If you don't like my peaches, don't you shake my tree."

It was getting late. One door from the kitchen led to the living room; it was always open. The other led to the garage; it was always closed.

"Tell you a secret," said Junior. "A military secret. We're all getting shuffled to the National Guard. Then I'll get my promotion. Meanwhile I can sleep on the couch."

He was drunk. Clay fished another Kent out of his mother's pack. There were only three left. He rolled one to Junior across the table. It rolled off and hit the floor.

"The wedding's tomorrow," said Clay. "Then I have to hurry back."

"My name is Hurry," said his mother. "I'm always in a harry." She picked up her cigarettes and went to bed.

"You can have your broom back," said Junior. "Room back."

"That's okay. My father kept a cot in the garage. I think it's still there."

"Really?"

"Really, it's okay," said Clay. He retrieved the Kent from under the table with his foot while Junior found his room and shut the door behind him. Then he smoked it. Then, for the first time in years, for the first time since his father had died and for years before that, he opened the door to the garage.

It was filled with silent radios.

φ

Donna's father gave her away. He drove all the way down from Indianapolis in his girlfriend's Camaro, and stayed sober through the ceremony, which was held in the redbrick Baptist church at the edge of town, where Donna still attended.

"She wanted traditional," said Bobby Lee. He was wearing a tux. Donna was wearing rose and so were her bridesmaids, one of whom, to Clay's surprise, was Black. Her name was Lily Mae and she worked with Donna at Owensboro-Daviess County Hospital. Clay was even more surprised when he met her husband.

"Ice."

Ice nodded and that was all.

"Long time, man. I thought you'd be in the Army or something."

"Cause I'm colored?"

"No, because we were both in ROTC, or something."

"You're not in the Army."

"Forget it, man. Nice to see you."

"Likewise, I'm sure," said Ice, and shook his hand, and edged off toward the wall. He was the only Black man at the wedding.

"She's nice," said Bobby Lee, later. "He's a bit of a stick."

"What are you doing after the reception?" Clay asked. "I have something I want to show you."

March in Kentucky can be warm or cold, depending. It was warm, but cold as well, out of the sun.

The Ohio was high, and the snags and bottles swept by fast, like runaways. Bobby Lee didn't get there until almost four, in his father's old Olds.

"It was weird," said Clay. "My father never allowed me in the garage when he was alive. At least I never went. The radios are still there, stacked against the wall. Nobody wants them, I guess. There was a cot, but it was too cold to sleep out there. I found this in a drawer."

It was a pistol, an automatic.

"This is a 1911," said Bobby Lee. "A Colt .45, the real thing, not some Brazilian knockoff. Probably Navy issue. It's worth something."

He handed it back but Clay didn't take it. "I want you to have it. It's a wedding present."

Bobby Lee shook his head. "That's not right. It was your father's. Did you find a clip?"

"I didn't look." Clay put it back in his bag and they shot a few bottles with Bobby Lee's .22.

"What about your honeymoon?"

"We've already had it. Donna is pregnant. I have to get back to Nashville. I'm teaching a course—it's part of the fellowship. And I have orals in a week."

"The Fugitives, still?"

"The South shall rise again."

"Let's all hope not forever," said Clay. He aimed and fired and missed. "I still never brought you a wedding present."

"I don't want a wedding present. That's Donna's thing. Showing up was enough."

Clay aimed and fired again.

"This is for Donna, then. Tell her Harl sends his love."

That night Clay borrowed his mother's (or was it Junior's?) Lincoln and cruised the empty streets of Owensboro. South, past the DDI, then north on Frederica to the river, then south again, back through town. *Don't,* he told himself.

Do was his reply.

He bought a pack of Winstons and parked in front of The Southern Kitchen. At ten after ten Ruth Ann came out, locking up.

She walked over to the Lincoln and, instead of getting in, leaned at the window, like a carhop of old.

"I heard you were here," she said. "In town, I mean. I didn't expect to see you here."

"Just wanted to see you," he said.

"Are you sure? I'm getting married."

"I heard. Congratulations."

He leaned over and opened the door.

"Don't be getting ahead of yourself," she said. But got in. "Got a cigarette?"

He showed her the Winstons and tapped out two.

"Just like old times," Ruth Ann said. "But not exactly. I'm pregnant."

"I heard." They were heading south on Frederica; they passed the DDI, at the edge of town. The fields and swamps and woods beyond gleamed black, just like old times.

"Heater work?"

"It's a Lincoln," Clay said. He turned it up and she leaned, leaned against him as he rattled over the iron bridge toward the Panther Creek bottoms. Leaned into him.

The Greyhound back to Denver was so full that people were standing in the aisles, and Clay gave his seat to a pretty girl who was nursing a baby under a raincoat so no one could see.

He found that he could sleep, sort of, on his feet, the bus rocking him like a cradle.

The trees fell away like half dreams in the night, and they rolled into Denver at dawn. Soldiers were checking IDs at the station, but they let Clay by with shrug. Hippies didn't need IDs. Their long hair was enough. They were checking for recent AWOLs, aka deserters.

The Mexicans were muttering. The new "Madre" government had sent free buses to Denver, Los Angeles, and, it was rumored, Chicago, to accommodate all those who wished to return to the mother country. The Exit Stamp had been replaced with a twenty-five-dollar exit fee, and it was said that you could board with a ten-dollar bill for the National Guardsman who was checking your papers. But that accommodation was now in trouble, as Hispanic AWOLs were finding themselves with free transportation to a non-extraditing country (Mexico had declared US AWOLs political refugees).

Clay watched all this from a safe distance, afraid he might be searched and the 1911 found. But long-haired gringos like him fit none of the categories.

Triple A was setting up at a Denver club called The Mosh. "The wandering hillbilly," said Merry. "Someone was just here, looking for you. I was supposed to give you this when we got home."

It was a postcard, a motel freebie: Holiday Inn.

"Yes, of course I was there," Becca said. "It seems like I'm always there." It was the same Holiday Inn, the same tiny bar. The same bored bartender, watching *F Troop* reruns. "Close, not that close, but we got our own little section for staff, not the same as VIPs. It was cold as hell, cold for DC. Spitting snow. It was horrible. There was no gunshot, no sound, no nothing. At least I never heard it. He had his hand on the Bible and his head just sort of jerked to one side and then he fell to his knees like he was praying. MLK grabbed the Bible before it fell and kept trying to hand it back to the Chief Justice, who hit the dirt, an old Army man. But you probably saw it all better than me if you saw it on TV."

"We saw it. I hear they never show it anymore."

"It's considered evidence now. There was no sobbing, no screaming, not at all like before; it was like everyone expected it. We were all backing away, falling over one another. I could hear Ginsberg at the mike, reading his poem."

"'Howl.'"

"Yeah. Strangely appropriate. Shouting it into the mike, which had been abandoned, left to him: 'I have seen the best minds of my generation destroyed by madness . . .' But you of all people know that poem. Until they cut off the mike. We were all backing away, falling over one another. I went home, just like before. To Rhode Island. Then to Block Island. Talk about deserted, in the winter. I broke in but couldn't get the furnace going. My dad came out and got me. I sat around for a week. But I still had a job. I went back to DC and they sent me to California.

Everybody wanted to act normal. It was weird. More normal than ever. You're awfully quiet."

She set her Shermans on the bar.

"The other thing, the EmCee thing, the Ginsburg thing, was apparently a false alarm. We're getting lots of false reports, I think deliberately. I'm working for MLK now, but I'm not sure what we're doing.

"I was in New York for a few days. That was weird. The cops were on strike and it was suddenly real easy to get a cab. California was even weirder. They're talking secession in LA. All those new immigrants. Reagan is learning Spanish. San Francisco was even weirder still. It's all about Oakland, of course. It's like a concentration camp. They bring the men home but they won't let them go home. The Army is guarding the Army. They asked for MLK but Reagan wouldn't let him land. They are burning piles of uniforms. The Diggers are giving away Black Panther T-shirts. It's like a siege. The soldiers, then the soldiers guarding the soldiers, then the demonstrators, then the cops, then the curious. Concentric circles. I stayed away.

"I did see Ira. His so-called Caravan is part of the T-shirt thing. They're printing them at a commune up in Marin. He has a new girlfriend and, guess what, she's Chinese. We even had a fight. He's hanging out with the Hells Angels, the idea being that everyone who's against authority should work together. You want another beer? I still have the old expense account."

"You're sure it was a false alarm?

"Positive. We're back at Go on the amnesty thing. I'm not sure MLK knew about the amnesty negotiations. That was mostly between RFK's staff and Humphrey, and who knows what the Hump is thinking now. Everybody's just holding their breath, waiting on the Supreme Court and this Commission. Had he been sworn in, that's the question. I'm only here for one more night. I don't have a roommate anymore. Want to stay over?"

Clay finished peeling the label off his Bud. It took a lot of concentration to get them off in one piece. He had a wet little stack of three.

"You're awfully quiet," she said.

"Triple A's heading back tonight."

"I get it," Becca said. "Gone again, she's back again."

"It needs a clip," said Harl. He handed the pistol back to Clay, who put it away in the blue folder at the bottom of his sleeping bag.

"Donna played the beautiful bride," said Clay. "Your father was there. So was Ice. Remember the Black kid in ROTC? We were on the rifle team together."

"Sort of," said Harl. "I didn't pay a whole hell of a lot of attention to the OHS Rifle Team."

"You and everybody else. He's not a kid any more."

"Was he ever?"

"He's working for my mother now. She's got him doing transmissions in the shop. Round Man is shitting a brick, I'll bet."

Round Man was her service manager.

"I'll bet."

Transmissions were considered white man's work.

"It's March that is the cruelest month," said Lowell. "The old man got it wrong."

With most of the snow gone, the dome was cold and drafty and everyone huddled in blankets around the stove, or stayed in bed like Plain Bob and Plain Jane, who were together again. "All they did at Libra was fight," said Annie. "Palomina asked them to leave. Except Palomina doesn't ask."

Evicted from his bed, Clay made a pallet on the floor between Lowell and the stove and directly below Dove, who sulked above them all on his scaffold, which was in the day the coldest and at night the warmest spot in the dome. Clay and Lowell shared a bottle to pee in. Some mornings it froze. Most mornings it froze.

Please crawled into bed with Annie and Harl.

Gasoline was $4.99. Neither the wonder truck nor the weeper

could make it down Johnny's road anyway. The Extended Emergency had been further extended while the Supreme Court considered what the papers were calling the "Presidential Primacy" case. MLK's march on Washington drew an estimated hundred thousand, half of whom were turned back with tear gas.

In the big rally at the Lincoln Memorial, four Hueys landed, scattering the crowd and trapping the speakers at the rail-splitter's feet. MLK got away, but two of the impeached justices were "detained" with subpoenas to a Grand Jury investigating irregularities in judicial proceedings.

Meanwhile, the troops disembarking in Oakland were tearing the insignia off their uniforms, discovering that being home wasn't the same as being mustered out.

And the Panthers were calling themselves the King's Men.

TWENTY-ONE

"Sounds like four-wheel drive," said Annie, perking up her oversized ears.

Clay pulled the door open just in time to see it rounding the Rock, slipping sideways in the mud. It was a new Dodge Power Wagon. On the side, it said SANGRE DE CRISTO DISTRICT SHERIFF in gold on green.

"District?" said Roads, pulling on his striped pants. Lopez was already out of the truck. He still wore his Pancho Villa moustache but his hat was smaller, and green instead of white.

Lopez was fat where Roads was thin. The two leaned against the fender of the Dodge and smoked and talked. Lopez shared his ready-mades. That seemed like a good sign to Clay; Harl, who always stayed out of sight when official personnel were near, wasn't so sure.

Lopez tipped his smaller hat and turned around without backing up, leaving a big circle in the mud.

"Courtesy call," Roads explained. "It's about the herb. Lopez says we're to cool it for a month or so. Things are getting a little strange in town."

"How so?"

"They've been federalized. He's now either *in* the National Guard or *under* the National Guard. He's not sure himself."

February is snow. March is mud. April on the other hand, especially toward the end of the month, is sticky clay and the roads are almost passable.

Even Johnny's. "Worth a try," said Roads.

Clay helped him strap the chains on the wonder truck and they sent Annie into Burg with the last of the girl money from the bottom of The Can.

"Glue," Dove whispered hopefully as they watched her round the Rock.

"She'll make it," said Roads. And so she did. She was back before dark with cornmeal, sugar, sardines for the pregnant Please, Bugler, and mail. The Hollywood money had arrived. Twelve gauge deer slugs for Roads, and a water pump for Clay in a faded cardboard box.

"Glue?" Dove whispered hopefully.

No glue. "But guess who I saw in town?"

"Yosemite?"

"Little Richard?"

"Guess who actually did what he said he was going to do, bought a farm, the old Ortiviz place on the river, where the Texans were raising hay last year?"

"Gantz," said Roads. "He must have failed his bar exam."

"And guess who was hanging on his arm?"

My service manager, your old friend Round Man, quit because of Ice, who is colored, but he won't say that. I had to promote Ice to service manager and I'm not sure he can handle it. He's not a people person.

"You can say that again," said Harl. He was standing on a cardboard box to keep his feet out of the mud, reading Clay's letter, watching Clay put the new water pump on the weeper.

"Hand me my Cadillac."

The Cadillac had a soft sound, like spring.

Libra was Earth: oil painters and their ladies, log houses, adobe and railroad ties and blood floors, rules and dispensations,

lines of sight. The Rocks was Air: geodesics and plastic foam, pancakes and jerky, flatheads and herb. Triple A was Fire: the hum-
bucker signal and Stratocaster buzz, blistering solos and color TV.
Ortiviz on the other hand was Water.

"It comes with water rights," Gantz explained. Ditches from
the river, open every Thursday, ten to four. "We can grow food."

"You mean hay," said Harl.

"These potatoes will grow," said Gantz. He showed the
Rockers the page in the catalog. "Winnipegs. I ordered them from
Canada."

Even Alameda looked optimistic.

Roads was rolling a joint to celebrate. "Water is the sacra-
ment here south of the Arkansas," he said. "That's the ancient
dispensation, ancient as the pueblos, as ancient as the Creator
himself."

"*Her*self," said Annie, as Please looked on approvingly, very
pregnant, smelling of sardines.

"Whatever," said Roads.

Clay and Lowell drove down in the weeper to look the
Ortiviz place over. Gantz was proud to show it off. Water rights,
and a single bottom plow, and even a tractor in the pole barn, a
questionable Ford that hadn't run in years. Twenty acres of hay
and pasture land in a bend of the river at the bottom of the valley,
only a mile from Triple A. Twenty more acres of piñon and cedar,
rock and scrub.

"Even a saddle," said Gantz. He pulled it out into the sun
and set it on a fence. He went to look for neat's-foot oil. He had
traded his leather pants for new jeans.

The old adobe four-room house had been empty for years,
ever since the old folks had died (it was their younger preacher
son in Colorado Springs who had sold the place), and the double-
wide under the cottonwoods next to it had fallen into semi-ruin
since their oldest son had been drafted and divorced, both in the
same month, two years before. The hay field had been leased ever

since to the Texans who ran the feedlots up the valley under the wall of the Sangres.

"Hay?" said Lowell. "Who can eat hay?"

"The winnipegs are on order," said Clay. "Meanwhile, Gantz wants to get a horse. He already has the saddle."

They could see him up by the barn, rubbing the saddle down with oil. His rubber gloves gleamed.

"And play cowboy. Like Johnny."

"Johnny's not playing. Unfortunately."

"Neither are we," said Alameda, who had overheard. She stepped out of the back door of the camper in a new western shirt with pearl snaps and brand new Justin boots. She even had a pack of Marlboros.

She even gave Clay and Lowell one each.

She even almost smiled.

"Too many carburetors," said Rotella. "They're fighting each other."

The vanderbike would run but it wouldn't idle. Clay had taken it out from under the dome and ridden it down just for fun. Johnny's road was almost dry. It was spring!

"There are only two."

"One too many," said Rotella, hanging up her screwdriver; each had its own place on the wall of the barn. "Take it up with the Japs."

Indigo was in the loft playing with the trap set. The noise in the barn was deafening. Rotella put her fingers into her ears. Clay pulled the bike out into the sun and followed her into the Big House for coffee and to check the news on TV. The news was deafening too: a big jailbreak in New York. Attica, a prison upstate, had revolted and asked for UN protection, which was promised but only partially received. There was a battle in which four New York state troopers were killed. Humphrey came to their funeral. MLK sent chartered buses from Canada and the prisoners made their way to New York City, where they were now under the protection of the United Nations, which was initiating proceedings against the US for human rights violations.

Merry gave Clay a week-old *Times* for Lowell.

When Clay got on the bike his left knee stuck to the tank. The Confederate flag on one side of the tank had been painted over with black paint.

"House paint!"

"Indigo's on some kind of toot," said Rotella. The drums were rattling louder than ever upstairs. "It's only on one side. Look on it as a compromise."

"House paint!" said Harl when Clay got back to the Rocks. "It's not Indigo's fucking bike. It's not mine either. It's Bobby Lee's and I might have to return it someday."

"Robert Lee," said Clay. "Robert E."

"So fucking what. That's ancient history. It was his room-mate's bike anyway, and we were no fucking slave owners, and neither were our ancestors, mine for sure."

"I'm a Bewley," said Clay. "We always had colored help."

The weeper was steaming.

"I thought you fixed this thing," said Lowell.

"I thought so too," said Clay.

They pulled into the muddy lot by the Ortiviz barn just as Gantz was leaving for Burg. "Good luck," he said. "I hope you brought a battery. I left you a can of gas."

Gasoline had jumped to $5.29 since the Saudis had thrown out the royal family. They were camped at the Ritz in Paris with the shah. Meanwhile, the potatoes had arrived from Canada. The ground was almost dry enough to break, but the tractor wouldn't even turn over, much less start, according to Gantz.

They watched him drive off, with Alameda scowling by his side, then muscled open the barn doors. There in the shadows was an ancient red-belly Ford tractor with a new gas can sitting beside it.

"A classic," said Clay, brushing the bird shit off the seat.

"Is that good or bad?" Lowell lifted the can, trying its weight. "I'm putting half of this in the weeper," he said.

The Ford's tires were cracked with age but up. They pushed it out into the sun and tried the starter.

Nothing. Just a click.

They jumped it from the weeper.

Nothing. Just a click.

"Bad starter," said Lowell. "We should have told Gantz to bring one from town. He has plenty of money."

"Maybe not," said Clay. He remembered a story Hosey had told him, about a red-belly that had sat in a Daviess County barn from Pearl Harbor till Hiroshima. The engine was locked; the pistons rusted in the cylinders. This one had been sitting since the eldest Ortiviz son, the one who had inherited the farm from his overage parents, had been sent off to the war from which he never returned.

Lowell fetched a lamp from the house while Clay pulled the plugs. They poured kerosene out of the lamp into each cylinder, then sat on the fence to let it work. "That old man was full of fixes," said Clay. He showed Lowell his Cadillac. It gleamed in the sun. There were birds singing in the fencerows. It was spring.

"We're smack in the middle of nowhere here," said Lowell. "Wonder what Andy would think?"

"Same thing you're thinking, I'll bet." Clay tried the starter again. It groaned, it moaned like an old man waking up from a long nap, and the engine kicked, then spat, then spun, then ran. A little back-and-forth unstuck the two-stage clutch as well and awakened the primitive hydraulics.

"A little whale oil does the trick," said Lowell, the New Englander, and they left the tractor out of the barn for Gantz to find and headed down the county road for Triple A, where Lowell was hoping to meet the bus, with Merry at the wheel, back from Denver. The band's schedule was erratic these days.

"So who's going to plant all those potatoes?" he asked. "Who's going to harvest them?"

"Free labor," said Clay. "Gantz figures that hippies will be pouring into the valley again as soon the weather warms up. Like migratory birds."

"Peasants," said Lowell. "And Gantz the Baron. But he's in for a disappointment. We're not going to see a flood of homeless hippies this year. Not with the Emergency and the interstates all closed. That's all over—for now, anyway."

"Maybe not," said Clay. "The birds are arriving already. Look."

The bus wasn't back from Denver. Instead, in the lot between the Big House and barn were brightly painted trucks, three in a line, all Chevys.

"Ira!" said Clay.

"Ira," said Lowell.

"California is getting seriously weird," said Ira.

"Tell me about it," said Lowell.

Rotella was admiring the trucks. "They are all the same," she said.

"All 235s," said Ira. "Makes maintenance simpler. That's the secret of the Caravan."

Ira's was the most familiar: the Hells Angels skull still showed through new paint on the plywood camper, overlaid with Day-Glo paw prints of the coyote, Ira's new totem, the trickster. The other two were just as bright with sunbursts and tarot signs. Colorful hippies were emerging like clowns from tiny cars. The women ran for the Big House and the bathroom, while the men peed in the bushes.

"We barely coasted in on fumes," said Ira. One of the men was negotiating a trade with Rimshot, already siphoning gas out of the pink Caddy. "Kick and the others are heading on to Taos. Ling and I thought we might hang here awhile."

Ling was his Lady.

"Calliope," said Clay.

φ

"California is getting seriously crazy," Ira said. They'd had to pay an exit fee to leave. They came on back roads, all the way across the mountains, since the interstates were all but closed. "They only check for stickers at the exits, but that means that once you get on you can't get off. We lost one truck in Durango, a mud hole as big as Rhode Island. We lost another to the cops in Reno, but that's another story. April is the cruelest month. Looks like you're overheating."

"Tell me about it," said Clay. He had refilled the weeper before leaving Triple A, but it was already steaming, halfway up Johnny's road. The new pump wept as badly as the old one.

Ling, Ira's new lady, wore a bright Mao jacket, and if Clay had expected her to speak with a high Asian lilt, and he had, he was disappointed, but only for a moment. She was all-American, a California girl: Santa Barbara, in fact, where her father was a plastic surgeon; then Stanford; then Berkeley for medical school.

"A doctor? A real doctor, not a PhD?" Clay was impressed.

Ling patted the doctor's bag on her lap. "I did my residency in the Haight, most of it. Then I got sidetracked."

"Ling ran the free clinic in the Haight," said Ira. "We didn't get along at first, and then we did."

"Pride and prejudice," said Clay.

"Yeah, and she's Darcy," said Ira proudly.

"It's a flying saucer!" said Ling as they rounded the Rock and the dome flew into view.

"A calliope," said Clay.

"What's that?"

"A kind of a steamboat," said Ira.

"Lowell was right about the Angels," said Ira, when dinner was over. "Remind me to tell him so. It got ugly. We were delivering people to the march in Oakland, and they freaked. Some of the Weather clones were carrying a Vietcong flag, and the Angels freaked on them. The Panthers stepped in—they have their own macho shit. It was bad."

"Weather clones?" Dove muttered. "Where's Lowell?"

"There wasn't room in the truck for four," said Clay. "Lowell stayed over. He said maybe Merry would drive him up in the morning."

"I'll bet."

"The Caravan thing was getting difficult," said Ira, "so we found a squat in Marin. An old farmhouse, a righteous place under a little mountain called Humpback, after the whale. That's whale country, you know, Point Reyes. Whales and cattle."

"Dairy cattle," said Ling, holding her nose. It was tiny, like her hands and feet, almost lost in her broad face.

"Then two weeks ago, short one day, at about eight in the morning, the shit hit the fan."

Ira and his sidekick were having coffee, getting ready to do some work on the trucks, all 235s, when eight Harleys came up the road, "in a storm of sound," he said. "They parked the bikes and Kick and I went over to greet them, and they walked right past us, without a word, into the house, and started trashing the place."

"Literally," said Ling.

"They threw all the mattresses out the door. They pitched the stove out, still burning. The stovepipe fell down. The children were crying. The women were watching."

"We were waiting on you," said Ling. "You were armed. You could have stopped them."

"Not likely," said Ira.

"They were probably armed too," said Plain Bob.

"Don't they always carry guns?" asked Annie.

"What am I going to do?" said Ira. "Shoot somebody over a stove?"

"It wasn't just about a stove," said Ling. "First they shot Kick's dog. Then they shot Susan's dog. Then they shot Juan's dog. *Bang bang bang.*"

"They never touched the trucks," said Ira. "That was the point, I think. We got the message. We split and here we are."

"How many are you?" asked Roads.

"There are only Ling and me for now. Kick and the others

are heading south to check out the Taos communes. They want to grow stuff."

"You should talk to Gantz," said Roads. "He just bought a farm, the old Ortiviz place. They're going to grow stuff. They need souls."

"Peasants," said Harl.

"I like it here," said Ling, looking up. "There's something about a round space that frees the soul."

"Grow what?" asked Ira.

"Potatoes," said Roads.

"Hay," said Harl.

"It's time," said Roads. Clay and Ira helped him set out his plants in the upper meadow, along the water line, where they would be fed by the leaks. It was Little Richard's old job. Nobody missed him, "not even Annie," said Clay.

"And here's Lowell," said Ira, when they got back to the dome. He was sitting on the deck with the *Times*.

Revolutionary Mexico had been given a seat on the Security Council, along with the United Arab States, at the insistence of the Soviets. The US voted both for and against; there were two US representatives, Humphrey's Goldberg and Jackson, who had been sent by MLK to represent what he called his Niagara Convention. The UN had voted to seat them both, and Humphrey had responded by recalling Goldberg, who had responded by resigning, though he hadn't gone over to MLK.

"Yet," said Lowell. "Where's Dove?"

Annie opened the door to show him. Dove was high on his scaffold, putting on his prom dress. Ling was cooking something on the stove while Roads looked on. The smell was awful.

"It's a Chinese herbal thing," Ling said, pouring it into a bucket "An ancient remedy, used for closing wounds. That yellow-green color is bamboo; the smell is panda blood, or so they say. It's a powder. I've always been afraid to try it, but it might solve Dove's problem."

Harl was already passing up the triangles from under the dome. Dove dropped a rope for the bucket. Clay tossed up a brush and a broomstick. Ira beamed and rolled a cigarette.

"It sure stinks," said Lowell.

"You oughta know," said Dove, and went to work.

Clay rode into Burg with Annie in the wonder truck. While she checked the mail, he laid a water pump on the counter at Lopez Auto Parts.

"Is that the *viejo* or the new one?"

"Does it matter? The new one weeps just as bad as the old one."

"It's old too. The seals dry out just sitting on the shelf. I told you I couldn't guarantee it."

"True."

"Tell you what, amigo. I'll give you a couple of cans of Prestone to keep it right."

The Hollywood money hadn't come. They made do with girl money and headed home.

"There was a cross leaning in the corner behind the anti-freeze," Clay said. "Made of timbers, six feet tall at least. And I'll swear I saw a crown of thorns behind the cash register."

"Welcome to Sangre County," said Annie. "He's Lopez's cousin, you know. They're all Penitentes. Wait till you see their Easter parade."

"I'll pass."

As soon as they turned off onto Johnny's road, Annie took her hands off the wheel and rolled a cigarette from the Bugler can. The ruts were deep and the wonder truck knew the way.

"Uh-oh. Heeere's Johnny."

He was on Color TV, heading down from the upper meadow. Clay waved but Johnny didn't wave back; he kept his head down as if he were riding into a stiff wind. Clay felt sorry for him.

Annie didn't. "I'll bet that bastard smashed our plants," she said. "I'll bet he rode back and forth over them on his stupid horse."

Turned out he had.

"That's the cowboy way," said Roads. He had extras; they had time to replant.

"They can't impeach the entire fucking court," said Harl.

"Sure they can," said Lowell. "They just did."

Congress had voted Articles of Impeachment against the Supreme Court for defying a Presidential Order to issue a decision on the rendition by the Ides of March. They were still deadlocked, rumored to have come to blows, almost, all those Old Men.

"What's legal?" asked Annie, discouraged. "They are the ones who make the laws."

The country was coming apart. The fighting at Oakland had turned fatal. The SS *United States* was scuttled in the harbor. It had been burned by the men who had not been allowed off. A boatload of antiwar supporters was turned back by the Coast Guard, while the soldiers burned, or jumped, or jumped burning. Hunter Thompson in *Esquire* described it as "a scene from hell."

Meanwhile Ortiviz was coming together. Ira and Ling moved into the adobe, covering the knocked-out windows with plastic sheets. Plain Jane and Plain Bob cleaned the mold out of the double-wide with a mop. While Alameda sulked in the International camper, Gantz counted his winnipegs and waited for the fields to dry.

TWENTY-TWO

"SHIT."

"What?"

"Those fuckers."

HUMPHREY DECLARED PRESIDENT
Supreme Court Decision Unanimous

"What do they mean by 'unanimous'?" Clay asked. Five of
the judges had quit rather than answer the impeachment charges.
Two of these had gone home; three had gone over to MLK's
Niagara Convention, which was certifying itself in earshot of the
falls, under the protection of the Canadian government.

"Now what?"

"Now the shit hits the fan," said Lowell.

Humphrey had offered the vice presidency to MLK, who
refused it and promised to march on the White House in protest.
Buses were pouring into DC from Atlanta. The ones from Canada
were in a convoy protected by renegade Army regulars who, like
the Panthers, were calling themselves the King's Men.

"It looks like a guided missile," said Annie.

"It's my ride," said Lowell.

It was coming around the Rock, silent as a ghost, eggplant
purple, with a rocket ship grille.

"It's a Studebaker Champion," said Clay. "A 1956. Almost as
old as the weeper."

Merry called it the champ. Rimshot was in LA again, and
Merry had bought it at Lopez Motors in Burg, to replace the pink

Caddy. $650. While he was explaining this, Dove came in from the outhouse and climbed his tower without a word. Lowell was leaving.

"A family funeral," he explained while he packed his bag, a maroon-and-silver *Vogue* tote. "I'm catching a ride to Denver with the Triple A bus. Then I have to fly to Boston. The funeral's on Sunday."

"Fly!?" said Annie.

"They sent the money weeks ago. It wasn't unexpected. It's my Uncle Jedediah, who got me into Harvard. I owe him."

"You split, remember?" Clay reminded him. But Lowell was already out the door. Then Clay saw his sleeping bag, unrolled. He checked the White House envelope in the blue folder in the bottom of the bag. Three twenties were missing. That left $280.

He caught up with Lowell as he was tossing his tote into the back seat of the champ.

"You might have fucking asked," he said.

"I didn't want to complicate things. It's EmCee's money, Clay. I know she would approve."

"Still . . ."

"I'll make it up. We all have our secrets, okay?"

He stuck his hand out the window. Clay took it. It was Lowell who had saved her life, and now she was dead.

The champ was a straight six. Merry started it with a grin. "Listen to it idle. You can hardly hear it run."

"It's a flathead," said Clay. "Like a possum at midnight."

The United Nations gave Israel twenty-four days to abandon the seized territories or be expelled from the UN. The Israelis responding by fleeing in record numbers, joining the refugees from South Africa, which was now under ANC rule.

There was fighting in Denver between the National Guard and the Olvidados, a Mexican street gang. Mexico was threatening to send troops to protect their nationals. Even Allende weighed in, from Chile.

The weeper was weeping more than ever now that the

weather was warm. Clay could hardly make it from the Rocks to Ortiviz without adding a quart of Prestone along the way.

Humphrey's Congress voted to censure MLK for not accepting the VP spot. Humphrey vetoed the censure, still hoping for a compromise. Elements of the 23rd Infantry Division in Oakland elected new officers and headed for Canada in a convoy of trucks requisitioned at gunpoint from the Alameda motor pool.

The National Guard fell back and watched. Some cheered.

Dove moved down from his tower. Ling's Chinese glue was holding and he seemed happier with Lowell gone. His prom dress still hung near the top, still stiff with glue.

"*Twas* is not a word," said Annie.

"'Tis so," said Roads.

"'Taint," said Harl.

They were playing Scrabble.

"I'm going to bed," said Clay.

He slept alone in the honeymoon bus, which had never been reclaimed by Plain Jane and Plain Bob. The engine was still at the edge of Rotella's forty-horse pile at Triple A, but the six-volt battery held a charge and the radio worked. Wheeling, West Virginia, was especially good, late at night, like the jukebox at the 4-Way. Del Rio, Texas, wasn't bad.

Truck driver music. *"Listen to those steel belts whine."*

It was warm but windy, so Clay sat in the weeper where he could roll a cigarette while he waited on Dove. Sagrado Shell was on what the locals called a mesita, one of those rocky little benches at the foot of the mountains that looked like landfill and often in fact was. Down the hill on one side was Burg: snot-colored adobes with cottonwoods watching over them like big shaggy dogs; a bar/movie theater/diner/hotel, the Royal Western; a coal-colored county courthouse with a green National Guard truck out front, taking up two parking spots; and to the east, the interstate, all but empty of traffic, like a Chinese Wall protecting the town and, who knew, perhaps the mountains as well from the long dry swell of the plains.

Down the other side, closer at hand, in a dry bend of a dry creek, was an encampment of VW buses, pup tents, and plywood around a bright new green tent, an octagon the size of Libra's community dome, with a wide yellow arrow painted on it, pointing straight to Heaven.

Or maybe Mars, Clay thought.

One Way looked more like a refugee camp than a commune, which was, Clay supposed, the idea. The few kids stirring all looked under twenty; the girls chased babies while the men (boys?) were busy disassembling picnic tables for firewood.

Dove held up two fingers and Clay rolled him a cigarette and passed it into the phone booth when the door squeaked open. Sagrado Shell had long been closed but the pay phone still worked.

Down the hill a white Ford Ranger crossed the dry creekbed and stopped in front of the big green tent. Four-wheel drive with a fat yellow arrow on the door. Yosemite got out on the driver's side; Little Richard, on the other. Yosemite looked straight up the hill, straight at Clay, and held up two fingers in a V, smiling. He had a beard like Moses.

Dove was hanging up.

They headed home. The weeper had no plates, but Sagrado Shell was on the west side of Burg, and on the country road it didn't matter.

"You look pleased. You get through?"

"Yes and no."

The Tel Aviv number hadn't worked—either the country code or the number itself was wrong—so Dove had called Cleveland to check the number with his mother, and wouldn't you know it, his father had answered. They hadn't spoken in two years, not since Dove had announced at the dinner table that he was "gay," the new word for queer. On his father's fiftieth birthday, which was probably, he now realized, a mistake.

"Anyway," prompted Clay.

"Anyway, I guess I caught him by surprise. He said, 'Hello, son, how are you?' 'Son,' he said. Then he said, 'There's someone here who wants to talk to you.' Then he just hands off the phone, and there she was."

"Your mother?"

"My grandmother. In Cleveland, and she says 'Dov, is that you? I knew that was you!' And she sounded great! She's been there almost a week. She had to fly out through Russia."

"Cool," said Clay, watching the temperature gauge. The trick was to catch it before it hit the peg and got too hot to refill while running.

"Some of the old folks stayed, she tells me, but she doesn't trust the Arabs. She says they stole her TV. The UN is resettling them in Germany but she has a thing about the Germans, which you can't blame her. US and South Africa are the only other countries that will take them in. South Africa, imagine that."

"Imagine," said Clay.

"It's turning into a race war," said Merry.

"It's always been a race war," said Clay.

"You sound like Lowell."

No one had heard from Lowell. The King's Men, greeted by cheers in some communities and silence in others, had been fired on in Oklahoma and then in Missouri on their "long march" to Niagara, growing as they went by opening prisons on the way.

The Niagara Convention (a third of the old US Congress, with newly elected additions from every state but Georgia, more than half but less than two-thirds Black) sent them gas money, and Canada paid their salaries, even while MLK was dithering in the mists of the falls.

A last-minute attempt by the National Guard to stop a column in Michigan resulted in four deaths, a downed helicopter, and a Security Council resolution declaring ten miles on either side of the Canadian border under ten thousand feet a no-fly zone.

"Bring the war home!" said Merry.

"Now you're the one who sounds like Lowell," said Clay. Or EmCee, he thought. "Be careful what you wish for."

It was time to plow. Clay looked on proudly as Ira pulled the starter and the red-belly started with a miniature roar.

"Easy!" said Clay.

"Behold the Lord of the Manor," said Ira.

Gantz emerged from his camper, where he had been changing his cowboy hat for a farmer's cap, and replaced Ira in the seat. Clay showed him how to raise and lower the plow, a simple one-bottom. The hydraulics looked good.

The red-belly Ford bucked once, twice, then obeyed as Gantz aimed it out of the barn lot, toward the edge of the field. Ira hung on. Clay followed on foot.

Plain Bob and Plain Jane waved from the double-wide's board-and-block step. Alameda scowled from the back door of the camper, left behind. Ling brought a coffeepot out to the adobe's crumbling porch. Ira joined her.

The red-belly Ford ticked happily, shaking the damp clay off its lugs like a big dog. Gantz dropped the plow. The earth groaned, then sighed like a girl. It had been a long winter.

The first furrow leaned to the east; the second bowed to the west; the third cut through them both, approximating a straight line. Gantz laid down a fourth as straight as a string. Then another, then another.

Sequences, thought Clay. Farming is all about sequences, and so is Gantz.

"How'd it go?" Roads asked that evening.

"Pretty good for a guy who couldn't pass his bar exam," said Clay.

Your cousin Junior has gotten his promotion to Major, but guess what? He's now in the National Guard!

φ

"Denver is mean," said Merry.

They had missed their new gig at the Club Cowboy, turned back by a checkpoint just north of Castle Rock. Denver was now under Military Emergency (ME), which no sticker could penetrate. The fighting, which had begun at the abandoned Greyhound station, had spread outward in concentric circles, like ripples from a rock thrown into a pond, until it had touched the suburbs themselves.

Fighting in New York too. The Puerto Ricans were blamed. They had added insult to injury, applying for separate representation under the UN's new Postcolonial Mandate; then welcoming Che to San Juan in the largest public demonstration since the Nationalists were released, even as refugees were flooding into Miami.

"My father-in-law was Puerto Rican," said Rotella.

"I never knew you were married."

"For a few weeks, in Albuquerque. Hand me your Cadillac."

They were finally assembling the forty-horse, fitting the recycled heads onto the salvaged jugs.

"A Puerto Rican in New Mexico?"

"Why not?"

"No reason," said Clay, who had always thought that the Puerto Ricans were like the Jews, New York City their briar patch. But even that was changing, according to Palomina, who had a card from Cicero. The refugees from Israel were all heading straight for Texas or LA. New York was all blue helmets. Atlanta too.

It was time to plant. All the Rockers, even Roads, even Dove, were down for the ceremony. Gantz drove the tractor, pulling a two-bottom plow set high, while Plain Jane and Plain Bob followed behind, dropping cut-up winnipegs into the two long shallow trenches. Harl and Clay came last, pulling a plywood four-by-eight to cover the potatoes with old dirt made new.

Ling and Annie cheered.

Ira and Roads sat on the fence, overseers. Merry and Rotella sat on the hood of the champ, smiling in the sun. Dove sulked with Alameda on the porch of the adobe. It was a beautiful spring day.

"Who invited them?" Ling asked Annie.

It was a new Ford Ranger with a yellow arrow on the door and Little Richard at the wheel. The bed of the truck was filled with One Wayers sitting at attention, three girls with rakes and five boys with hoes.

Roads went to meet them. Clay and Ira followed.

"We came to help," said Little Richard. "We saw Gantz in town and he told us what was happening."

"It's all under control, thanks," said Roads.

"We're all good neighbors," said Little Richard. "It's all one valley."

"They can watch if they want to," said Roads.

"But they stay in the fucking truck," said Ira.

"Don't be such a shit," said Little Richard. But he went back to the truck and looked on almost amiably while the potatoes were planted. He leaned against the fender, smoking, while the kids in the back knelt with their hoes and rakes upright like spears.

"I think they're praying," said Roads.

"For us or against us?"

"God only knows."

Lowell was back. "We missed you," said Annie. "How was the funeral?"

"Some of us," said Dove.

The Rockers were sitting on the deck of the dome, watching the sun go down over Blanca, sharing a six-pack of Walter's and a plastic bottle of Cutty Sark. Lowell's treat. Plus sardines for Please, more pregnant than ever.

"Funerals are all the same," he said. "Boston was mean. Everyone is holding their breath."

"Did you get to New York at all?" Clay wanted to know.

"Barely. Both the tunnels and the George Washington Bridge were closed for almost a week, since the attack on the UN building."

The first missile took out a lounge on the fourteenth floor. Eleven died. No one claimed responsibility but the NYFD was demobilized after refusing to respond, and renegade elements were thought to be responsible for the second missile, fired from Queens, which had missed and taken off the top of the American Prudential building on Thirty-ninth and Fifth Avenue.

The city was now under UN mandate and blue helmets were everywhere.

"So does that mean New York City is no longer part of the USA?" Clay asked.

"It never was," said Lowell. "Isn't that what we loved about it?"

"Quod erat demonstrandum," said Ling, who was visiting to check on Please, who pulled on her panties and ate another sardine.

Her little teats were big as tangerines, her belly as bright as a pumpkin.

"Brought you something," said Lowell. It was Clay's poems, the xeroxes that had been returned by *South* magazine. "I wasn't about to leave them on the table in the diner. Read them, you'll be surprised."

"I will?"

"They're not bad."

Clay put them in the blue folder with his mother's letters, EmCee's twenties, Ginsberg's nickel, and his father's 1911. He wasn't ready to read them yet.

Roads was back from Taos and the news was good. The Oklas had made it through in time for the solstice, and he had the sacraments to prove it, nestled like newborns in a little round paper bag. They had driven on the interstates, where they were often mistaken for Mexicans and stopped—but just as often, Roads said, confused with crackers and waved through.

"Crackers?" protested Harl.

"It's the hats."

The solstice meeting was held at Ortiviz. The long poles were brought down from Libra, wrapped in the cloud-colored canvas like bones in a wedding dress. Assembled, the tepee was twenty feet across and twenty-two high. The smoke hole was just wide enough to let a few stars in. "It's time," said Roads.

Ling, who disapproved of drugs, and Merry, who had had enough of peyote, stayed in the adobe as Ground Control. The rest filed into the tepee.

Gantz was Fire Man, sitting at the right side of Roads. Annie was Pipe Lady. Little Richard, who had showed up with his totems, his feathers, and his beads, having left all the Jesus kids behind, was cut a pass and named Drum Dude. Roads, the Road Man, rattled the bag: "Take and eat."

They took, they ate, they puked; they took and ate again. The smoke hole swarmed with stars. Dove wore his prom dress, cleaned in the creek to kill the smell. Clay wore his Emily's Taxi jacket.

Annie, her broad breasts painted like racing hot rods, stuffed tobacco in the clay pipe Roads handed her and sent it circling around the fire. The circle grew larger as the night wore on, and the hippies made room for their guests, the ghosts: the horse soldiers and buffalo hunters, the dead in their faded blankets, even the doomed in their gimme hats. Clay looked for EmCee, but she didn't show, not even her shadow. The bag came around again, take and eat. Please began to cry and Annie led her out on all fours past the fire. Roads took the drum from Little Richard and started to play, louder and louder until even Harl was singing, even Alameda. The smoke hole turned blue, stirring the stars away.

As they came out the sun was just gleaming off Blanca's lone glacier. Dove was limping; his foot had gone to sleep. The sky was a blue bowl, empty except for one long white scratch: the red-eye from NY to LA. The men stood in a line and peed toward the east. Inside the adobe, a baby squalled. Ling was on the porch, drying her hands on a towel.

"It's a girl," she said.

TWENTY-THREE

"WHAT'S HER LITTLE NAME?" BRENDA ASKED. SHE HAD COME UP TO see the baby.

"Pei," said Ling.

"Peyote," said Roads.

"Don't listen to him," said Brenda. "And don't tell Johnny I was here. I just wanted to take Color TV out for a ride and see the new baby. Johnny's been feeling lowly, anyway. He's gone to Pueblo to the hospital. They're keeping him over night."

Annie made Brenda some herbal tea. She drank it politely but Clay could tell she didn't like it. She twirled it in her cup politely, then set it aside to hold the baby in her wide lap. "We had a baby once," she said. "But only for a year."

That was all she ever said about it.

"They are growing," said Lowell.

"The vines are growing," said Harl. "The potatoes won't."

"They might," said Clay.

They parked the weeper, still steaming, in front of the adobe.

The Ortiviz place was looking like an actual farm. The fields were fenced; the barn door opened and shut; there was even a yel-low-and-blue oilcloth tablecloth on the kitchen table in the adobe.

Ling even wore a calico dress.

"It's dark in this kitchen, friends," said Ira. With one hand he banged the coffeepot on the table and with the other he picked up the Ortiviz Bugler can. He wore his hair in a ponytail these days. His shirt matched Ling's calico dress, almost. He led them out to the porch, which faced east.

"The problem with Gantz," said Ira, "is that his boots never hit the ground. He's either in Burg with Alameda, shopping at the Safeway, or riding around on Trigger, looking for stuff to landlord about."

They could see him in the distance, tall on his horse under his hat.

"He named his horse Trigger?" Lowell asked, amazed.

"We did that," said Ling. "Roll me one of those."

"Since he bought that horse he hasn't done a lick of work, not that he did any before."

"He bought the place," said Clay. "That's something." He had come down to fix, or at least check out, a hydraulic leak on the red-belly Ford. Harl and Lowell were just along for the ride. They were wiping the dirt off the lines when Gantz rode up on his horse, at a gallop, and skidded to a stop.

"Need some help down by the river. The fence is down and there's a cow in the field, trampling the potatoes!"

They followed him on foot. Ling left the porch and came along too. Alameda looked out of the back of the International camper, then went back inside, slamming the aluminum door behind her.

"It's huge," Gantz called back over his shoulder. "I think it's a bull."

"That's no cow," said Lowell. It was walking in a circle, making a path through the tender young potato vines, then stooping its shaggy head to toss them up with its wide horns. "That's a fucking buffalo."

Lowell told the story that night, over dinner at the Rocker dome. "There was a huge hole in the fence, and there it was. We couldn't do anything with it. Gantz's horse was afraid of it too. Trigger."

"He named his horse Trigger?" Dove asked from above. He ate alone. He only came down when Lowell wasn't around.

"It's a sure sign," said Roads. "A gift of the peyote, like Pei here." He handed the baby back to Please and rolled a joint. "Things are looking up. The buffalo are back."

"Not exactly," said Harl. "It had a tag in its ear."

"A cowboy came to get it," said Lowell. "Apparently the Texans keep a herd up near Westcliffe. They sell them to the national parks."

"A real cowboy," said Clay. "In a pickup truck."

"He herded it off down the road with the truck," said Harl. "They don't pay attention to horses."

"Of course not," said Roads.

Please handed the baby to Clay while Annie unbuttoned her blouse. After she was fed, Pei liked to sleep between Annie's big breasts. She almost never cried. She sucked and snorted and snuggled, opening her eyes only once or twice a day to look around the world, new to her, with some wonder.

"Gantz thought it was a cow," said Clay. "I recognized it right away from the nickel Allen Ginsberg gave me."

He showed it to everybody, again.

Ran into your old girlfriend yesterday, Miss Trailer Tramp. She is still working at the Southern Kitchen. She's pregnant. She's marrying Danny Rose—I don't know if you remember him? He's a policeman now.

"Rose was always a bit of a cop," said Harl.

Clay folded the letter and put it into the blue folder. It was getting full. Someday, he thought, he should put the letters in order, separate them by season. They were like leaves—falling from the tree that was his mother.

"There's a helicopter in Burg," said Annie. "Parked on the courthouse lawn, next to the National Guard trailer."

"What kind?" asked Harl.

"The kind with the big propeller on top. No letter from Mother. I had to spend the girl money on gasoline. And Merry sent you this."

She handed Lowell the *Times*.

The World Court, at the instigation of the Bolivaran Assembly, had voted a war crimes indictment against the Humphrey government for human rights violations. Humphrey condemned it as interference in internal affairs, a violation of sovereignty.

"Torture," said Clay. "That's a new one."

"Not exactly," said Lowell. "Torture has always been an unacknowledged but reliable instrument in the imperialist toolkit."

"You oughta know," muttered Dove from atop his tower.

"I like the Clark Kent guy," said Annie.

Allende, Chile's new leftist president, did look a little Clark Kent–ish with his thick glasses, deceivingly mild manner, and, of course, hidden powers. It was he who had assembled the Bolivaran Assembly, which included Argentina, Venezuela, Cuba, and now Mexico.

"Plus Puerto Rico," said Lowell. "It's official. They left the USA last week and joined the Bolivaran Assembly as an independent nation."

"Puerto Rico? I didn't know they were part of the US."

"They weren't," said Lowell. "And now they aren't."

"Either of you two seen Merry?"

Lowell was a silhouette, standing in the big square doorway of Triple A's barn.

Clay shook his head. He was sitting on the forty-horse. Rotella was torquing down the heads. She claimed she could get within four foot-pounds using Clay's Cadillac. Clay checked her with an actual torque wrench.

"You're amazing," he said.

"Aren't you going to check them all?"

"Nope. No need."

A new silhouette appeared in the door. It was Merry. "Either of you two seen Lowell? I heard he was looking for me."

"He's looking for you. Give us a hand here."

After loading the finished forty-horse into the bed of the

weeper, they went into the Big House for coffee. Rimshot was back, watching the news with the kids. They were beginning to prefer it to cartoons.

"They like the funny faces," said Lowell, joining them.

Humphrey's chairman of the Joint Chiefs of Staff had threatened air strikes if the King's Men crossed the border back into New York state. Humphrey had fired him, caught between the Niagara Convention and the United Nations, and convinced that all this could and would be settled peacefully, with MLK as his veep.

"Not likely," said Lowell. "When things reach a certain point, you have to have an army to settle them peacefully."

Humphrey had an army, the National Guard, but it was hemorrhaging deserters even as the King's Men (formerly the 23rd Infantry, and elements of the 4th) were picking up recruits and "draftees" from prisons. The UN promised back pay.

Charles, crowned king after his mother's suicide, had monitored the Northern Ireland plebiscite and then come to Canada to arrange asylum for the Orange refugees, though some said it was all a ploy to prevent Quebec from leaving Canada. He and the Dalai Lama had tea with MLK. And Ling's Chinese glue was holding the top twelve triangles in place.

"They always hold in the warm weather," said Dove, the pessimist. "It's the cold that makes them fall."

At first Clay thought it was Little Richard. It was the One Way Ford Ranger, with four-wheel drive. Even so, it slipped, it slid, it scooted around the Rock. Someone else was driving.

Clay was putting the forty-horse into the honeymoon van; he eyeballed the clutch, hoping the pilot shaft would go. The Ford pulled up in front of the dome, at the foot of the steps, and two women got out. One was white, a kid of about nineteen in a long dress. The other, the driver, was an older Black woman of about forty. She was dressed like Becca: like a lawyer, like a Realtor.

"Hello, the dome!" she said.

Clay set down his Cadillac and headed over to cut them off. Annie and Roads were in the upper meadow, pinching buds. Harl was at Ortiviz with Roads, criticizing the potatoes. Lowell was down at Triple A with Merry. Dove was washing his prom dress in the creek.

"Hello. Are you all lost?" he asked.

"Lost? We once were lost," the older woman said, "but now we're found." She stuck out her hand. "Just a friendly visit, sir." Her smile widened ominously.

Clay pointed at the fat yellow arrow on the door of the truck. "You're from One Way. Thank you but we don't need a visit."

"This is Andrea—she is from One Way." Andrea blushed and dropped her eyes. "I'm Rebekah with a *K*, from For the Children, in Colorado Springs."

"And?"

"We're not here to visit you, though we are always glad to see you. We're here for the children."

"There are no children here that need visiting. Or saving. Or praying over."

"Are you sure, sir? Children can't always tell us what they need."

"Fucking positive."

"What about that little one?"

Clay looked behind him. Please was standing on the dome's high deck with Pei on her shoulder.

"We don't pray over the children, sir," said the woman who called herself Rebekah. "We pray *with* them. Every child's life is a prayer in itself, often a silent prayer We are just a helping voice."

Please started down the steps, holding the baby out like a prize.

"Don't," said Clay.

But she did. He watched helplessly as Please handed the baby to Rebekah, who kissed her on the forehead, then covered her tiny soft skull with her hand. She closed her eyes and mumbled a prayer.

The white girl, Andrea, mumbled along.

Then she handed the baby back to Please and they both got back into the Ford and left, grinding the gears on the truck mercilessly as they turned it around.

"Don't you ever do that again!" said Clay.

Please burst into tears, then handed him the baby and ran back into the dome.

It was smiling.

"Hey, Pei," said Clay.

Chop chop . . .

"Looks like a bug," said Clay.

"A Huey," said Harl.

They could see it far below, apparently following the county road that was almost visible from the dome's half moon deck. Like a big insect—but more predator than prey, Clay thought.

"What are they looking for on the county road? Aren't they supposed to be patrolling the interstate?"

"They're just booking hours," said Harl. "Flight time. Training. The county road gives them something to follow, something to do."

"Seems pointless," said Dove.

"Seems Army," said Harl.

"Aren't they the National Guard? Not the Army?" Roads had just come out, wiping his hands on his rag, looking for the Bugler.

Harl scooted him the can. It was almost empty.

"It's a horse," said Annie. She had such ears! She pulled on the rope to open the door and stuck her head outside.

Clay joined her, wondering, Johnny?

No, it was Gantz, with Alameda on the back, hanging on for dear life. He left her tying Trigger to the weeper while he came inside, looking for Roads.

Roads was already boiling water for coffee. He stirred in the grounds and banged the pot on the counter to sink them, cowboy style.

"Ran me off my own farm," Gantz said. "Ira and that damned Ling. Plain Bob and his so-called lady too. They woke me up at dawn, banging on the side of the camper, and ran us out. I'm going to town to get the sheriff. They pulled a gun."

"Where's your truck?" asked Clay.

"I couldn't find the keys," said Gantz. "I'm going back to get it with the sheriff. They pulled a gun"

Alameda was in the doorway, scowling.

"Wait here," said Roads. "Let me go talk to them."

Clay drove him in the honeymoon van: its first trip around the Rock. The engine sounded okay for a VW, like a slow suicide. "It has a radio!" said Roads.

"But no first gear," said Clay. And already it was popping out of second.

Plain Jane and Plain Bob were serving breakfast: sausage (Jimmy Dean) and eggs. "Gantz bought all this," Roads said, pouring himself a cup of coffee from the Mr. Coffee on the back of the woodstove, "and the farm as well. What makes you think you can run him off?"

Ling explained.

"So he was bossy," said Roads. "That's not a crime."

"This is a collective farm," said Ira. "The potatoes belong to everyone. The sausage too."

"He wouldn't cook," said Plain Jane. "He wouldn't clean. All he did was drive into town everyday."

"All he did was ride around on his horse and watch other people do all the work," said Ira.

"He said you pulled a gun," said Roads.

"That was me," said Ling. "I wasn't going to shoot him. I just showed it to him." She showed it to Roads. It was a little Czech 9 mm. Her father, the neurosurgeon, had given it to her when she had signed on to run the clinic in the Haight. He didn't trust hippies.

"Let me see it," said Clay. It was loaded. He pulled out the clip.

"Good God, girl!" said Roads.

"Take him the truck," said Ira, tossing the keys onto the table. "And tell him he can have his farm back as soon as the potatoes are finished."

It was almost noon when Clay and Roads got back to the Rocks. Gantz and Alameda were gone.

"They couldn't wait," said Lowell. "I think they're going to get the sheriff."

"*Dum de dum dum,*" said Harl.

"Then somebody needs to take Gantz's truck down to Triple A and leave it there with the keys in it," said Roads. "I don't want Lopez coming up here in some helicopter and finding it here."

"I can do that," said Lowell.

"I got over you," said Dove. He was dismantling his tower. He was handing the pieces down one at a time to Harl.

"There was nothing to get over," said Lowell. He was back after two nights at Triple A, breaking up with Merry. He slept that night with Dove in the "corner" by the coats. His old spot near the stove, cold now in the summer, was taken. Plain Jane was back without Plain Bob. Ling had suggested they separate for a few days. There was nothing to do at the farm anyway but cultivate the vines, and Ira handled that with the tractor.

Clay was sleeping in the honeymoon van. Third gear was gone as well. It had been demoted to architecture again. He ran the engine once a week to charge the battery. He kept the folder under the mattress. He couldn't seem to get around to reading the poems. Radio was better.

"A ride to One Way? You got religion?"

"I'm a doctor, Clay. I have responsibilities. There are two new babies at One Way. I delivered one two weeks ago."

"They invited you?"

"Never mind that. I'll treat you to some gas."

Ling sent Plain Bob to the barn to get it. Ira looked on, shaking his head.

Clay had just driven down to have a look at the potato vines, but what the hell. The weeper had no plates, but One Way was on the north side of Burg, just off the county road. Plus he liked being with Ling; he liked her silences.

Plus the weeper liked the county road and Clay enjoyed the singing of the tires on the asphalt. And there it was: the long view out of the valley onto the eastward-leading Great Plains. There was no traffic, of course. Then:

"What's that?" Ling asked.

A rhetorical question. It was a truck, a familiar Ford Ranger with a fat yellow arrow on the door, parked crossways on the narrow road. There was a blue light blinking on the dash, and a man standing beside it with a gun.

"What the fuck?" said Clay. It was Little Richard.

He stopped.

Little Richard set his rifle into the back of the truck, standing up, and walked toward the weeper. He was wearing his usual regalia, filthy leather pants and worn ribbon shirt. Yosemite watched from behind the wheel.

"You've heard us talk about Yosemite," Clay said. "That's him in the truck."

"I figured," said Ling.

Little Richard approached, looking embarrassed. "Hey, Clay."

"Hey what? What's this?"

"Just a courtesy stop. Volunteer. Do you have any cigarettes?"

Clay handed him the Bugler can.

"Can't smoke at One Way," Little Richard said, rolling one. He had never been very good at it. His hands were shaking. "Looks like you're overheating a little."

"What the fuck is this all about?"

"Well." Little Richard tapped the end of his cigarette on the windshield of the weeper, apologetically. "You don't have a sticker," he said.

"So what?"

"You can't go into town without an EE sticker. I don't make the rules."

"That's for sure. The sticker's for the interstate. I'm not on the interstate. And I'm not going into town anyway. Not that it's any of your business."

"No need to get ugly," said Little Richard, handing him back the blue-green can. "I am trying to handle this in a friendly way."

"On what authority?" Ling asked, over Clay's shoulder.

"Volunteer security," said Little Richard. He reached into his pocket and pulled out a billfold and opened it. A flag sticker on the inside of one fold said AMERICA ON ALERT: HOMELAND SECURITY.

Clay laughed. "That's not a badge, it's a fucking sticker."

"The badges haven't come in yet," said Little Richard. "Look, Clay, don't be such a shit."

"He can't help it," said Yosemite, who had come out of the truck and joined him. "Put that cigarette out and let me handle this."

He was carrying the rifle from the back of the truck. It was an M16, military issue. After the .30-30 it looked like a toy with a plastic stock.

"Just a courtesy stop," said Yosemite with a smile. The Moses beard was trimmed but his moustache was bigger than ever. "I am a federal deputy, and this man is my deputy."

"Then move your deputy deputy's fucking federal truck," said Clay. "This is a county road."

"Not any more. Perhaps you people don't read the papers but this county has been federalized under the new Extended Emergency. That includes the roads."

"All the counties everywhere," said Little Richard.

"I read the papers," said Clay. He didn't, actually, since Merry had stopped bringing them up to the Rocks. He hadn't expected the Extended Emergency to extend this far, this soon.

"We are operating under National Guard authority here, and I'm afraid we can't allow you to pass without the proper authorization papers. You don't even have plates, much less the proper sticker. If you like I will escort you into town, and you can speak with the captain yourself."

"We're not going to town," said Ling. "I am a doctor, on call. I don't think you have the authority to interfere with me."

"I know who you are, Dr. Ling," said Yosemite. "Are you an American citizen?"

"That's none of your business, *sir*."

"May I see your birth certificate, please."

"It might be about the new babies," offered Little Richard.

"There is a clinic in Colorado Springs," said Yosemite. "That's only an hour up the interstate."

"Let's get the hell out of here," said Ling.

"Tell Roads hello," said Yosemite.

"And now," said Clay as they turned around, "you have met Yosemite."

Riots in LA, where the lines of cars stretched for blocks and people were fighting to get to the pumps. "Even when gasoline is expensive it flows freely in riot situations," said Huntley, and Brinkley agreed.

Gas was $6.22.

Riots in Atlanta and DC too, sparked by the departure of the Interim Congress to Baltimore and then quelled by the arrival of the King's Men, who seized the White House "on behalf" of MLK, who declined from Niagara, still hoping for a compromise.

Then the third rocket was fired at the UN, this one from Hoboken; it missed and wiped out a block in the east forties. Declaring for the UN (without being asked) the US Army, aka the King's Men, moved on Jersey. Instead of fighting, the National Guard pulled back to Fort Dix, the rival convoys passing on the New Jersey Turnpike.

Cicero was back, with a new VW bus with a sliding door and a 1600cc engine. He had sold the gallery. He showed Clay and Rotella what was left of the UN money after buying the van and bribing his way through the interstate checkpoints. "They call them blue bills," he said. "Nobody is sure what they're worth.

They're worth less the farther west you go." He showed them the sliding doors and the 1600cc engine.

Rotella was unimpressed. "Same old air-cooled boxer," she said. "Just another Dixie Cup."

"There they are again," said Clay. Three vapor trails, like ducks, in formation, heading east to west.

Then on the southern horizon: three more, west to east.

"MiG-21s," said Harl. The UN had declared the entire US a no-fly zone after an Air National Guard strike on the Jersey turnpike from Fort Dix.

They watched in silence for long time. The peyote brought them too, thought Clay.

Careful what you wish for.

TWENTY-FOUR

"THE GIRL MONEY IS GONE," SAID ANNIE. SHE SHOOK HER HEAD AND shook The Can. She hadn't heard from her mother in weeks.

"Maybe I can have a little talk with Lopez," Roads said. He opened the trap door into the open storage space under the dome and brought up a black plastic bag. "Is there any gas in the wonder truck?"

"It doesn't have a sticker," said Clay.

"I'll stop by the NGs and get one. That'll make everybody happy. Courtesy call."

"Don't do it," said Harl. "It's a trap."

"Come on, girls, let's all go."

It was dark when Annie, Please, and Pei returned, dropped off by Cicero in his new VW bus. Pei was crying, her little face smeared with snot. So was Please. They had busted Roads.

"They? Who? For dope?"

"I guess," said Annie. "The National Guard. They call it 'detained.' They were very cool about it."

She was the only one not crying.

"Cool?"

"They are set up in a green trailer on the courthouse lawn. The trees have been cut down and the helicopter is parked on the grass. The benches are all in a stack.

"Roads went in to get the sticker and do his make-nice and we waited in the wonder truck. And waited and waited. Finally this kid comes out, in uniform of course—they're all just kids— and said we had to leave and that Roads had been detained. He leaned in and took the keys out of the truck. We couldn't lock it or anything."

"You took the dope, I hope," said Harl.

"I wasn't about to do that. I couldn't anyway, he was standing right there."

"You could have said it was a diaper bag."

"Well, I wasn't about to," said Annie. "So there we were, stranded. Luckily Cicero came by and gave us a ride."

"I told him," said Harl.

"This is bad," said Clay.

"It wasn't all that bad," said Roads when he arrived at noon the next day, walking up the road from Johnny's. "They held me overnight and let me go with a desk ticket. I saw Brenda at the Safeway and she gave me a ride as far as Johnny's. She was buying Spam for Johnny—that's all he will eat. I think he's had a stroke but she won't call it that. He just sits and watches TV."

"You saw him?"

"Through the window. In his sad chair."

He set the plastic bag and a can of Spam on the kitchen counter.

"They let you keep the dope!?" Clay was amazed.

"It wasn't about the dope. They let me get my stuff out of the wonder truck but they kept the truck. It was all very weird. It was 'sir' this and 'sir' that. I felt like I'd been knighted. I spent the night in the jail but they didn't even close the cell door. They said Lopez had the keys but he was gone somewhere. He came by later but didn't lock the door. He brought me a pack of Marlboros."

"So, Sir Roads, what are the charges?"

"That's the thing, I don't know. They don't either. They're waiting on some kind of papers from Denver, and when they hadn't come by noon they let me go. They made me sign a thing that said I'd come back for a hearing, but they couldn't release the truck till then. And guess who explained all this? It wasn't the captain, who's this old dude who used to run the stockyard in La Junta who doesn't even keep his shoes shined. It was Gantz. He's their legal adviser."

"I thought he failed his bar exam."

"So we were told. He's pretty tight with that bunch."

"So where are the Marlboros?"

"I gave them to Brenda for Johnny. The Spam is from her."

"Looks like a bug," said Harl. "From above. From below they look like green angels."

Chop chop . . .

"A loud bug," said Clay. There it was again, visible in a notch, then another, marking the route of the county road five hundred feet below. *Chop chop chop*. For three mornings now they had watched it from the deck of the dome.

"An ugly bug," said Annie.

"It's a Huey," said Harl. "Ugly is as ugly does."

"Where's the wonder truck?" asked Merry. He had driven up in the champ with a peace offering. Roads came out with the coffeepot and told him the story. "So when's this hearing?"

"It was last week. I wasn't going to go down there and eat their pancakes again."

"What about your truck?"

"There's the problem," said Clay.

"I don't own that truck," said Roads. "It owns me. It's like an old dog. It'll find its way home someday."

Lowell and Dove came out and sat on the deck, one on each side of Merry. The three seemed almost jolly.

"French is the new Spanish," said Lowell. Quebec had joined the Bolivaran Assembly. Humphrey and MLK were talking again, through King Charles of England.

There was hope for a settlement, still.

"As you see," said Ira. He held up a potato the size of a golf ball. "We'll be eating potatoes before the first snow."

"That's only a month or so away," said Clay.

"A little snow won't kill the vines," said Ira. He had been reading agricultural magazines; they were stacked by his and Ling's bed in the adobe. He even wore coveralls, like Annie's: "But without the prize inside," he said.

Snow seemed far in the future, like Death. It gleamed in the distance on Blanca, but here in the present, late summer, Plain Bob was sitting on the low step of the double-wide enjoying his coffee in the sun, in the nude. Alameda came out and lit her cigarette off his.

"Where's Plain Jane?"

"Libra," said Ira. "This is all Ling's doing. Come take a look at the red-belly. It'll start but it won't idle."

"Honey," said Clay, "you in a world of trouble."

Your cousin is home but not home. I saw him last week up from Hopkinsville for only a few hours. Old Hickory barbecue has changed hands for the worse, he agrees. Junior was called down to Fort Campbell where the colored soldiers burned some trucks.

"So now he's a fireman," Clay muttered. He folded the letter and slipped it into the blue folder, along with his poems and EmCee's money. And his father's 1911 .45.

Humphrey was out.

"Good riddance!" said Annie.

"Careful what you wish for," said Clay.

Humphrey, who had "resigned for health reasons," was "under observation" at Johns Hopkins, leaving the federal government under the direct control of the EE Military Coordinator, a General Haig, whose first move was to pull the National Guard out of Fort Dix and into Denver, which was now declared the capital.

"Denver?"

"It's like chess," said Harl. "They apparently get one move." The UN's no-fly rule was suspended for three days, and US jets—the ones that hadn't been disabled on the ground by sabotage—were brought into Denver from Alaska, from Guam, and from Florida, while MiGs looked on from on high.

Harl rode the vanderbike down to Triple A to ID the planes. He came back more angry than disappointed. There was nothing on TV but cartoons.

"You're leaving again?" Annie liked to see people coming, not leaving.

"Don't you want to help harvest the potatoes?" asked Harl. Everyone knew he didn't.

"Another funeral," Lowell said. "An uncle in Wainscotting, a family favorite. It was all very sudden."

"How will you get there?" asked Annie. "There are no flights and the buses are for military only. There's no money in The Can anyway."

"Leave the man alone," said Roads. "He knows what he has to do."

Dove and Lowell said good-bye this time. That took awhile. Clay was waiting at the honeymoon bus when Lowell came out alone. He lifted the mattress and opened the folder and took out EmCee's White House envelope and gave Lowell three twenties. That left $220.

"You sure have a lot of uncles."

"Thanks," said Lowell. "This'll be the end of it, I expect."

"Thank EmCee."

"I always do. Have you read the poems yet?"

"I'm working up to it. I hear they're not bad."

"Tell Ira so long for me. Tell him to behave. And here comes Merry in the champ."

Lowell stuck out a hand. Clay walked around it and took him

in his arms, then let go, then watched as they drove away around the Rock.

Then he climbed the steps to the dome.

"At first I thought it was a buffalo," said Ling.

"Aren't they extinct?" asked Dove.

"You been in your tower too long, Goldilocks," said Ira. Even though the tower was gone.

"Let the lady tell her story," said Roads.

Ling told the story. Ira's snoring had awakened her just before dawn. Then she heard something stomping around on the front porch of the adobe. Afraid it would break through the old boards, she went outside to run it off and saw two NGs tacking a document onto the frame of the screen door. "You should get dressed, ma'am," one said.

"I am dressed," said Ling, but she went inside and pulled on her jeans. By now Ira was awake, and Plain Bob and Alameda too, and Kick and his lady too, who were visiting from Taos. They could hear the high rattle of a diesel in the field, where Little Richard and the One Wayers were plowing the potatoes under. A green Dodge Power Wagon with a flatbed trailer and the One Way Ford Ranger sat side by side at the end of the driveway. Yosemite sat behind the wheel of the Ford. He even raised two fingers in a wave.

"We stood on the porch and watched," said Ling. "There was nothing we could do. It was like vandalism."

"They brought a John Deere up on a flatbed," said Ira. "They left the red-belly in the barn. They were still going by ten o'clock by Ling's watch, so we just split. My truck wouldn't start, so Kick gave us a ride up here to the Rocks."

"And Gantz?" Roads asked.

"He rode up at some point on his horse," said Ling. "We left him there, sitting on the porch watching them destroy the potatoes."

"I saved a few," said Plain Bob, rattling a paper bag.

"And Alameda?"

"We left her there, sitting on the porch with Gantz."

The potatoes were the size of golf balls. They had them for supper that night.

They were calling themselves Redeemers. They wore masks on TV and talked about freedom.

"The freedom to burn things." Rotella said.

They burned bridges in Indiana, barns in Idaho, buses in Detroit, cars and crosses in Georgia, and two kidnapped King's Men in a locked shed in Illinois. MLK called them misguided pawns; the UN called them terrorists.

"Terrorism in the defense of liberty is no vice," said Haig. "It's time the silent majority spoke up for America."

"Got a light?" muttered Clay.

Pei was learning to crawl, always returning to her starting place. "She's doesn't know straight lines," said Dove. "She's a dome baby."

"Like you," said Roads.

The dome was crowded and busy. Roads rattled pots and pans. Plain Bob and Plain Jane were building a new bed—a better one, they all hoped. Harl was using the Scrabble set to teach Please to read, perhaps even to talk. Annie and Ling were sorting through the coats, already thinking about winter. Ira was cleaning Ling's little Czech pistol, which had never been fired.

Dove was in his prom dress, trying to read *Fanshen*.

"Do you miss him?" Clay asked.

"Of course," said Dove. "I guess. But I missed him even more when he was here."

Chop chop . . .

At first it was a dream. And then it wasn't.

Chop chop . . .

Clay sat up in the honeymoon bus, where he was sleeping. Had he overslept? It was as bright as day, then even brighter, then dark again, as if the Sun and the Earth were tumbling together, tangled in a fall. The *chop chop* was familiar from a thousand movies:

Trouble.

Clay got out of the honeymoon bus and ran up toward the dome. Roads was on the deck, pulling on his striped pants, looking both puzzled and fierce. Harl was in the doorway behind him.

"What's going on?" Clay asked.

"You tell me."

"It's the Huey."

The chopper hovered overhead. The spotlight picked out the wonder truck, then the weeper, making them both look shabby and small. Then the dome, dazzling them all.

It pulled up higher, and the light scattered enough for Clay to make out two trucks rounding the rocks. The green Dodge Power Wagon, with the white Ford Ranger right behind it. They made a wide circle in the lot until they were pointed out again, then stopped.

A truck door slammed.

"What's going on?" Ling asked.

No one knew. The light on the deck was so bright that it made the world beyond invisible. Clay shaded his eyes and saw a figure walking toward the dome. He couldn't tell which truck it had gotten out of.

Chop chop . . .

The Huey pulled up even higher. The light dimmed and Clay saw six One Wayers in the back of the Ford pickup, three on each side. They sat upright, looking festive and spooky in white, like hunting dogs. Clay couldn't tell the boys from the girls.

The walker walked into the light. It was Gantz.

"What's this all about?" roared Roads. Ira tried to hand him the Mossberg but Roads shook his head. "What do you want?"

"I'm sorry, Roads. I'm not at liberty to disclose that information. I'm not here on my own behalf." Instead of coming up the steps, Gantz knelt and laid a manila envelope on the bottom one. Then he hurried back down toward the trucks.

"What the fuck," said Annie.

The Huey swung up and away, its *chop chop* fading fast, as the trucks sped off around the Rock. One of the One Wayers ran to catch up and Clay saw that the white was a tunic, like a sandwich board, with a fat yellow arrow on the back.

The honeymoon bus was burning. It was lit up inside—maybe just a mattress fire! Harl grabbed the fire extinguisher from inside the door and ran down with Clay, but by the time they got there the tank had ignited with a *whoosh!* so they backed away and watched it burn.

"Those little fuckers," said Harl. It was like a little sun.

Ling brought the Bugler can and they sat on the deck and watched it burn awhile, then went inside for breakfast. The smoke stank. Annie handed Clay the manila envelope.

It was two subpoenas, one for Clay and one for Lowell, both to the Mid-Atlantic EE Military Commission, dated August 15, two weeks ago.

"It's bullshit," said Ira.

The honeymoon bus burned till noon, then flickered out. It was cool by late afternoon. The pistons had melted in the jugs. The mattress was a blackened corpse. Clay lifted it carefully. There was nothing left of his folder but the clasp and Ginsberg's nickel, which Clay polished with spit, then pocketed. EmCee's twenties and Clay's mother's letters and his poems, all were ash. The 1911 was just a heavy silhouette, black as night, like a cartoon gun.

He left it there.

There were dull orange streaks in the sky, and even as Clay watched, one split into two, and those two into two more. They would have looked even better at night.

"What is it?" Annie asked.

"War," said Harl.

Indeed. Only hours after Haig's ill-advised nuclear threat, the UN had struck the Nike missile bases in North Dakota. Then as a warning, as a corrective, after a ten-minute warning to minimize loss of life, they had taken out Haig's Air National Guard on the ground near Denver: first the planes, then the aprons and the runways, and finally the hangars themselves. All this was done between midnight and dawn.

It was daylight now.

They were mopping up the USAF guidance/surveillance satellite grid, which had ceased to be a secret since a section of the Air Force had gone over to the Niagaras—or as the Redeemers called them, "the niggers."

"Take care not to piss them off," said Roads, taking in the entire sky with one long sweep of his arm. Washed blue by day, it looked no deeper than a sea.

"Who?"

"The quarrelsome gods."

Rimshot was back, in his pink Cadillac. "California has seceded," he said.

"We knew that," said Merry.

"No, again. Northern California has seceded from Southern California."

"Jesus," said Annie who had ridden down in the weeper with Clay. "What about Oregon? Washington?" She had an aunt in Oregon. An old aunt with a glass eye. She had given up on her mother in Mazatlan.

"Who knows? San Francisco is cool though. There are two Japanese cruisers in the harbor, flying the UN flag. The town is filled with sailors. It's a boom. The SS *United States* is still in Oakland. Grounded, and leaning over. Still burning, they can't put it out. We came across on 50, through Reno, which is jammed with people, most of them from Vegas. It's fucking cowboy wild."

"Is that good or bad?" Clay wondered.

"Then we came through Vegas. The mob runs Vegas. They're selling bottled water. Somebody blew the dam."

"My father helped build that dam!" said Please when she heard the news that night. She started to cry. Her father had taken her, once, to see the dam. She was six. It was Valentine's Day. He stopped in the very middle and left her in the Pontiac with an envelope with a heart drawn on it in pencil, and jumped. Flew, almost, it seemed like to a little girl.

No one knew what to say. It was the most any of them had ever heard from her.

"I still have the valentine," she said.

TWENTY-FIVE

THEY WAITED TILL DARK AND ROLLED THE VANDERBIKE ALMOST TO the Rock so it wouldn't wake Pei when it started. The little 350 sounded sweet; it wouldn't idle, but that didn't matter. It would run. For safety's sake, they bypassed the town entirely. Two rough cattle guards and a stretch of sandy wash, and they were looking at a dark adobe house, between two cottonwoods, atop a low bluff.

"You sure this is the place?" Ira asked.

"Pretty sure," said Clay. "I was here one time with Roads. I think."

They parked the bike in the weedy yard and knocked on the door. It swung open, unlocked. There was no furniture in the house.

"Even better," said Ira. Clay wasn't so sure.

They went around back. There was a huge dish pointed at the sky, as if TV came from outer space. *Star Trek* maybe.

The wonder truck was parked between a VW bus painted with flowers that looked bright, even in the moonlight, and a new Dodge half-ton.

There was a double-wide on concrete blocks with a step made of concrete blocks, lights on inside.

"Should we knock there?" Ira asked.

Clay shook his head. "If that's his mother-in-law's place, he wouldn't want us waking her up."

"Then we just take it?"

"It's ours, isn't it?"

The battery was almost dead. "I guess that proves he hasn't been driving it," said Clay. It turned over once, twice, slowly. Then groaned and died.

A light came on in the trailer. The door opened and there stood Lopez, framed in the light, buckling on a gun belt.

"Shit," said Clay.

"What can I do for you boys?" Lopez asked. He was as big and square as usual.

"Got any jumper cables?" Ira asked.

"Not what you need," said Lopez, in his soft Hispanic drawl. "You need papers, and this."

He held out a coil wire, then pulled it back.

"Come on," said Clay. "You know this is Roads's truck. Those assholes are just fucking with him. You know that."

"Got a cigarette?"

Ira gave him a ready-made. An enormous fat woman appeared in the trailer door, blinking.

"Go back to sleep, Mamacita. Just a couple drunks."

"Give us a break, Lopez," said Clay. "Roads needs his truck. Those assholes probably don't even keep track of this shit. If somebody were to steal it they wouldn't even know."

"Or fucking care," said Ira.

"Fuck those greenhats," said Lopez. "They're gone anyway. They left me to mop up. Then the Mexicans moved in. Hell, I'm a Mexican! Isn't that right?"

"You don't need no stinking badge," said Ira.

Clay shot him a look. It was too soon to say which way this was going.

"Are you smoking again, *hijo*?" asked the woman in the door.

"*No, Mamacita. Nunca más.*" Lopez cupped his cigarette and, with a nod, led Ira and Clay around the side of the house, to the front.

"We still have to respect the law, boys, isn't that right?" He took one last drag and threw the cigarette away.

He threw one leg over the little 350 and grabbed the handlebars and bounced the front forks up and down, once, twice. "Tell you what," he said.

φ

"A tank," said Annie, back from Burg. "A Mexican tank."

"What the hell is a Mexican tank? Mexico never made a tank."

"It had a picture, a stencil really, of the Virgin of Guadalupe on one side of that top thing and Che on the other. That's what makes it a Mexican tank. Plus all the Mexicans soldiers sitting around on it."

"Turret," said Harl. "It's an old Patton. There's it and a couple of trucks, they're all parked on the courthouse lawn. They even put the benches back."

"What about the NGs?" Clay asked. The fucking greenhats.

"Gone with the wind," said Annie. "They pulled out last week all of a sudden, according to the Nice Lady who is running the Lopez grocery. She's not giving out girl money anymore but she's taking it. There's been a lot of looting. They had an armed guard sitting there with a shotgun. She let me have half this stuff on credit. Do you need any of this flour, Dove?"

"You know I don't or you wouldn't have asked." His glue was holding.

"What about that chopper?" asked Roads.

"The Huey is still there," said Harl, "but the rotors are gone. Somebody is using them for fence rails, or maybe the NGs took them with them to disable it. Haig has pulled them all up to Denver anticipating some big showdown. I asked the Mexican captain about it; the soldiers wouldn't say anything, wouldn't even look me in the eye. Of course maybe they don't speak English. He said they were under UN mandate. This is apparently an unresolved territory. They are there not to occupy Burg but to keep anyone else from occupying it. It's all temporary until the plebiscite, which Haig claims is never going to happen."

"So what about the One Wayers? Any sign of Yosemite and that crowd?"

"Their camp is still there at the edge of town," said Annie. "But it looks like most of them moved up to Ortiviz. They call themselves the Crusaders now. We saw a few of them looting the Safeway. They left the Bugler."

Three cans, and one of Tops, which no one liked.

EmCee was back. Clay hadn't dreamed of her in months, and now there she was again. In the dream (and in the dream he knew it was a dream) she was sitting on the hood of the Ford, like Ruth Ann, only it wasn't really a Ford and they were waiting for Old No Show, and there he was, putting his cold hand on Clay's ankle, all bony fingers . . .

Clay rolled over, out of the dream, but the hand held on.

He sat up. That usually did it with dreams, but the hand held on.

Someone was kneeling at his feet, in the dark. There was just enough light from the high arc of windows to see a finger waving like a reed in front of dark lips.

"Lowell?"

"Shhh. Where's Ling sleeping?"

"For Christ's sake." Clay pulled on his jeans. "Outside. She and Ira are in his truck. We towed it over from—"

"Meet me outside on the deck." It was a whisper. "Bring a flashlight."

"I thought you were in Massachusetts."

But he was already gone. Clay found his Emily's Taxi jacket in the dark, then a flashlight with more difficulty. Lowell had left the door open. Clay managed to close it without a sound.

The full moon peered over the top of the mountain, curiously. Lowell and Ling were already heading around the side of the dome, up into the rocks and the piñons.

"Come on," Lowell said.

Clay didn't need the flashlight. He followed them up the long path through the upper meadow, still soggy in spots where the water line had leaked, toward the dark tree line of the National Forest. Ling was carrying her doctor's bag. Lowell tried to take it but she held onto it. Nobody said a word.

At the top of the path, by the upper tank, a Dodge pickup was leaking steam from under the hood. A man got out, holding a rifle. No, it was a woman with short hair, in dark shiny coveralls. She covered her face against Clay's light, then uncovered it and took Ling by the arm.

It was EmCee.

It was EmCee.

She took the flashlight from Clay's hand and led Ling to the truck. Clay followed. Lowell was already leaning over the bed of the truck, pulling at a tarp.

"EmCee."

"Clay." She took his arm and handed him the flashlight. It was sticky. "We need your help."

"I can see that." He pointed the light at the hood of the truck, then back at her face, her hands, her blouse. "You're bleeding."

"Not me." She led him around to the back of the truck. Lowell was in the bed, kneeling between two bodies covered with a tarp. He pulled it back gently. There was blood everywhere.

It was Becca and some guy. It was Ginsburg. Ling was already kneeling in the blood, opening her bag, pulling up Becca's skirt, pulling at a tourniquet that was already tied around the top of her thigh. EmCee held the light.

"It's mostly hers," Ling said. "His is mostly internal."

"What happened?" Clay asked stupidly.

"We're going to need a stretcher, some kind of carry," said Ling. "There's no road down from here."

"Truck's done for anyway," said Lowell.

"I'll go wake the others," said Clay. "See what we can put together."

EmCee handed Lowell the light and turned to Clay as if seeing him for the first time. She took his hand in both of hers. She was missing a finger.

"Clay!" she said. "God bless you."

Φ

"Prison?" said Lowell. "He was never in prison. Prisons have rules, visiting areas, soda machines. He was at the Air Force Academy."

Clay shivered. He had heard the rumors. "Is that what happened to his hands?"

They were careful never to say his name: EmCee's orders.

"You don't want to know."

"How did you get him out?" Ira asked.

"We didn't," said EmCee. "We waited until they brought him out. Clay, roll me one of those, will you?"

Lowell had been wounded too: shotgun pellets in his left hand; one had gone through the webbing. It was now all wrapped in gauze instead of a torn T-shirt. EmCee was missing a finger on her right hand, but that was an old, old wound. Becca was snoring on morphine, the deep flesh wound in her right thigh neatly wrapped. Ling was bending over Ginsburg, who had taken a shotgun blast in the side; Clay had looked at it once and then looked away.

Roads was making more coffee. They had already gone through a pot. Annie was counting eggs.

"Even the Academy is not the end of the line," Lowell said. "They shuffle their high vals around, two or three at a time. We waited until a move was underway."

"How did you know when they were bringing him out?"

"There are ways. It wasn't just him we were after. This wasn't just our operation."

"Does Merry know?" asked Dove.

"Know what? I haven't seen Merry."

"Does Merry know that you were lying to us all along? To everybody. About everything."

"Get over it," said Lowell. "And not about everything."

"Will you boys shut up!" said EmCee, glaring at Lowell. "Ira, you could boil some water if you want to help. Ling will need some sterile stuff. Dove, you can tear up some shirts for dressings."

Ginsburg groaned, then screamed. Then groaned again.

Φ

"That one straight across the valley is called Fu Manchu; you'll see why when you see its long moustache when the snow comes. Those two out at the edge of the plains are the Huajatollas, the Breasts of God. The one on the left, the north, is twelve thousand something."

Clay saved the biggest for last: Blanca, which brooded over them all at the end of the valley. "There you see," he said, "the southernmost glacier in the continental USA."

"It used to be me," EmCee said. "Showing you the world. Now it's the other way around. Now we're even."

That was the last thing Clay wanted to hear. "I had some money for you," he said.

"Lowell told me what happened. Clay, you did your best. You always did your best."

That was the last thing Clay wanted to hear. Even sitting next to him she looked so far away. Maybe that's what I loved about her, he thought.

Even sitting next to him she looked as unattainable as ever.

They were mostly colored, which helped, I guess. I think they would have burned the dealership but Ice was able to talk to them. There are white gangs too. Gangs with flags!

"Thanks," said Clay.

"Thank the Nice Lady," said Merry. "That's the end of it though. The post office is closed—she's cleaning it out. Has anybody heard anything from Lowell?"

Clay shook his head.

"Nothing for me?" asked Annie. She was sitting on the deck in front of the door. "We'd ask you in for coffee but we've got a very sick baby and Ling says no."

"How's the champ running?" Clay asked. He led the way down to the car.

"Like a possum at twilight. The American way."

"Let's just hope you don't need parts."

"Why so?" Merry looked alarmed.

"They'll be hard to get," Clay said. "Studebaker went out of business ten years ago."

Merry groaned. "Why does nobody tell me things?"

"We should try and do something with that truck," EmCee said. It was still there at the high end of the upper meadow, by the stock tank, at the edge of the National Forest.

"Nobody uses that National Forest road," said Clay.

"Still. Somebody might spot it."

"I'll go with you," said Harl. They trudged up the water line, past Roads's ruined plants, high enough to see the long reach of the plains through the notch to the east.

"Was she always like that?" Harl asked.

"Like what?"

"She says jump and everybody jumps. How long were you two together?"

"Long enough. Then not long enough."

"Well, there she is."

Harl meant the truck. It was a dark-red Dodge with a slant six that bullets had bounced off of. Perhaps, Clay thought, it was the slant. Not so the radiator, the windshield, the driver's door. They rolled the truck into an arroyo and covered it with piñon branches.

"I'm amazed they got this far," said Harl. "From Springs, over that old road."

"Don't be believing everything they say," said Clay. "A lot of times, with Weather, explanations are designed to mislead."

"According to Lowell, there is no Weather."

"Exactly."

They started back down.

"How long you think they'll be here?"

Clay shrugged. "I think that's up to the war hero, not EmCee."

φ

"Fire," said Annie. She was teaching Pei the words for things. Her theory was that as soon as she learned a few words she would start to talk. Meanwhile, she was a very silent baby. Like her mother.

After the Halloween bombing of a synagogue in Omaha and a UN base in Little Ferry, New Jersey, the World Court in the Hague declared Haig a war criminal. He responded by calling for an uprising of Redeemers, some of whom proved their mettle by butchering twelve UN soldiers at a checkpoint south of Chicago, the first international loss of life since the fighting in New York. It was said that Haig had nuclear weapons in a mountain near Colorado Springs, but no way to deliver them. It was said that Humphrey was dead, killed by his own Secret Service.

There were no papers anymore: all the news came on the radio from Cuba and Canada. The back two-thirds of the honeymoon bus was a blackened ruin, but the radio in the dash had survived. Clay pulled it out and jimmied it into the wonder truck with alligator clips. He made a bed in the back.

There was a bad smell in the dome. It was getting cold but Ling's Chinese glue was holding, so far.

"It's the infection," Ling said, pulling off her gloves, which were boiled and used over and over. "We need antibiotics. Other stuff too."

Clay drove her into Burg in the weeper.

The Mexican soldiers lounged on the courthouse lawn, smoking cigarettes around their tank. The Huey had been stenciled with Che's picture, but it still lacked rotors.

The Safeway was empty, looted. Walgreens was locked up tight, with a yellow tape on the door.

"I hope you brought a crowbar," Ling said. Clay sprung the door and they slipped inside. Ling filled her backpack with bandages, sulfates, drugs, moving fast. Clay grabbed a carton of Camels. They were heading for the door when Ling stopped short.

"What's that noise? Sounds like a chainsaw outside."

Lopez was waiting for them, mounted on the vanderbike. It still didn't idle. He had painted it black and Clay had to admit it looked better. There was a grinning skull on the tank.

He blipped the throttle. Clay gave him two packs.

"Let's get the hell out of here," said Ling.

The first snow came early, silently, in the night: just a powder. The Rockers awoke to find a white silent world, looking clean, with the familiar junk buried under six inches of new snow.

Ginsburg was dead.

EmCee and Lowell wrapped him in a blanket, the one Please had arrived in, and they buried him at the bottom of the upper meadow, just on the other side of the piñons. EmCee ordered Becca to stay behind but she came anyway, limping only a little. Her leg was better. She held on to Clay's arm.

Roads said a prayer.

"He knew he never had a chance," EmCee said.

"Star," said Pei. She was better with words than her mother. But it wasn't a star. It was Libra, the community dome. They couldn't see it from the deck but they could see the light it made, burning, from four miles away.

Cicero and Palomina, Plain Jane and Plain Bob arrived on foot, carrying what they could. They dried their boots by the stove. "Fire," said Pei. They had even burned Cicero's new van.

"We didn't hear them coming," said Cicero. "But we saw them driving off in that Crusader truck." His paintings had gone up with the dome. Clay rolled him a cigarette; he had never gotten the hang of it.

"They can't stay here!" EmCee whispered to Roads.

"They belong here now," said Roads.

ϕ

It was crowded in the dome, cold in the wonder truck. Clay was listening to the radio, wrapped in two sleeping bags, when he heard a knock at the door. Then it clicked and swung open.

It was Becca, wearing his Emily's Taxi jacket. "May I come in?"

"Please."

And nothing else, not even shoes. She took it off and curled up in bed with him, and he warmed her feet with his hands, first one and then the other. "Who's that we're listening to?"

"Marty Robbins," said Clay.

TWENTY-SIX

IT WAS OVER. IT WAS TIME TO GO. CERTAIN CALLS HAD BEEN MADE BY Lowell with the phone at Sagrado Shell.

He came back up with Merry in the champ and pulled Clay aside. "I have something for you," he said. It was the 1911 .45. Lowell had taken it apart and cleaned it up. The walnut grips were blackened but the rest gleamed. He'd added a clip with bullets nestled in it like puppies in a box.

"It was my father's," said Clay. He helped Becca pack. She was dressed like a hippie now, in a long skirt and a headband. "I have something for you," she said, pressing a small box into his hand.

EmCee and Ira were back from Ginsburg's grave.

Palomina and Annie were helping Roads clean the kitchen. Please straightened her bed. Cicero had a headache. Ling brought the coffeepot out to the deck.

Dove and Clay watched Merry turn the champ around, with much slipping of the clutch. Luckily, there was little snow. They all got in: EmCee, Lowell, Becca. They drove away, they disappeared around the Rock, and they were gone.

Pei waved from Harl's lap.

Dove was looking fierce. Clay opened the box and gave him a Sherman with a lavender tip. He had to light it for him.

The second snow stuck. So did Dove's triangles. Roads killed a turkey for Thanksgiving. "Could have been a buffalo," he said. "I saw tracks in the upper meadow, and a wallow in the snow."

φ

Edna's son Ice (how did he get that name?) is now working
for the UN. And so am I. The dealership was taken over for a
motor pool and I found out only later that he had encouraged it.
I was about to fire him but thought better of it, since they are
paying us in the new blue bills.

"Don't thank me," said Annie. "Thank the Nice Lady. The
post office was burned but she's keeping the Lopez grocery open,
and she's getting mail again."

"The Mexicans are gone," said Ling, who had ridden into
Burg with her. "They took their tank with them."

"The NGs are back?"

"No way. Not them or the Mexicans either. We drove by the
courthouse. It's all boarded up. The whole town looks boarded
up. The helicopter is still there, looking broken down, but that's
all."

"So who's running Burg?" Roads wanted to know. "Who
brought the mail?"

"The UN," said Annie. "Two guys in a blue truck last week
but they didn't stop to talk. According to the Nice Lady, they
didn't speak English or Spanish either. They were in a big hurry.
She is so nice. She said she couldn't take the girl money anymore,
but she took it anyway. She even gave me some change. Look."

Blue bills: three of them, a ten and two ones. They passed
them around and Roads dropped them into The Can.

"So who's running Burg?" he asked again. "Any sign of
Lopez? Even Gantz?"

"No sign of Gantz. Lopez is in the grocery, as we speak, with
a shotgun on his lap."

"How does he look?"

"Like anybody looks with a shotgun on his lap," said Ling.
"We saw a few of those One Wayers in their Crusader tunics at
the courthouse. They were standing around the helicopter. I think
they had been siphoning gas but didn't want us to know it. We
didn't stop to talk. We saw Yosemite heading into Burg on our

way out, but he didn't stop to talk. And guess who was in the truck with him?"

"Alameda," said Plain Bob.

"Poor guy," said Ira.

It was colder than ever, especially at night, but Clay stayed in the wonder truck with the radio. The truck driver music still came in clear from Wheeling and Del Rio. The news came from Radio Free America in Montreal, mixed with static, rumors, and snatches of French.

The UN had seized control of most of the interstates and opened them at least partially to bus and truck service. They were closing in on Denver, still under Haig's control, which extended all the way south to Colorado Springs, where the Redeemers had cut the overpasses, laying them down over the lanes like barricades.

It was rumored that Haig still had a few planes, and nukes too. MLK was said to be in Georgia, trying to block its secession as a Black state.

The east-west trains were rolling but they carried only troops, most of them from Nicaragua, Poland, France. The British were mostly in the east. The Canadians were administering the northeast. Except for Denver and a narrow strip along 80 running east all the way to Kansas, the Redeemers controlled only Texas, where trailer cities were receiving refugees from Israel, South Africa, and the Deep South, which was burning from both ends.

Utah was a Mormon state once again, declaring a sort of Swiss neutrality, which the UN was prepared for now to honor. Polygamy was found, on careful reexamination of the sacred texts, to be lawful after all.

"They're not so bad," said Annie, whose mother had had a Mormon boyfriend, a stunt man, who had very patiently taught her to drive in his Camaro. "The men, anyway."

"I'll bet," said Ira.

φ

Clay was rolling a cigarette when he heard a distant rumble and looked up. Three jets in formation, heading north.

"MiGs?"

"Tupolev Bears," said Harl.

Cicero was amazed. "How can you see that high?"

"Civil Air Patrol," said Ira. "He can even see the stars."

There were more flights that afternoon, all in threes. The UN was flying out of its new base in Dakotah, arranged with the new Oglala Council, which used its "provisional" UN seat to request the withdrawal of US forces from nearby Minnesota and Nebraska. Skirmishes broke out along the highways as Indians from all over the country, mostly Oklahoma and California, used their UN passes to maneuver their jalopies north.

"There goes our solstice meeting," said Roads.

It was a cowboy.

"A real cowboy," said Annie. "In a truck."

He parked in front of the dome wearing a bandana against the cold over his nose and mouth like a bandit; he said he was looking for cows. The heater in the truck, a Chevy Apache with stock sides, was on the blink.

One cow in particular, with a yearling calf in tow. "If it was just one, they wouldn't have bothered sending me."

Roads invited him in for breakfast while Plain Bob and Harl hauled the two carcasses from behind the dome up into the trees. Annie even allowed him to spy her tits. He took off his hat and put on his glasses. His name was Sergio and he was from Pueblo, and ever since his wife, Juana, left him (this was the cowboy part) he had been working for the up-valley feedlot Texans, who were driving their cattle out to La Junta, where, in accordance with the Christmas cease-fire, they would be loaded on a train for Dallas. He had been a steel worker back in the day but he had always wanted to be a cowboy, and now he was going to Texas at last.

They would need cowboys on the train and he had always loved trains.

"I remember you," said Clay. "You fetched a buffalo down at the Ortiviz place, down by the river."

"That was me. I hated those stinkers."

Harl and Plain Bob were back, looking cold and innocent. "We haven't seen any cattle," said Roads. "But there's something here that might interest you."

They put on their coats and Roads led him through the piñons to the upper meadow. Clay went along, curious. A buffalo, little more than a yearling itself, was rooting in the snow along the water line, looking for something left over to eat.

"We got rid of ours in the fall," the cowboy said. "Look at that ear, it's never been tagged. I can't imagine where that came from. Hell, you can shoot it."

"What the hell was that all about?" Clay asked as they watched the cowboy drive off.

"Just wanted to be sure," said Roads. He thumped his frozen gloves together; it was like applause. "The buffalo are back!"

"Where in the hell did you get that?" Roads asked.

"It's not loaded," said Clay. He placed the 1911 on the dash. He placed the clip beside it. "It's just for show, in case those Crusaders start asking for papers again."

"Well, put it in the glove compartment," said Roads. "I don't want any trouble. I just want a look-see."

The wonder truck wouldn't start, so they were taking the weeper into Burg. It would be Roads's first trip since his "detainment."

"I hope you know this is stupid," said Clay as they pulled out onto the county road. Annie had objected too.

"I just want to see the Christmas decorations," said Roads. "Nobody's going to bother us."

Toward town, the road was clear. The prairie wind had blown away the snow. They drove downtown to the courthouse square. Someone had hung a wreath on the Huey and there was a manger scene on the lawn. Roads insisted on parking and getting out. Clay stayed in the truck and rolled a cigarette.

A group of Hispanic men, twelve in all, was marching around the courthouse, dressed in gray hopsacking robes. Four of them carried a huge cross. It looked to Clay like the one he had seen in the auto parts store, leaning against the wall. The rest followed, some whipping themselves with ropes, one with a strand of barbed wire. One carried a drum.

The One Wayers watched from the courthouse lawn. There were ten of them, including Little Richard, all in white tunics, shivering in the cold. Their truck was parked on the grass, which someone had cleared of snow. They didn't seem inclined to join the parade.

"Penitentes," said Roads. "There's Lopez."

Clay couldn't tell which one was Lopez. The marchers all looked alike.

When they came back around, Roads joined them. That makes thirteen, Clay thought. But they didn't seem to mind. Roads walked behind, matching his steps with theirs. They disappeared behind the courthouse, and when they reappeared Roads was beating the drum. He handed it off without missing a beat and got back in the truck.

Little Richard lifted two fingers in a wave as they drove off. They stopped at the Lopez grocery on the way out of town.

"Some celebration," said Clay, topping off the radiator. "I thought Christmas was about joy and stuff."

"They know what they're doing," said Roads. "It's all one, the birth and the death, all one event to them. We missed our solstice so that will have to do." He opened the new Bugler can. "I see you got some mail."

I got your address from your mother. She is sick, you know. She won't tell you but she is.

"Damn," said Clay. Had Brenda turned off the power or was the power out again? Either way, the house was cold. There was no electricity. The TV sat silent and resentful in the living room like Johnny after his stroke.

He had hoped to spend the evening watching TV. No such luck. He pissed in the toilet and flushed it. That was fun.

He went out to the barn to throw the horses some hay and look for some companionship. No such luck. The horses, Color TV and the lame little mare Brenda called Beauty, stood side by side in their separate stalls, ignoring each other like Rockers in the morning in their two-stall unisex outhouse.

The Rockers had agreed to watch over Johnny's while Brenda spent Christmas Eve with him at the Home in Pueblo. Since the burning of the Triple A bus, even the locals were freaked.

"I don't even care about the house," Brenda had said. "But if something happened to Color TV, that would be it for Johnny."

Roads understood. Clay volunteered. He had never cared for Christmas Eve anyway. The only Christmas present he remembered was the train set, which only went round and round. It came with no little houses, trees, or stores, like Junior's, which even had a drugstore with people inside on the stools.

He went back inside and sat in Johnny's butter-leather chair and decided to worry about his mother. He owed her that much, but what could he do? The interstates were closed again as the UN forces gathered around Denver, closing the noose even while negotiating with Haig. Ice had written in his precise printed hand. Did that mean things were really bad, or was he just trying to make Clay feel guilty?

John Wayne stared down from the wall. The chair felt cold and medical. Meanwhile the Rockers were gathered around the roaring stove, or snuggling in their beds together: Harl and Annie, Please with baby Pei, Plain Bob and Plain Jane, Ira and Ling. Cicero and Palomina . . .

Dove was at Triple A with Merry; their mourning had brought them together. And Roads, always alone yet never alone, he was a crowd in himself . . .

Christmas Eve. "Fuck you, John," said Clay, just to hear a voice. He went back out to the barn and climbed up to the loft over the horses. It was just as cold but it had a warm smell of piss and straw. That was better than nothing. It was starting to snow. The low clouds were almost warm, and the flakes were big and fluffy. He spread a horse blanket over the straw and wrapped himself in another one. He had a book in his backpack, *Dhalgren*, but he didn't want to light a lamp in the straw, so he used it for a pillow. He did risk a cigarette, one of the Shermans, which he only pulled out when he was alone, which, come to think of it, wasn't often these days.

It was the horses that woke him. The house was on fire.

TWENTY-SEVEN

"SHIT!"

Clay opened his backpack and rammed the clip into the 1911 and fired two shots into the air. He swung down from the loft. The only sound was the merry sound of dry wood burning; he could see through the windows that it was already too late. The curtains were dancing with flames. John Wayne was already turning black.

He ran to the front and saw taillights disappearing into the thick snow that was descending like a white blanket. He fired into the air once more. This time he felt the kick. They were heading up the road, not down.

"Hold still," he said to Color TV. There was a saddle on a sawhorse but he didn't know where to begin with it. He managed a bit and bridle, then threw on a blanket. The other horse was going nuts, kicking at the back of its stall, so he turned it out. The road was lost in the snowdrifts but he could see the tracks. There were two sets.

"Shit!"

He could hear engines racing, wheels spinning. They were stuck. The last thing Clay wanted to do was catch up with them, so he pulled the reins and rode up into the piñons. Johnny had a trail here, a shortcut along the top of a low ridge. The trail was lost in the snow but Color TV knew it. He started to run.

From the ridge top, Clay heard shouts; looking down, he could see two trucks bunched up at the log the Rockers had dragged across the road. Several figures in the light of the trucks were moving it. They all wore white with fat yellow arrows, front and back. They were singing.

Someone was waiting on the deck of the dome. Clay slid off

the horse before it stopped and ran up the steps. It was Harl, a blanket over his head, with Roads's Mossberg in one hand and a flashlight in the other.

"I heard shots."

"That was me." The door groaned open, just a crack, and Ira came out carrying a flashlight. There was the sound of commotion behind him.

"Turn that out."

"They burned Johnny's house," said Clay. The snow was thick, hanging in the air, not falling, and there was no sign of the fire at Johnny's beyond the low ridge, just the sound of wheels spinning, trucks grinding, moving again, approaching. There was a dim glow in the general direction of the Rock, like a low moonrise.

"I hear fucking singing," said Ira.

Years later, remembering that night, Clay had a clear image of the white Crusader Ford Ranger rounding the Rock, with two rows of kids in the back, in white, boys on one side and girls on the other. Bouncing and shining in the light of the still-unseen truck behind like a load of angels, guns upright between their knees. But where could that image have come from? There was nothing to see. The snow was as thick as fog: the fog, Clay thought, of war.

He could barely see his hand in front of his face.

"They can't see us," said Ira. "Let's go down and shoot out their tires."

"Too late," said Harl. "We want them to leave, not stay."

Clay realized suddenly that, aside from the log, there was no plan at all. He hoped Johnny's horse would find its way home.

Inside the dome, two lamps were lit. Annie held one high. Dove, back somehow, looking grim, held the other. Pei was quiet in Please's arms; it was Please who was crying. Cicero and Palomina were covered with snow. They had been sleeping in the tepee at the edge of the piñons, above and behind the dome.

"They just burned Johnny's house."

Ling muttered something in Chinese: A curse? A prayer?

Roads was moving a bed, opening the trap door in the floor. It was almost never used. "Annie, take Please and Pei downstairs; take blankets. Dove, you go with them."

"Fuck that," said Dove.

"Ling, you should go down with them. The sides are open so stay out of sight. Take your bag. Where's Ira?"

"Here." He and Harl were in the open door, looking both ways at once. The fire in the stove roared in the draft. No one wanted to leave the warmth of the dome.

Tat tat tat tat . . .

There was a crash, high above, and glass fell like bells glittering on the floor, the beds, the rumpled scattered rugs. Annie set her lantern on the floor. Roads tossed Clay a flashlight and he shined it down the hole and saw boxes, tools, a trunk, a roll of roofing: peaceful, easy stuff. Someone handed him a baby. He handed her down to Annie, who went last; then dropped the flashlight down to Dove, heavy with D cells, an easy catch.

Tat tat tat tat . . .

"Fuck," said Harl. "That's an M16, they are way ahead of us."

Roads set his lantern on the floor. "That's just to scare us," he said. "They want to burn us out, not shoot us. You boys need to be outside. Make them think."

Cicero and Palomina were gone, leaving the door open behind them. Clay looked out. Dim lights, two sets, then darkness. A wheel spun, then stopped. An engine raced, then died. Silence fell like dark snow.

Roads took his shotgun from Harl. It was suddenly, alarmingly, dreadfully cold in the dome with the door wide open. Tiny orphan snowflakes were drifting down from the shattered arc of windows high above. Ira held Ling's 9 mm across his chest like a duelist, waiting for the signal. Harl was ramming a clip into a .45, a 1911 just like Clay's but shiny. He used his bad right arm like a stick and held the gun in his left.

"Where the hell did you get that?"

"Your EmCee. She said we might need it, and here we are."

"They will try to come around," said Roads. "You guys need to be outside. Watch the sides and the back; they won't be coming up the steps."

Clay followed Ira around to the low, uphill side of the deck and jumped down to the ground. Harl went the other way. Under the dome he heard voices, shuffling; there was a light, then it was gone.

There was a light below, almost bright, even through the snow. It split into four.

"They're lighting fucking torches."

Ira fired once, twice, and the torches scattered; one split into two again. Now there were five.

Clay fired once. *BLAM!* The 1911 kicked so hard it almost flew out of his hand.

Harl appeared, a looming shadow. "Get away from the dome! If they return fire they might hit somebody." Then he was gone. Clay looked for Ira, but he was gone too.

He ran up toward the piñons—invisible, but he knew where they were. They stood waiting like friends. Below, the torches spread out serenely, almost festively, the only thing visible through the snow. Two left, two right, one bobbing straight up toward the dome.

Tak tak tak tak . . .

There was a scream, a low, honking, terrible scream.

Tak tak . . .

Then silence. Clay could only see three torches now, all moving left. His jeans were wet to the knees. A shape hurled out of the darkness, almost on top of him.

Ira. "They fucking shot Johnny's horse!" Then he was gone, and Clay was alone again. He didn't know how many shots he had left. He was afraid to pull out the clip. His hands were numb with cold. He could only see one torch now—no, two: both on the far side of the dome. The snow was thinning and he could see the shapes holding them, ratlike, just arms and legs.

Krak krak . . .

That would be Ira's little nine. Another torch joined the two from somewhere. Where was Harl? Clay ran down out of the trees, slipping in the snow. Now he could see the shapes of the Rocker trucks with a torch bobbing between them.

BLAM!

That must be Harl, behind him. He looked around and saw another torch in the piñons, where he had just left. He could see it in the twisted shafts of the little trees. They were closing in on all sides.

BLAM!

Nothing happened. *You're wasting shots,* he told himself. He tried to run up the hill toward the piñons but his feet were like stumps, it was like walking on stilts, and the snow was blanking out everything again. Now there were two torches, and no trees.

He heard a baby crying. It was a curiously comforting sound. He had no idea what to do or where to go.

Then he heard feet scraping on the steps. He was closer to the dome than he had thought. He found the steps, and there was someone above him. There was a shout:

"Roads!"

It was Yosemite. Clay couldn't see him but he was right behind him, starting up the steps.

Tak tak tak . . .

BOOM!

Yosemite almost knocked him down, his leather hat flying, then fell flat on his back, half on the deck and half on the steps all covered with snow. His face was gone. Clay ran past him up the steps. Roads was backing up slowly, through the door, into the dome. He sat down fast and hard.

"Get out of here," he said.

"It's me."

There was a light. It was Ling. She was leaning over Roads with a flashlight in her mouth. Roads was holding his hand over his heart like he was saying the Pledge of Allegiance, except his hand was darkening as the blood covered it like a glove, pulling itself on.

"Go," said Ling.

The door was wide open. Someone was pulling Yosemite down the steps; he had him by both arms. Clay almost shot him, then didn't, and he was gone. Up the hill, the tepee was burning. Two shapes, Cicero and Palomina, were pulling things out into the snow. There were three torches circling to the left, one to the right, descending out of the piñons. Clay dropped off the deck into the snow and edged up along the dome to cut it off.

Something rattled under the dome behind him. The baby had shut up. A torch was approaching, only a few yards away, a bright smudge through the blowing white wall of snow.

"Get out of here!" Clay shouted. "Stop or I'll shoot."

As if to confirm his threat he heard two shots from the other side of the dome. One loud, one a thin crack: Harl and then Ira. He could already tell them apart.

"I'll shoot," he said again.

The torch kept coming, pulling a figure behind it.

"Don't be a shit, Clay." It was Little Richard. A light beamed out from under the dome, finding his white tunic, then his face. He carried a torch in one hand and a gas can in the other. The light found it: two-gallon, red.

"Clay," he said. "I'm not here to hurt you."

"I have a gun."

"No, you don't."

Clay showed it, held it up, but Little Richard kept coming.

"You're not going to shoot me. I helped build this dome."

He pushed past Clay, ignoring the gun. Then there was a *BOOM*, the loudest Clay had ever heard, and Little Richard fell backward into the snow. He started to get up, then sat back down.

Annie emerged from under the dome, head down to miss the beams. She was carrying Roads's Mossberg. Dove was behind her with the flashlight.

"Oh, no," she said. She handed Clay the Mossberg. Now he had two guns, one in each hand.

Chop chop chop . . .

Clay realized he had been hearing it for a while. It was getting closer. Down the hill he could hear a truck trying to start. It rattled—a diesel? He could hear shouts and wheels, spinning in the snow.

"Shit," said Dove. He kicked the can but it didn't move. He picked up the torch and shoved it into the snow, fire first.

The *chop chop chop* was louder than ever. The world lit up, as bright as day all of a sudden. Annie was leaning over Little Richard. There was a black hole in his tunic, getting bigger and bigger. He was saying something. She was nodding. It was like a scene from a movie.

"Shit," said Dove again.

The chopper was coming down, only a few yards away, hidden in a furious swirl of snow. Clay pulled Annie to her feet and they just stood and watched. What was the point in running?

The rotors slowed to a crawl and they saw two men get out— no, three. One held a rifle, one carried a medical kit, and the other was clapping oversized gloves together with a *whump whump* sound.

They all wore blue helmets.

TWENTY-EIGHT

"You look like a pirate."

Junior was not amused. Perhaps it was the occasion. He was waiting outside the bus station in the Lincoln with dealer plates. Clay almost didn't recognize him; he hadn't seen him out of uniform in years.

"You drive like a pirate too."

The eye patch didn't slow Junior down. *Two-D, but you correct,* Clay thought.

"You know us pirates."

"I'm sorry I didn't make it in time. I had to hitchhike to La Junta to get a bus since Denver's a mess. Then it was three days to St. Louis. I've been on the road for five."

"Nothing works right anymore," said Junior. There were burned cars along the highway, numerous on the outskirts of Evansville, where the Blues and the Redeemers had traded blows, then thinning out as the highway narrowed to two lanes due east across southern Indiana.

"Corn looks good," said Clay, though it didn't.

"She got your letter," said Junior. "There's nothing to apologize for, considering. It all happened so fast. Slow and then fast."

Highway 60 ran straight as a string between the Indiana cornfields, looking untouched except in places where a downed fence or a burned barn stood as a reminder of the fighting that had raged, then smoldered, back and forth across the river.

"You're lucky you missed it," said Junior. "But then you've always been lucky, haven't you?"

"We saw some if it."

"Now it's all zones. And you got your president. And we've got a mess."

"Administrator." And it was you who made the mess, Clay thought, but he didn't say it. What was the point? Junior was the only family he had left, back here anyway.

The Lincoln was the only car on the highway. Even the trucks were scarce, mostly local. There had been more traffic in the Midwest Zone, and the blue helmets were friendlier too. This area was still in dispute between Atlanta and St. Louis.

The 4-Way was still there but the sign was dark and the restaurant was shuttered. Raccoons prowled through the semis in the lot. Most of them looked abandoned. "This used to be a big truck stop," said Junior.

"I remember."

"Now it's a checkpoint."

"I see."

A surly Black man came out of a trailer by the restaurant with a clipboard. His blue helmet had a King's Men sticker on it. Junior showed him some papers. He looked at the dealer plates and waved them through.

"They run everything," said Junior.

The bottomlands were still flooded. The highway south ran as straight as the highway east had run. It was dark, and the water was silver, like a setting for the trees, dark as pencil drawings, hickory ash and oak, speeding by near the road and more slowly far away. The road ran on a high levee, broken in one place where they had to crawl through, with the water sloshing over the hubcaps. Then Junior turned off and edged down toward the muddy riverbank.

The bridge was gone. Clay saw why Junior had been speeding. They had barely made the last ferry, along with a waiting semi and a Ford pickup with stock sides filled with doomed hogs.

"Fuckers shut it down at sundown," said Junior. "You can beg or you can even threaten, but it won't do any good. You will sleep in the car, *sir*, you will wait here, *sir*. It's all *sir* with them these days."

Wasn't it always that way for you? Clay thought.

A sign on the ferry said NO SMOKING in three languages, one of them Dutch as far as Clay could tell.

"Roll me one of those," said Junior.

Downtown was dark, but Likens Drugs was still open. So was the Old Hickory barbecue. So was the Barrel House liquor store.

Clay woke up in clean sheets, in his mother's bed. The birds woke him up. There weren't many birds out West, not at 6,600 feet anyway.

His letter was on the table beside the bed. She had never opened it.

Junior was in the kitchen, straightening up. The almost empty bottle of Kentucky Tavern was on the table, where they had left it the night before. Junior had slept in Clay's old bed.

"Coffee!" said Clay.

"There are ways." Junior was in a better mood.

Clay turned on the TV. The northeast was threatening to go with Canada. Redeemer Texas and Southern California were protesting disarmament. Haig had turned up alive, part of a prisoner exchange. The amnesty apparently covered even him.

MLK, the UN's Interim Administrator, was promising plebiscites. "Don't hold your breath," said Junior from the bedroom. "He's just a figurehead."

He came out wearing his National Guard uniform. An act of defiance. "Your mother liked it," he said.

"So'd your dad."

"The chapel at the funeral home was burned. There'll be a graveside ceremony at eleven, just for family, then a reception here at the house at noon. Scooter couldn't make it; his dad is too sick to travel."

Clay found his father's blue suit in his mother's closet. She had never thrown it away. Necktie too, the same as before.

There were more cars in town. It seemed almost normal, but reduced. The magnolias and the dogwoods were in bloom.

Ice was at the graveside; he had driven out in the wrecker. The three shook hands. The funeral home arrived in a Cadillac hearse with nothing but a preacher and an urn, which was all they buried. "She never made it out of Kentucky," Clay said.

"You did though."

"I know she was very proud of you, Ray," said the preacher.

The house was packed with people. That was a surprise.

"Mostly from church," Junior said. "She sang in the choir."

"I never knew."

"There was a lot you never knew," said Junior. He shook a lot of hands. No one seemed bothered by his uniform even though they had all supposedly been put away after the amnesty. It went with the eye patch, Clay thought.

Bobby Lee came in with Donna, with a baby in her arms. They had come on a bus from Nashville. "They're running again," he said. "I'm teaching three classes; I cut one."

"The Fugitives?"

Bobby Lee laughed. "Freshman comp. Maybe someday the Fugitives. Maybe even literature."

The baby was a boy, Robert Penn, already called Bobby P. Donna said her daddy had died. She asked about Harl. Clay told her Harl was fine back in Colorado. Things had been reduced to the truth.

A wrecker pulled up in front. It was Ice, with his wife and child. "He thinks it's his private car," said Junior.

His wife, Lily Mae, was sweet. "I sang with your mother in the choir," she said. "She had a beautiful voice. She could have been on the radio."

"She was, once," said Clay. "My father heard her on the radio before they met. The story is he wrote down her name and looked her up in Calhoun. He was here with the TVA and she thought her prince had come."

Junior was opening another bottle of Kentucky Tavern. The kitchen table was crowded with salads and various ham dishes and little triangular pimento cheese sandwiches.

Clay didn't feel like eating. He opened the door to the garage and closed it behind him. He had left the drawer that had held his father's 1911 open, and he closed it.

The radios looked on silently. Clay wondered if they were worth anything anymore. He didn't even know where to turn them on. He sat down and cried for a while until the door opened.

It was Bobby Lee. "Sorry. I'm not going back till tomorrow. Let's go down to the river? I'll pick you up."

Clay nodded. After a while he went back into the house. People were leaving. Junior was shaking hands, busy.

Clay hugged him from behind.

"What was that for?"

"We saw some of it," said Clay. He told Bobby Lee about the battle at the Rocks. "We buried Little Richard next to our friend from New York. I don't know what they did with Yosemite. They just hauled him off."

"Yosemite Sam," said Bobby Lee. He took aim at a plastic bottle bobbing by, just arrived from Louisville or perhaps even Cincinnati, and fired.

"You missed."

"No shit." He handed the pistol to Clay, a .22 that looked like a cowboy .45. "What about Roads, your Wizard of Oz?"

"Roads would have died if it hadn't been for the blue helmets. The other two were already dead. They took Roads to the hospital in Pueblo and he should be home when I get back."

"Back to Utopia. Isaac and the others."

"Ira. And Dove and Annie and don't forget Harl. We have a baby and a doctor too. You all should come for a visit."

"I'm not so good with utopias. And the others, your Zelda, your Lazarus girl?"

"I have no idea where they are."

"I'll bet."

"No, seriously, it's too soon for that."

Here came a picnic cooler someone had lost. Clay fired.

"Missed," said Bobby Lee.

"That was a hit," said Clay. He gave the pistol back to Bobby Lee and rolled a cigarette.

"So you say. There wasn't all that much fighting around here. Most of it was north of the river. All the Redeemers did here besides sulk was blow the bridge. Who would have thought the South would be less violent than the Midwest? I think MLK going to Atlanta helped. He had the UN with him and that kept a lid on things."

"The South shall rise again."

"But not as they knew it," said Bobby Lee. "Kentucky will probably go with Atlanta, for sure. We like looking across borders. What about the people you killed? Is that under amnesty?"

Clay shrugged. "There'll probably be a hearing at some point. Right now we don't know if we are part of Mexico or the Protectorate. They're mostly just interested in keeping the lid on things while they sort it out."

Here came a beer can. Falls City, from Louisville for sure. "Lids are good," said Bobby Lee.

He aimed and fired.

"We have a little place the mountains," said Clay. "It's real pretty there."

"I'll bet," said Ruth Ann. "I always knew you never belonged here. I always knew that, you know."

"Belonging is complicated stuff," said Clay. "I'm sorry to hear about your husband."

"The ghost?"

"Huh?"

They were at Old No Show's, sitting on the hood of the Lincoln. Ruth Ann put on her bra while Clay rolled her a cigarette.

"Rose was like a ghost," she said. "We never had much to say to each other. Then when I lost the baby he blamed me. To tell the truth I'm better off without him. At least I have a job."

"The Southern Kitchen."

"Business is good. All the blue helmets eat there."

"I have a better idea. I go back tomorrow."

"I know." She finished buttoning her blouse.

"Why don't you come with me?"

"Is that what this is all about?"

"It could be."

"I'm astonished you ask. Though not surprised."

"Astonished is good. It's really a pretty place. You'd like the view."

"As good as here?" In the distance, toward town, they could see lights, though not as many as before. Above were the million stars, brighter than before.

"Better."

"You used to say there were vast intelligences out there," Ruth Ann said, looking up. "Do you still believe that?"

"I'm sure of it." Though he wasn't.

She slid off the hood of the Lincoln. Even in the dark she was pretty. The bugs were loud.

"Tomorrow's awful soon," she said. "You'll be coming back. Meanwhile, I'll think about it."